Gareth Clarke

PORTRAIT OF GERARD

HZPublishing

Copyright © 2025 by Gareth Clarke

All rights reserved. No part of this book may be reproduced or used in any manner without written permission of the copyright owner except for the use of quotations in a book review. For more information, address:
garethclarke137@gmail.com

HZPublishing

Portrait of Gerard

'And what shall I love if not the enigma?'

- Giorgio de Chirico

1

She was as beautiful and desirable as any woman would ever be. Long, lustrous golden hair, swaying like a breeze rippling through a cornfield on a summer's day, eyes pure, powder blue, gentle, true. She turns to me, her perfume like forgotten days of June, her lips a soft, caressing touch, and so on.

Anyway, to put it simply, our own company was sufficient - we needed no other. What we did need, though, was some other source of income. In spite of the fact that we were both working, the mortgage was starting to weigh heavily. Our incomes were reasonable, but I certainly didn't earn a fortune. I don't know exactly how much Melanie was paid - apart from shared expenses, financially we remained independent - but there's little doubt she made a lot more than me.

She's highly focused and dedicated to her work; even at home most evenings she has her face pressed to the screen. She's good at her job and knows she's good, and I've no problem with that. I'm not one of those guys with a hang-up about the woman in their life being brighter or more successful or earning more than they do. But my lack of ambition and limited earning power sometimes seems to sit uneasily with Melanie.

I freely admit I'm not ambitious. I've never wanted to put all my focus and energy into one specific area. To me a job is just that - something I can do, without too much effort or involvement, make a little money, then walk away at the end of the day and forget about it entirely until the doors open next morning.

Around nine o'clock on Friday evening there came a loud, insistent rapping at the front door. I looked over at Melanie, her face glowing a strange, alien white in the glare of the computer screen.

'Are you expecting anyone?'

'Not that I'm aware of,' she replied, without looking up.

The knocking began again, this time even louder and more insistent.

'Could you answer the door, Robbie - I really must concentrate.'

Yeah, fine. It's not as if I was doing anything important. Not once during our conversation had her fingers faltered at the keyboard.

In the gathering dusk a short, slight figure stood clutching what appeared to be three or four large paintings. From the small, thin face two of the brightest, most intense blue eyes fixed me with an unwavering gaze.

'I'm Gerard,' announced the apparition in a metallic, rasping voice.

'I'm sorry, you're…'

He put down what I could now clearly see were indeed canvases, wiped a hand on his trouser leg and held it out. For one so small and thin his grip was remarkably hard.

'I've come about the room.'

'Oh, I see. You must have spoken to Melanie.'

'No.'

'Ah. Well, you must have seen our advert in the local press. But we didn't put an address in the advert. So how did you...'

Gerard, clutching his pictures once again, edged into the hallway.

'I'm delighted to see you've kept the original window frames.'

'Well, we just haven't had a chance to - '

'And this,' he said, nodding towards the coloured glass panelling in the front door.

'I couldn't have contemplated taking the room if you'd had God-awful plastic windows put in. Nothing, but nothing more surely destroys the aesthetic appeal of a building than defacing it with the wrong type of windows. I despise plastic windows more than any other single thing in this world.'

His voice was shrill and harsh.

'You know, it might be better - '

'If aesthetics is not the driving force in society, then any higher civilization becomes an impossibility.'

'Yes, I see, but I've just realized the time - '

'So few people appreciate the importance of detailing. They look at a building and think the windows are not important.'

'Quite. Well, it's been - '

'They're vital, absolutely vital in maintaining aesthetic cohesion. If you deface a landscape with pylons, or wind generators or motorways it's like taking a pen and drawing a line across a beautiful painting.'

'You're probably right. Now - '

'All aesthetic pleasure is lost. You could argue that the landscape is 95% intact, just as you could argue that a fine Victorian building like this would be 95% intact if you put in plastic windows.'

'You could indeed. So - '

'Yet 95% of the aesthetic enjoyment would be lost because the building would have lost all aesthetic integrity. Absolute aesthetic cohesion must remain the absolute priority.'

'Absolutely. Now perhaps it's time you - '

'Robbie?'

Never was I so relieved to hear Melanie's voice.

'Yes,' I said, with only a hint of high-pitched desperation. 'I'm in the hall.'

A moment later the golden vision appeared.

'Melanie, this gentleman has come about the room. I know it's getting quite late so I was thinking - '

'Hi, I'm Melanie. Won't you come through.'

Yes, that's more or less what I was thinking. In the living room, without a word Gerard arranged the four canvases in a group, then turned to Melanie.

'I thought you would want to see a few examples of my art.'

'You're an artist?'

'Of course. I've taken the liberty of bringing four of my works, each of which is an illustration of a different facet of my art.'

Once glance and I recognised the style immediately as that of de Chirico. Each painting was a poorly executed pastiche, the lack of real ability shining through in unmistakeable fashion. But in place of the piazzas and classical allusions of de Chirico were the red brick mills and terraces, factories and warehouses of a Victorian industrial landscape. The streets, for the most part devoid of people, were lined with stone setts. Gas lights stood like wary sentinels, while in gaunt and lonely railway stations steam trains puffed smoke into empty skies. And amid the deep shadows and strange, sloping perspectives were tall white marble statues, looking quite incongruous in their unfamiliar setting.

Crowning this collection was a portrait of a mannequin, its head a large white egg, limbs like long, inflated balloons, apparently about to mount a racing motorcycle. A warehouse jutted into the picture from the left, throwing a near horizontal shadow across the middle ground of the picture, while in the background against a dark sky I was able to recognise Lutyens' cathedral.

'These are really something, Gerard,' I said, though what that something was I didn't elaborate. The little artist responded with a knowing smirk. Melanie was examining the paintings with intense interest. She turned to Gerard.

'This wonderful figure here,' she said, pointing. 'It looks rather like a dummy, Gerard.'

'It is a mannequin,' replied Gerard coldly.

'Surely it's the same thing,' I said.

'It's wonderful,' continued Melanie hurriedly. 'In fact all your paintings are simply wonderful.'

Her face was shining with a glow of admiration, her golden hair tumbling across her shoulders, head tilted slightly to one side, her expression warm and eager, her smile gentle and encouraging. She had never looked more beautiful or desirable. The little artist could hardly fail to be flattered by the attentions of his admirer, or impressed by his own power, and he rose to the occasion magnificently.

'My paintings speak of pain and loneliness and loss. They are the empty, haunting spaces of the mind, filled with troubled dreams.'

I looked at Melanie, sitting open-mouthed in wonder, as if at the feet of a prophet who had just offered her the key to the mysteries of the universe.

'This is my inheritance - I am the heir of de Chirico.'

I released a shout of laughter which I tried to hide by coughing, which unfortunately turned into a genuine coughing fit. Finally, red-faced, I waved my hand at Gerard to continue. With an irritated glance, as though I'd disturbed a carefully composed speech, he resumed.

'It is my task and my challenge, one facet of my life work, to continue to develop this inheritance for the modern age and to make it relevant to the England of our time.'

The horrifying thought flashed into my mind that this was a set-up. Maybe there were hidden cameras somewhere recording our reaction. Or alternatively friend 'Gerard' might just be making the whole thing up for his own gratification. Either way, as a hoax it was an elaborate one - the paintings, bad as they might be, were real enough. Or maybe he was just completely mad. Inclining for my own peace of mind to the latter theory I decided to humour him.

'You know, Gerard, there's just one slight problem. I'm afraid the England of our time has no steam trains any more. It's a shame, but there it is.'

'That's not the point at all,' he snapped. 'They are symbols of the fragmentation, the pulling apart of communities and lives in an industrialised society. Mass transport systems necessarily have that effect. A steam train is just a picturesque and aesthetically pleasing way of presenting that particular symbol.'

'I loathe symbolism. It's possible to read anything or everything or nothing into symbols. They can be explained quite persuasively as meaning one thing by one expert then shown to mean something completely the opposite by another. It's portentous and pretentious. Art appreciation becomes not what works visually but a contest at spotting hidden meanings.'

'You have no understanding whatsoever! Art, indeed life itself, is entirely concerned with symbols, either explicitly or unconsciously. Every component of every work of art, be it painting, literature, music, architecture or whatever means something different to every person who looks at it or listens to it or reads it. And if the meaning is different for different people then each object represented or each phrase or melody becomes in fact merely a symbol with a subtly different meaning, depending on the context of the listener's or observer's or reader's own experiences. Where something has no exact, specific meaning it must necessarily be regarded as a symbol to which an infinite number of different meanings and values can be attached.'

'That's precisely the point I was making. If a work of art is regarded simply as a collection of symbols, each meaning something different to each listener, then it ceases to have any meaning at all. My point is that a great work of art is devoid of implied symbolic significance because its meaning is clear and explicit and therefore much the same for any observer.'

'Much the same? In other words not the same! If words and meanings are not used precisely, it's far better that they're not used at all. The odd grunt would suffice.'

Cheeky little sod!

'You're playing with words, Gerard. Quibbling over semantics,' I concluded, rather weakly.

Melanie, who'd been showing signs of increasing unease and irritation, now stepped in, suggesting that Gerard firstly view the basement, being the nearest of the rooms available.

She led the way, opening the door and switching on the single bulb, before politely inviting Gerard to go down first. He took a few steps, then suddenly turned and looked back up at me, his eyes livid in the cold light.

'Why should objects mean what we take them to mean?'

I could think of no response.

'Why should we be descending these stairs? What meaning does it have?'

'To get down to the basement?'

'Ah, but why are we descending rather than ascending? Why should one mean one thing and one mean another? Why should we attach assumptions and preconceptions to our actions?'

Again, any meaningful response was beyond me. I could sense Melanie twitching a little beside me, but I couldn't look at her face without conspicuously twisting my head round.

'When you see a building, for example, it triggers a series of predictable responses. You see its size, its function, its age, condition, architectural style. Even its history and possible future. But why? Why see these meanings? The building will have depths of meaning beyond any you may imagine. A hidden, secret soul. And what is true for a building is true for everything within our experience. Every word we utter, every note we hear, every rustle of leaves or bark of a dog or sweet confection in a baker's shop. Everything has hidden meaning - meaning beyond the visible and obvious. It is the function of the artist to interpret these meanings - to capture the unfathomable, the enigma of existence.'

He set off once more. I really wanted to catch Melanie's eye, but she kept her gaze fixed resolutely ahead. We managed to reach the bottom of the stairs before he turned to me again.

'The artist sees, senses, feels, as if the object and sensations have never been seen, perceived or felt before. He sees them free of all associations - like a child, a young child experiencing something for the very first time, open-mouthed in awe and wonder. Its significance, its portent incalculable. Its meaning opaque, indecipherable. There are no reference points. There is no checklist of correlation. Its meanings are infinite, or finite to the point of invisibility. Only the seer, the prophet, the artist can interpret these signs, these images, these symbols, so that others may say, Ah, yes! Of course! That is what it means.'

The basement is a large space with many interesting subdivisions and hidden recesses. A little natural light comes in from a window at ground level.

'Ah,' he said, 'now this…'

And with obvious satisfaction he began to stride around, eyes gleaming. Running his hands in a strange, exploratory fashion along walls and exposed sections of woodwork. Inspecting the various little compartments and cubby holes of the basement, including two small alcoves where we'd managed to cram in a bathroom and kitchen.

I expected him at any moment to cry out as a hand collected a splinter. But finally, in a tone of great moment, he declared the room suitable to his purposes. And leaving the canvases - unaccompanied by any form of monetary deposit - left as abruptly and unexpectedly as he'd arrived.

2

A harsh, cold light washed down the narrow stairway. I wasn't desperately keen on going down there, though sometimes I seemed drawn almost involuntarily in search of some key or sense of meaning to the Gerard episode.

The room was full of shadows and dark corners. An unmistakeable feeling of foreboding and unfinished business. Canvases still lay stacked in piles against every free space of wall. An easel stood forlornly like some angular beast of burden. Still a strong smell of oil paint and turpentine. The endless piles of books and papers. And the inevitable posters of de Chirico - mannequins, piazzas, chimneys, statues, steam trains, rubber gloves, poets and philosophers.

I'd wanted to clear the whole damn place out straight away, but Melanie had insisted that everything be left just as it was. And now his lair had more than ever become an unhealthy, haunted place, with the morbid aura of a shrine. Or was Melanie in fact secretly awaiting his return - still clinging to hope in the face of cold reality?

Nobody ever came forward to claim his things. Despite our best efforts we never traced any living relative or friend. It was as if he'd simply materialised from some hidden place to wreak his own special brand of havoc, before disappearing as swiftly, and certainly as surely, as was possible.

And in the months following his death, I began sorting through his personal effects. Sifting out and destroying much that would have presented his character in a less than favourable light.

My one guiding thought in this process was to be true to what I believed would have been Gerard's own wishes in displaying his accomplishments. Needless to say there was much, especially among the vast horde of juvenilia, that demanded a ruthless approach. Its publication would plainly not have enhanced Gerard's reputation. And there were other things too, sometimes of a quite revealing character, that I decided were too personal to publish.

One discovery - a real find - was a spool of about five or six minutes of cine film, with Gerard silently gesticulating, shouting, pulling faces and generally running through his repertoire as demagogue in embryo. Seeing my old friend, like some spectral vision, going through his paces in the cloying darkness of his lair - well, let's just say that rarely has any specific five minute period of my life given such pleasure.

A cache of literally hundreds of photos, found with the film, also showed Gerard practising his dramatic poses. And glancing through these I was struck by a sudden inspiration. Selecting a couple of full face shots, I drew a line down the centre of the image, bisecting Gerard's face. The contrast revealed between the two sides of the face was startling.

The right hand side, Gerard's right, that is, was a study in concentrated, staring intensity, seemingly representing the full power of his will, an almost demonic force. The other side was nothing but a blank. No expression, no emotion. No past or future - just an empty vessel.

Examining these apparently opposing poles in Gerard's character, the thought crossed my mind that this might be the key to understanding this strange, unique personality. Was the blank face in fact the real Gerard, a man without roots or past, for whom the absence of personality was, in truth, his true personality? The right hand side by contrast representing the power of the human will to create on a blank canvas whatever construct of past or personality it chose - the power of free will defying a deterministic universe.

What pleasure there is in probing what lies behind a mask! The eyes and face reveal much, or sometimes nothing, but remain imperfect mirrors of the soul. More, of course, is revealed by the way we communicate, not just in what is said or left unsaid but in the manner of expression - the phrases used, tone of voice, inflection, use or deliberate non-usage of colloquialisms or local vernacular, even obscenities. But always the absolute reality of personality remains elusive.

Where Gerard is concerned there are particular difficulties in trying to differentiate between the layers - to ascertain where one mask ends and another begins.

Was there ever any substantial reality to the persona behind all the successive layers at all? Was there, in fact, ever any personality to Gerard or was he, as the photographs seemed to show, simply a construct? A faceless man, like one of his mannequins. The more I thought of it, the more certain I became of this idea of Gerard as a construct fashioned by the effort of his own will out of nothingness.

And when I came across a letter among Gerard's effects it set me thinking again along these lines. Why should he have gone to all the trouble of inventing events, situations, stories, plans and schemes? I now believe it demonstrated a compulsive need to put something in place, simply because there was nothing else there. In a very real sense Gerard didn't exist. But with sufficient self-knowledge to realise this he assembled a quite complex superstructure of fantasies allowing him, starting with a blank sheet, to become whoever and whatever he chose. A truth constructed from his will and imagination - an edifice built upon the thinnest of thin air.

The letter was unaddressed and unstamped, as if it had been written and then forgotten or discarded. It is, however, dated, though I would suggest the date itself is meaningless.

26.3.83

My dear Mr. Ghaffari,

I am sending this letter in greetings to yourself, and to your esteemed wife of whom, though of course I have never seen her face, I have the most fond recollections. Greetings also to your pleasant daughter, Anahita.

It seems a long time since we last communicated, therefore I thought I would take this opportunity to renew our acquaintance. I'm sure you recall, as I do, and with equal pleasure, the many interesting discussions we had ranging over the whole field of social, artistic, political and commercial life. You will remember that underlying these discussions was the constant, and understandable, preoccupation with the relations between your country and Iraq. I hope that what I have to tell you might provide a fresh psychological insight into the ruling elite of that state, and that with your many political connections both at home and elsewhere some good may come of it.

I was recently part of a trade mission to Iraq. We were a group of successful entrepreneurs invited over by the Iraqi Trade Minister. I forget his name - nice man - moustache, glasses, military uniform. I noticed he'd been awarded several medals. But it was high-powered stuff - we were introduced to all the members of the Revolutionary Council, including the President himself. Contrary to general opinion, Saddam Hussein is a charming man, absolutely charming. Quiet, modest, restrained in his expressions, powerful and well-informed in his arguments. I was fortunate to have quite a long discussion with him about trade links between our countries, the potential for economic growth in Iraq, quotas, oil prices, free trade, the European Union.

He was knowledgeable and eloquent on all these subjects. In the course of being wined and dined during our stay, and although the majority of our time was spent visiting various factories and installations, towards the end of the visit our party was invited to a museum of modern art staging a series of what one might term conceptual tableaux - a species of performance art, and certainly more than merely illustrations of some event from history as one would expect from a traditional tableau.

The event comprised a series of perhaps nine or ten works, mainly though not exclusively using the human form, each draped by a large, encompassing black shroud. After a lengthy and opaque introduction to each exhibit by the artist, an assistant would then step forward and dramatically whip off the sheet revealing the figure or figures.

And the first of these was quite startling. A tall personage, dressed in Western clothing, dark dinner suit and tie, all quite normal. Except that on their head was a mask of such demonic impact that it drew gasps from the audience. You could actually see people instinctively huddle together.

It was Satan, with a ruddy, vicious-looking face, pointed chin and nose, protruding cheekbones, and long, sharp horns. It looked around, and seemed to hiss quietly as it surveyed the audience, and people literally cowered at its glance. Then the most extraordinary thing happened. The figure reached up with both hands, took hold of its horned head, and lifted it off.

And underneath the mask, standing on the podium looking hot and slightly embarrassed, was the President himself, Saddam Hussein! After the buzz of exclamations and gasps of astonishment had died down, Saddam apologised for gate-crashing such an important artistic event. In quiet tones he explained that he had been inspired to present himself as he suspected the world saw him. But, he said, like the mask, that image is an illusion, and underneath is a normal, quite ordinary man, dedicated only to working for the good of his country.

I thought it was an effective and clever piece of drama, brilliantly executed. After a while the excited chatter of the audience died down, and the other tableaux were revealed one by one, each drawing polite, respectful applause, though I'm not sure that the symbolism of some of the works was explicit to all members of the audience. I noticed many around me exchanging confused glances. People then had an opportunity to wander round, look more closely at the works, and meet the artists themselves.

And all the while, Saddam Hussein was mingling with the audience, flanked by his bodyguards, chatting pleasantly to slightly overawed members of the public. At one point he actually caught my eye, obviously recognised me, smiled and waved. I was deeply flattered to be singled out in this fashion.

The most extraordinary and disturbing episode of this event was still to come, however. At the end of the exhibition, in search of the exit, I found myself at the end of the room where there was a kind of creche. A thin, silver-haired woman, her face a picture of boredom and disinterest, was sitting there smoking a cigarette. She was presumably the creche attendant, though she took no interest whatever in the occasional cries and whimpers of her charges. I was about to turn away, when I heard a small voice calling, touched with desperation. I looked around, trying to see where the voice had come from.

'Please. Help me.'

It was coming from a blue carry-cot parked among many others. I went to it and looked inside. The memory of what I saw will remain with me for the rest of my days. The poor little thing was barely human. The top of its head appeared to be missing. The eyes, blue and staring, were almost in its forehead. I don't know where the voice came from because I couldn't see any mouth. But the worst thing was its stomach. It was open, like a huge, festering sore. I could hardly remove my eyes from the horror of it. Then the poor creature spoke again.

'Please, take my tee-shirt off. I'm so hot. Please help me.'

For a moment I stood there as its blue eyes clutched imploringly at me. Then I was overwhelmed by its dreadful deformities, the stomach like an open sewer. I turned suddenly away, and pushed my way out of the building into the cool, fresh air. I can hardly bear to think of it even now.

It promises to be a warm spring this year. How pretty the bluebells look! I wonder if you are planning a vacation this summer? I have booked a cottage in the Lake District for August. I shall use the time to recharge my batteries and prepare myself for the next stage of my development as artist. No doubt, however, I shall be drawn into a little light sketching. Slate is such a charming material!

I respectfully remain,

Your friend,

Gerard

Of course it's all the ludicrous, bogus detail that makes his tales seem almost believable. That's the trouble, you see - when he was alive he could do no wrong, and now he's gone he's become an icon. You can't challenge anything he said, you can't ask him to prove anything or account for anything. Not that Melanie would dream of doing that anyway. Even if he completely contradicted himself she'd just claim he'd had a revelation. What the hell was it about the little fake that she so admired?

3

There was an evening long ago, though chronologically only last year, when Melanie and I were relaxing in the living room at Fairfax House. Enjoying a nice, quiet time. Melanie's head was glued, not literally, to the computer screen. Meanwhile, mind sharpened by a couple of beers, I'd just come to a definitive judgement to the effect that the adverts on TV were on the whole more entertaining than the programmes themselves, and I was just contemplating sharing this revelation with Melanie when I heard the ominous thud of footsteps.

Gerard's basement flat was self-contained, so there was really no need for him ever to come into the rest of the house except to exit the place via the hall, and there was certainly no need to come into the living room. However, prompted by bitter experience I leapt up, trying to calculate whether I'd time to get out of the room and find a safe haven, or whether it was better anyway not to leave them alone together for any length of time. And I'd just begun to think how predictable my thought processes were in this familiar situation, when Gerard entered the room.

Without preamble or invitation he perched himself on the settee next to Melanie, drawing his legs up and crossing them, before starting to talk at me.

'Robbie, what sort of shape do you think society should take?'

'Well, I think the best shape would be a circle with a series of little indentations around the edge.'

Gerard, normally devoid of humour, burst into loud laughter. Melanie, as startled as me and presumably primed for a rebuke at my flippancy, instead managed only a weak, confused smile.

'That's a good one, Robbie,' said Gerard, still smiling broadly. 'But you know, there's an element of truth in there. Your circle is a fair diagrammatic representation of the basic unit of my new society.'

Further acquaintance with A New Society confirmed my belief that it was completely derivative, clearly based on the writings of Winstanley, Godwin, Morris and Kropotkin. Okay, there were one or two little modifications to take account of modern technology, but it was basically a copy. And totally unworkable, of course - as are all utopian models - relying as they do on either the perfectibility or tractability of human nature.

Melanie was looking at Gerard with shining eyes.

'You've designed a new society, Gerard?'

'Certainly.'

'Why, that's wonderful!' said Melanie. 'What's it called, your new society?'

'A New Society.'

I gave Gerard a gentle, sympathetic smile.

'Gerard,' I said, 'you don't think a more pithy title would be appropriate? Like maybe Leviathan, or Oceana, or City of the Sun, or maybe Looking

Backward? Or what about Republic? Or Herland? Or how about Utopia? There's a catchy title for you.'

Gerard's good humour evaporated a little.

'I'm well aware you're being facetious, Robbie. And, as you obviously know, all those titles have been used before. In any case, none of them, with the possible exception of Herland in certain specific aspects, have anything in common with my society.'

Melanie looked bleakly towards me for a moment before turning back to Gerard.

'What's your new society like, Gerard?'

She gave the words a kind of breathy sensuousness, like a nauseating parody of Marilyn Monroe.

'It will be a satisfying, peaceful and sustainable society. It will take the best of human nature and give it full rein to develop. I'll show you a leaflet I designed if you're really interested.'

I'm not remotely interested, you little prat.

'Have you really, Gerard? That would be fascinating.'

'I'll go and get it then, shall I?'

Oh God, no, please don't.

'Yes please, Gerard.'

Oh fuck.

Gerard jumped off the settee and went scurrying excitedly away.

'What are you encouraging him for? Why are you deliberately playing up to the little jerk after all I said about trying to curb his delusions and obsessions?'

'I am not playing up to him, as you put it, and why shouldn't I take an interest in all of Gerard's wonderful ideas? I only wish some other people would show some sign of creative thought occasionally instead of slumping in a comatose state in front of the TV every evening. And in what sense is Gerard's society a delusion? How can a blueprint for a hypothetical society be in any sense delusional? Only if he actually believed it already existed, which he clearly doesn't, would it be delusional. And how can it be an obsession when Gerard has been here for months and has never before mentioned his new society? And don't ever call him that again, do you understand?'

'That's a whole herd of questions, Melanie,' I replied, staggering a little after this onslaught.

Gerard came rushing back into the room, and tossed the leaflet casually towards Melanie, whose expression miraculously transformed into beatific goodwill.

'It just describes the main features. Of course, I'm working on a full exposition of my society, all the nuts and bolts details that communities will need to fully implement the concept. And, yes, Rob, I might indeed give it a more pithy title, as you put it, when it's finished.'

Of course you will, you supercilious little -

'This is fascinating, Gerard,' said Melanie, her eyes afire with enthusiasm, and began reading aloud.

> *The aim of this new society is to provide the best possible answer to the world's seemingly insoluble problems, in such a way that each individual in every land has an equal share in material benefits and equal opportunity*

> *for achievement and fulfilment. The only way of accomplishing this is through a form of society based on self-governing, self-sufficient communities.*

'Have you ever read News from Nowhere, Gerard?' I asked. 'I'm sure you'd find it most enlightening.'

Gerard gave me a look, picked up and replicated with greater intensity by Melanie.

'Of course I've read it. Any similarities between my society and any utopian text advocating self-governing communities are entirely coincidental. A New Society was conceived and developed completely independently, simply from an analysis of the human condition.'

You lying -

'Robbie, why don't we just let Gerard's society speak for itself,' said Melanie, before continuing.

I glowered silently.

> *Only if a community is self-sufficient can the people within it control their own lives on a practical level. If they are reliant on a national or international network of interdependent producers, then there needs also to be either centralized control of production and exchange, to match supply with demand, or else a market economy, with money as the only practical method of exchange, leading to accumulation of wealth and inequality. Either way, people are dependent, as in almost all present forms of society, on processes and events which they cannot control.*

'This is an amazing analysis, Gerard. You seem able to get to the root of problems with such clarity and simplicity.'

I felt a wave of nausea threaten to engulf me. Gerard had a peculiarly irritating smirk on his face.

> *A form of society based on self-sufficient communities, where small groups have virtually complete autonomy in the running of their affairs, is the only situation where people can effectively have control over their own destiny. Centralized...*

To be honest, though, my interest in Gerard's wonderful society was waning. The combination of the beer I'd drunk earlier and the whisky I was taking now for its anaesthetic properties was having a calming, soothing effect. I settled lower in my chair.

Gazing into the depths of the glass, I held it to one side against the light of the fire. A rich glow came from within, like a tiny yet potent beacon, seeming to promise a place where there was only warmth, trust and contentment. And as Melanie's voice continued I closed my eyes, trying to visualise what this wonderful place might be like. Though occasional phrases such as *defined by a written constitution* and *limited powers restricted to clearly defined areas and circumstances* continued to filter through my semi-conscious state, after a while I found myself in Scotland.

A remote glen, somewhere in the Highlands. An old, detached stone cottage, miles from habitation, with an unruly, pretty garden and large cultivated plot surrounding it. There was a glorious warm smell of turned earth and vegetation. And the even more glorious sight of Melanie, wearing a red tee-shirt and tight blue jeans, her golden hair falling around her arms, shaking the soil from a potato plant. She sees me watching her - a responding smile of love and sensual enchantment. A self-contained, perfect world.

Quite abruptly I found myself walking a narrow, grassy ledge. Both ahead of me and a few feet to my right the grass seemed to dip to nothingness. Stopping and gingerly turning my body I realised with horror that I was on the brink of a sheer drop. Retreat back along the wet, slippery grass seemed impossible. I couldn't understand how I'd got to that point in the first place. Isolated and terrified, I tried to calm myself while keeping quite still.

It was then I became aware of the presence of two buildings, one each to right and left. They appeared to be great warehouses, monumental in scale, rising out of the depths below. Great swathes of brickwork and stone, with row upon row of forbidding windows. My senses swam looking up at them as fluffy white clouds drifted past their great mass. Carefully turning my head to look straight ahead I was startled to see for the first time a dazzling white marble statue where I could have sworn there was nothing before. Impossible to miss, towering above even the warehouses, and surmounting a great stone column.

Far beyond and below a Victorian industrial city sprawled. Countless rows of terraced streets surrounded by grimy mills and warehouses, ugly public buildings and scores of tall, smoking chimneys. A light haze covered the city as the sun beat down relentlessly on the swarming, sooty streets.

It was clear that both statue and warehouses were symbols of industrial wealth and power, glowering down with menacing force at the city below. A city presumably built and controlled by the character in white marble. I looked more closely at the face of the figure. And the more I looked, the more familiar the features seemed to become. That intense, obsessive stare, the annoying self-satisfied smirk.

With a sickening thrill of recognition the identity became all too clear. Gerard - artist, genius, raving megalomaniac - was responsible for this great sea of self-glorification. But no longer little - this was Gerard writ large. Gerard as no doubt he would wish the world to see him. I could even hear that relentless, excited voice rising in pitch, rising shrilly towards some great climax, perhaps the peroration of a no doubt long and excruciating speech.

All countries would join together in a federation of nations, each nation self-sufficient through the equal distribution and recycling of resources

God, it was hot. But the sun seemed to have dwindled and was now radiating somewhere near my left leg.

and each having an equal voice in world affairs

I opened my eyes. My neck was stiff and my head throbbing. So it wasn't the sun, after all - it had all been a terrible nightmare. But I'd woken into something almost equally terrifying, and that relentless voice wasn't Gerard's, but Melanie's.

Common interests and responsibilities are acknowledged by the acceptance of the principles of A New Society as a guiding philosophy binding all nations in a true community, but without compromising cultural diversity

'I'm going to bed,' I said, walking unsteadily from the room and slamming the door. They could do whatever the hell they liked for all I cared. I stopped and listened for a few seconds, but the voice continued regardless. I don't think they'd even noticed me going.

4

'Do either of you have any idea where they keep the plans for cathedrals that haven't been built yet?'

I did an involuntary double take. Said I didn't know, it wasn't something I'd ever really thought about before. Melanie said that wasn't very helpful and asked Gerard which particular cathedral he had in mind. He replied, rather tetchily, that there weren't that many unbuilt cathedrals for which there were extant plans. Of course it was Lutyens' cathedral he was talking about and did she have any ideas about where the plans might be kept. I don't know how she managed to keep a straight face.

'I expect the City Council has a copy of the plans,' she said. 'I should think they keep a record of all plans that are submitted. And I suppose even a cathedral would need planning approval in the normal way.'

Gerard humphed and seemed put out at this for some reason. He settled lower in his chair, frowning.

'Of course, they might keep a copy in the cathedral,' Melanie added brightly. 'To show visitors.'

Gerard looked up, and the small, thin face brightened.

'Where do you think they might be kept, if they are in the cathedral?' he asked.

'Well, let's think. What about…um…what about the crypt?'

'The crypt! Yes, of course. The one part of Lutyens' design that the backsliding weaklings actually managed to complete. How is it that just a few hundred yards down the street, the Anglicans, in exactly the same position - building work interrupted by the war, shortage of funds and all the rest of it - how come they managed to keep going and stick to the grandeur of the original concept, with something that was almost equal in scale to the Lutyens design. As always it comes down to a failure of will, a lack of resolution, a lack of courage. The bastards ought to be strung up. By God, if I had my way...'

Being used by now to Gerard's tirades we just waited for the whirlwind of indignation to blow itself out and for his colour and twitching limbs to return to something like normal.

'Anyway,' he concluded, 'doubtless you're right. It all makes sense now.'

It might have made sense to my excitable little friend, but all I could see was the start of another of his overreaching obsessions.

Naturally, it turns out he's known both of Liverpool's cathedrals since the late seventies - twenty, twenty-five years or more ago (as he looks no more than thirty himself his chronology of events is strange, to say the least). Anyway, at that time the west end of the Anglican was still unfinished, so Gerard was able to advise the Dean and Chapter on some changes to the plans, a subtle remodelling, which of course they gratefully accepted. I'm surprised he didn't advise them to have the building realigned so that the stained glass might catch the evening light more effectively. Or maybe moved six inches to the left. No doubt the idea would have been yet more gratefully received.

How he had the sheer brass nerve to come out with this stuff I don't know, and what was the point? Unless of course it was all to impress Melanie. She bought the lot. The cathedral stuff, the TT races - a good story, I admit. The utopian master plan. The invisibility theory - another good one. And the thing is, in spite of yourself it was easy to be carried, if not away, then at least a small distance by his enthusiasm. The little face lit up by those bright blue eyes, arms waving, jumping around excitedly like a child.

'Have you any idea how tall it's going to be?'

We both shook our heads.

'Five hundred and twenty feet!'

Grinning triumphantly.

'Five hundred and twenty feet from the lowest step of the West Front to the top of the lantern on the dome. Do you know, that's as tall as Blackpool Tower?'

We said, no, we hadn't known that.

'Now, all we have to do is hide somewhere in the cathedral when they lock it up for the night, then make our way to the Crypt, find the plans, and wait for them to open the doors again in the morning.'

We looked at each other, both equally confounded.

'But why?' said Melanie at last. 'Why should we do that?'

Gerard threw up his arms in exasperation.

'To get the plans, of course. How else would we build it unless we had the plans?'

'Build it!' we chorused.

'Of course we're going to build it. Do you think that I will accept such a fabulous work of art being spurned and forgotten? All we need are the plans, and somewhere to build it. And I can tell you I have one or two ideas about that.'

'But, but…'

'But nothing. People are so easily discouraged by details.'

I decided it was time to insert a large spanner into the scheme.

'Sorry to throw cold water on this idea of yours, Gerard, but I think I ought to point out that it would take hundreds of people, with a huge variety of skills and trades, all working for the best part of a hundred years to build anything as ambitious as this cathedral of yours. I wonder if you've thought about that, Gerard?'

The blue eyes flashed angrily.

'Seeing only difficulties and obstacles is the preserve of the spineless weakling. All great human events, all creative impulses, have been shaped by the will of the strong man. The weak follow where the strong man leads, and the power of leadership is in direct proportion to the magnitude of will of the individual. This cathedral will be built in my lifetime because I have willed it to be so.'

'I see. But what about the cost? We're talking about tens, or more likely hundreds of millions of pounds.'

'Finance will follow where a great, generous artistic impulse is driven by an indomitable will. The money is the least of our concerns.'

'You know, I'm glad to hear you say that, Gerard, because something that's concerning me is that your rent is three months overdue. I wonder if your will could be directed to the task of procuring and handing over the required amount?'

This gentle prompt had quite a dramatic effect. Gerard jumped up, knocking over his chair, shot me a venomous glance, swore viciously and loudly exited the room.

'Ah well, I suppose that means we won't be getting the rent for a little longer.'

'That was completely unnecessary.'

'I agree. His behaviour is becoming more and more absurd and unbalanced by the day.'

'I was talking about you. How could you insult him like that!'

'Insult him? I was asking him for the rent, for God's sake. What does he do all day, shut up in that basement?'

'He's an artist, as you well know. Have you forgotten all those wonderful canvases he brought when he moved in?'

'Forgotten? I've still got the mental scars.'

'Why do you always find it necessary to denigrate Gerard and all his achievements?'

'Tell me something - why do your critical faculties disappear whenever the little master's name is mentioned?'

'I think it's simply jealousy. It's a very negative emotion, you know. You really ought to try and overcome it.'

With some difficulty I managed to contain my resentment.

5

'Imagine! Just imagine the city - the city as it should, and could, and shall be!'

He was once again perched on one of our settees, wearing an old pair of jeans and tee-shirt streaked with paint, holding court in excited, exuberant mood, eyes gleaming with excitement as his powerful vision brought every detail to life.

'Terraces as far as the eye can see. Row upon row upon row! The matchless beauty of it! The symmetry! The soaring lines of perspective! The rhythm of repetition! The consistency of scale! The understatement of the detailing! And - oh, the beauty, the wonderful texture and colouring of the bricks! All so perfectly, so tastefully done - notwithstanding that they were built as working-class dwellings. A majestic symphony of brick given cadence by great factories, mills and chimneys. Glorious! Glorious!'

The eyes were now staring transfixed at some mythical, idealised past, or possibly some equally illusory future.

'And to think that all this beauty could be consigned to filthy, smoking piles of rubble,' the voice that had been warm and caressing a moment before now shrieking in anguish, 'by the whims of a no-talent know-nothing scum of council bastards in thrall to the backhanders of any rapacious developer who might happen to cross their path. Look!'

Now practically screaming.

'Look at it!'

I gave a puzzled look towards Melanie meaning what exactly were we supposed to be looking at? She shushed me with a frown and raised finger to pursed lips. Well, what were we looking at? Did he really think that just because he went off on one of his interminable tirades that we must necessarily see what he sees, feel what he feels. It was difficult not to be antagonised by such monstrous egotism.

And there was Melanie, laptop open but for once ignored, her face a picture of ardent admiration. Long fingers toying absently with the silver pendant suspended on a chain around her neck that dangled provocatively towards her chest. Her whole being clearly in thrall, as Gerard would doubtless have put it, to the rapacious charms of the little master.

'I've got a good idea, Gerard,' I said, wearying of this preposterous tableau. 'Why don't you rebuild all the towns and cities of Britain exactly as they were in, say, 1850?'

Even I couldn't have predicted the hilariously galvanising effect of this light-hearted suggestion. Still high on emotion Gerard was off and running with an enthusiasm which threatened to engulf even his far-flung boundaries of hyperbole. There arose great marching armies of terraces, their murky standards issuing from legions of chimney pots while tall, forbidding centurions in the shape of mills and factories and warehouses maintained an iron discipline within the ranks. It was a glorious sight to behold, even if Melanie seemed somewhat less than amused by my gentle provocation.

As Gerard expounded on the possibilities, his vision stretched from Leeds to Bradford, Halifax, Keighley and beyond, and then across the Pennines to encompass Manchester, Warrington, Wigan and Widnes before coming finally to rest, inevitably perhaps, in the industrial heartland of Liverpool. And then he saw once more the massing rows of stone sett streets stretching down towards the river, and the great sandstone mass of Scott's cathedral with its mighty tower presiding over the city, and there - there at the other end of Hope Street...

Here words failed him for a moment. But instead of the expected lightning strike of righteous anger he became strangely businesslike, the focus of his mind abruptly shifting to his greatest obsession.

'As I see it, we are faced with two main possibilities. Firstly, either we find a new site for the cathedral. Or, secondly, we use the existing, and intended site - the site of the old poorhouse on Brownlow Hill, which is what Lutyens shaped his plans to originally.'

Though reeling slightly at the abrupt change of pace I gathered that we were back in the fantastical realms of Lutyens' cathedral. I decided an attempt should be made to reacquaint Gerard with reality, both for his own good and for any mild amusement it might offer.

'Well, I think your problem there Gerard is that there's another cathedral now occupying that site.'

'That thing!' He snorted contemptuously. 'That bloody wigwam isn't worth keeping. It's only a pathetic copy of Niemeyer's Cathedral of Brasília when all's said and done. And worst of all it's sitting on top of Lutyens' crypt like some giant bird dropping.'

'Whatever its merits, or demerits, you can't just wish the building away. It's there, and there it'll stay for a good long time.'

'Perhaps,' said Gerard mysteriously, 'and perhaps not.'

'What do you mean?' asked Melanie.

'You're aware, I suppose, that those stick-like struts on Gibberd's cathedral are functional?'

'I must admit I hadn't really thought about it,' said Melanie.

'Well, it's obvious if you think about the weight of the lantern - about two thousand tons. Those struts disperse the thrust of that lantern. There's nothing within the building taking that weight. Remove those struts, or even a proportion of them, and there is nothing to prevent the whole structure from crashing to the ground.'

'But wouldn't that damage the crypt, Gerard?' I said, deflecting my attention with difficulty from the sight of Melanie looking confused.

'And then there is nothing to prevent the completion of the greatest architectural work of art of this or any other century.'

'Or millennium,' I added helpfully.

'It is imperative,' proclaimed Gerard, his voice becoming crankily insistent, 'that I go to Liverpool as soon as possible!'

Oh, my dear friend, imperative indeed, and as you quite rightly say, as soon as possible. And forever, I trust. A little back-to-back down by the docks, perhaps. My mind raced at the prospect of once again having the house to ourselves, of being able to…

'We'll take you there, won't we, Robbie?'

I leapt in alarm.

'Well, I…that is I'm sure there are many other means of - '

'It is vital that we go as soon as possible. Not only do I need to assess the weaknesses of the Gibberd cathedral, but the future of an entire area of terraced housing is at stake.'

'We don't have a problem with that, do we Robbie?'

'Well, Melanie, we'll just have to see how we - ah, now, Gerard, am I right in thinking there was a photograph or was it photographs which you said demonstrated the vital importance of detailing - you know, street furniture and so on?'

Rather touchingly the little face lit up.

'I shall show you precisely what I mean. Just wait there a moment.' And he was away, scampering down to his lair.

'Why did you have to say that, Mel?' I said, as soon as he'd gone. 'We're not really going to go, are we?'

'Of course we are. We've just agreed to.'

'Yes, I know, but it was your idea, not mine, and anyway we could experience unforeseen technical difficulties. The car could develop severe engine problems, for example, or the gearbox could explode, or a brake disc could suddenly fracture, or - '

'Don't be silly. I'm sure that as a former racing driver Gerard would know precisely when somebody - '

'Former racing driver!' I couldn't prevent myself from smiling broadly. 'Who told you that one? No, don't tell me - let me guess!'

'You may choose not to believe it,' said Melanie with great clarity, 'but in fact Gerard raced cars to a very high level, and could certainly have gone on to become world champion, but in fact chose not to.'

I tried with limited success to contain hysterical laughter, while Melanie looked on resentfully.

'Here,' said Gerard, returning and jumping back onto his perch. 'I've found it. Look at this.'

He produced a thin volume folded to reveal a grainy black and white photograph. To me it appeared a typically desolate urban nightmare from the sixties. A semi-derelict terrace of shops, one end chopped off by demolition, side by side with several bleak concrete multilevel apartment blocks. In the foreground a woman wearing a dark raincoat and clutching a shopping bag, bent over against an icy wind, was about to step into the road.

After a few moments I passed the book to Melanie who studied the photo intently. Gerard, fidgeting around as we looked at the picture, could contain himself no longer.

'Well?' he asked, eyes ablaze and arms outstretched invitingly. 'Have you ever seen a more perfect representation of the aesthetic value of detailing?'

Melanie looked up and smiled encouragingly.

'Note the stone flag pavements, the road laid with stone setts, the Victorian post box in the foreground, the gas street lamp - setting off to perfection those wonderful Victorian three-storey shops, all with their original fronts intact. This is what could have been achieved! This is what *will* be achieved! Imagine those buildings cleaned and repaired, the roofs re-laid if necessary, windows reinstated to the original specification, again if necessary, the shop fronts repainted and gleaming. Think of the effect! Think of the beauty! Think - if every shopping street was full of such character, such variety.'

'What about those blocks of flats behind them, Gerard? I don't like the look of them very much.'

'Such things are of no significance,' replied the artist dismissively. 'They shall be swept away together with all else that can be of no aesthetic value.'

Amid all the uncertainties of an uncertain world, and despite all rational reservations, the absolutes of Gerard's universe were sometimes strangely compelling. I leaned over Melanie's shoulder to see the date on the picture. But then her nearness and exquisite perfume and the cascade of gold that was her hair combined to unravel my senses so that my one, my only desire was to be alone with her, to run my fingers through that golden sheen and stroke her cheek and neck, to put my arm around her and gently caress…

'There shall be terraces as far as the eye can see. Row upon row upon row! The matchless beauty of it! The symmetry! The soaring lines of perspective! The rhythm of repetition! The understatement of the detailing! The…'

Oh my God, I could swear it's the same bloody rubbish as before. And however aesthetically striking the symmetry of repetition might be I simply couldn't listen to that garbage again. I pulled away from Melanie and sat glumly next to her. This time the little genius seemed in danger of becoming more excited than ever. Sweat was pouring down his face as he danced around on the balls of his feet, crying out with anger and hatred one moment, whimpering and pleading in anguish the next.

No doubt performance art is as valid artistically and no less demanding than other forms of theatre, and there was little question that Gerard was a master. Some might have criticised the performance as overblown, but in my view bravura acting requires a daring and panache which few have the nerve to bring off. My reservations stemmed from an element of doubt as to whether Gerard was actually in control of his performance. Was it a calculated display or was he simply a captive of his emotions? The ability to abruptly change gears emotionally suggested a conscious striving for effect, though having thrown the emotional switch he certainly then seemed drawn into a dangerous realm of disconnection from everything around him. Was giving that impression itself part of the performance, part of a carefully calculated effect creating the illusion of being out of control, with the purpose of achieving the maximum emotional impact? The layers of deception within Gerard were so numerous and entrenched as to defy ready analysis.

And all my suspicions of craft and calculation were aroused when, emotional energy apparently spent, he began drooping and stumbling around the room, clutching at pieces of furniture for support. Prompting Melanie to leap out of her chair to support and comfort him, one arm laid protectively around those manipulative little shoulders.

6

The cool early morning freshness of an overcast Sunday found us standing outside Fairfax House, with Gerard clutching a variety of pads, pens, pencils, sketch pads, paint boxes, cameras and tripods.

'Right,' prompted Melanie brightly, 'who's going in the front? Would you like to drive, Gerard?'

'No, he wouldn't like to drive. The car isn't insured for any driver, it's specifically insured for you and me.'

'I thought the insurance policy covered any driver with the permission of the vehicle's keeper?'

'No, as I've just said it specifically doesn't cover any driver, with or without the permission of the vehicle's keeper, but only the two named drivers who, as I've just indicated, are you and me.'

'Are you sure?'

'Quite sure.'

Gerard was preoccupied with juggling his equipment. Suddenly he lost control of a camera which hit the ground with a loud metallic clatter. With an equally loud oath he threw the rest of the stuff down on the pavement and picked up the camera, followed by stormy mutterings as he closely examined it for damage.

'Have the terms of the policy recently changed then?' said Melanie, turning back to me.

'No, the terms of the policy have quite recently remained exactly as they were at the time of the inception of the policy.'

'Well, shall I drive then, and Gerard sit in the front and map read, as he knows where we're going?'

'No, I don't think that's a good idea.'

'Robbie, we can't stand here on the pavement all day. Make up your mind. We're going to be late for the service at this rate.'

Gerard, by now apparently satisfied that the camera was still intact, had gathered up his various pieces of equipment and was waiting impatiently.

'I should prefer to sit in the back,' he proclaimed, 'where I shall have the space to write and sketch.'

'There you are, Melanie. Problem solved. Now, why don't you drive as you're such a beautiful driver, in every sense, and I could read the map and direct you.'

'I don't think that's such a good idea, Robbie,' said Melanie, opening a back door and helping Gerard in with all his bits and pieces. She glanced round at me. 'You know we always get hopelessly lost when you map read, and then you get angry and blame it on me for not following your directions properly.'

'I never get angry or blame it on you for not following my directions properly, and what's more…'

The car keys arced across the roof towards my head. I just managed to sidestep in time, bent down and picked them up.

'For God's sake, Robbie, let's not make this trip any more painful than it need be. Can't we just enjoy spending some time together for once?'

'Look, it's not my choice we spend so little time together. And we're not together now, are we? Not with the mighty Thor stuck in the back there.'

'Just leave him alone, will you. Get in the car.'

Once clear of the great conurbation of Leeds and Bradford the motorway twists and turns for a while before passing Huddersfield to the south. Then at last leaves what could loosely be termed civilization behind and makes its way up onto the high moors. I experienced the usual euphoria at the release and escape into open space. The car felt good and I began to press on, relishing the high closing speeds between myself and vehicles we passed. Melanie sat impassively beside me. It began to rain, and I increased my speed further so that we were diving into plumes of blinding spray before rushing out again the other side.

'It's strange, isn't it?'

Melanie looked round.

'What is?'

Tall corridors of rain moved slowly south across the moor, the surface of the road glistening, almost floating upon it.

'How even a motorway can be beautiful.'

She gazed out at the great curving lines of road, a substantial elevation change separating the opposing flows. Here and there a farmhouse, once lonely on the flanks of vast wilderness remained, trapped and isolated in the midst of noise.

'None of this shall endure!'

A familiar hollow resentment gripped me at the sudden intrusion of that rasping voice. For a short time I'd found peace amidst the grandeur of the unfolding landscape and the noise and speed of travel. Melanie twisted round in her seat.

'What won't endure, Gerard?'

He peered out through the rain-spattered windows.

'All of this shall be swept away,' he replied with a nonchalant reverse sweep of the hand.

'Robbie, look what you're doing!'

For a couple of seconds I'd found myself studying Gerard in the rear view mirror. Looking ahead I saw we were closing rapidly on a line of cars in the middle lane, half obscured by spray. I flicked the car to the outside lane, feeling it go light as we skated over a patch of standing water.

'For God's sake keep your eyes on the road.'

'Everything's under control,' I said, my heart thumping rapidly in reaction to the sudden fright. After a few seconds to calm myself I glanced briefly in the mirror.

'Surely you're not going to destroy this landscape, are you Gerard?'

His head turned from viewing the scenery.

'It is necessary that the entire motorway network be dismantled, and the land restored to its natural state.'

'Oh...wouldn't that be a little inconvenient? Especially if, like us, you were trying to cross the Pennines to Liverpool?'

'There are several perfectly satisfactory trans-Pennine routes which - and here the A59 springs immediately to mind - fulfil that function, and with full restoration to their original alignments will be both functional and aesthetically satisfying.'

'I'm sorry about that,' I said, making my voice plaintive. 'I've always rather liked the M62. I've always found it quite impressive. What about you, Mel? Do you find it impressive?'

Clearly Mel was in something of a dilemma here in terms of just how impressive she should find something which Gerard had every intention of sweeping away.

'I suppose I haven't really thought about it particularly.'

Nicely judged. But why, just for once couldn't you actually support me.

'Will you please slow down, Robbie.'

Two wagons running line astern were throwing out great clumps of vapour which towered over the road like spray demons. I lined the car up for a surprise attack, edging our speed up past the ninety mark.

The car danced a little as it hit the slipstream of the lorries, then as quickly we were through into free air.

'I won't tell you again to slow down.'

'Okay, okay, I'll slow down.'

I lifted off abruptly, then concentrated intensely for the next few miles on keeping the needle exactly on the seventy mark.

It was for the rare and brief moments that we spent alone together that I adored Melanie, wishing only that they were less rare and less brief, and that she would learn to free her mind from endless preoccupations with work and material things. She was all I needed in my universe. Whatever became of everything else was a matter of complete indifference, provided only that she was there next to me. But I needed all of her there - body, soul and emotion. Not scraps and crumbs thrown at irregular intervals. I needed an intensity of commitment and desire to match my own, and such feelings seemed increasingly beyond her emotional register.

But more than anything I needed that viper in the back out of our lives. Coping with his madness was fast becoming unsustainable. Why were we on this insane expedition in the first place? How did we get mixed up with this nonsense and actually find ourselves going to Liverpool at the behest of this arch-lunatic? The sight of his imperious image in the mirror, sitting there like some Roman emperor in a chauffeur-driven chariot caused my mood to turn abruptly to anger.

'You know, all this rubbish about terraced housing and chimneys and whatever, it's all complete nonsense.'

Melanie's goodwill dissolved as swiftly as a Siberian summer.

'Why don't you just concentrate on driving, Robbie.'

'No, wait a minute. This wonderful society of yours is based on small communities that are self-governing and self-sufficient,' I said. 'Am I right?'

'If you'd managed to stay awake when Gerard was telling us about his new society then I'm sure any objections would have been answered.'

'Is that correct?' I persisted.

'Broadly speaking, yes,' came the reply from the back.

'Fine. And if these communities, and by extension this form of society as a whole are to be truly sustainable in terms of energy supply and food production, then that means much lower population densities than at present. Is that also correct?'

I looked in the mirror. Our eyes met briefly. There was a wary, thoughtful look on his face.

'I'm not denying that is the case given the level of technology appropriate to small, self-contained communities. Let me make it clear that for the human race to progress it is necessary for there to be an end to centralised government with all its corruption, vested interests and inequities. People must learn to take control of all aspects of their lives and thereby achieve true autonomy. This is the only path to freedom and progress. And for this to happen they must be self-sufficient in the basic tools of existence. There must be sufficient land for food and energy production, time for all necessary work, yet time also for artistic endeavour. Only in this way can the human race mature emotionally, psychologically, intellectually and artistically. And yes, of course, in this society the population density will necessarily be in direct relation to the capacity of the land to produce sufficient energy and food to sustain the system indefinitely. That much is clear.'

'So far, so good, except that I can't remember where I was now...okay, so we've acknowledged that population densities are going to be much lower because your society is not based on unsustainable use of fossil fuels. Right?'

'That is correct.'

'Fine. Right. Well, in that case there simply wouldn't be any need for the high density working-class housing that you love so much. Your society is based around low population densities and sustainable local communities. High density terraced housing is incompatible with that. It makes no sense. It did make sense when it was built, providing basic accommodation for the workforce of factories supplying the world with cheap mass-produced goods. But in your brave new world that form of housing would be a senseless anachronism. Besides which it's practically all been swept away now.'

'Of course there will always be lunatics bent on desecration of all that is sacred and beautiful! Yet life should be a continuum, an organic, integrated process of steady growth and renewal.'

The poor creature, clearly rattled, had begun pleading as if with some authority above and beyond this earth. Both hands were clenched in fists held close to his face, which was contorted with emotion. His voice was pitched to compete with the noise of the engine and the rain beating on the windscreen.

'The rate of change should have been slow. It should have been at a measured, incremental pace. Think for a moment,' he said, trying to pluck some argument out of the ether, 'think of the lives that were lived there. Think of all the Christmases when children looked out on a white wonderland of snow-covered roofs through casement windows glazed with frost. They sit in front of a blazing fire, play games and chatter excitedly while their mother prepares the house. She ensures that the grate is freshly black leaded. Mistletoe is hung on the mantelpiece. Stockings are hung which next morning will be full of tangerines, nuts and toys. As dusk approaches they go out to play, and have snowball fights on the gaslit streets as they make their way to wooden-fronted shops, interiors lit by gas, gazing through the windows at all the treasures on display. And on Christmas morning the tree is lit by candles, the tiny flames dancing and flickering in the baubles decorating the tree.'

'A pretty picture you paint,' I said. 'Yet in reality many of those children would have been in rags. Too poor even to have warm clothing or any kind of footwear.'

'That isn't the point!' said Gerard, now close to hysteria. 'This is now, not then.'

'Exactly. You've got a ridiculous, idealised view of the past. And harping on about it through rose-tinted glasses won't bring it to life again.'

'You have no understanding - none whatsoever! I am telling you it doesn't have to be like that. Can't you understand that? What you are saying has nothing to do with the buildings themselves or with the built environment!'

'The buildings don't exist anymore, Gerard. Can't you understand that? It's all too late. They've gone.'

'I accept nothing! Nothing! My society shall embrace beauty, and beauty shall embrace the form of the ideal urban environment. And I shall determine its form! And it shall embrace the vibrations of all living things, the symphony of leaves, the warmth and perfume of the air, yes, even the glorious texture of bricks! Life is too precious, too perfect a gift to be cast away in stupidity, boredom and despair!'

'Oh yes!' breathed Melanie in ecstatic agreement.

'Oh, for the love of God,' I murmured under my breath. 'You're in denial, Gerard. And it's creating a dangerous tension in your mind between the two models of society you hold so dear. One is incompatible with the other, yet you can't bear to loosen your hold on either one.'

'Will you stop it!' hissed Melanie. 'Just drop it. Look, this is where we turn off. Why don't you concentrate on what you're doing.'

'You're supposed to be the map reader. Anyway, I was concentrating. I knew full well we were turning off here.'

In fact it was probably just as well that she'd reminded me. The discussion lapsed as we turned off the motorway and began an uninspiring trek through areas of decay and dereliction towards the city centre. Gerard appeared subdued. He slumped in his seat, either lost in thought or sulking. After twenty minutes or so, we pulled up outside the Metropolitan.

7

Without a word Gerard, suddenly and magically reanimated, leapt from the car and bounded up the entrance steps leaving Melanie and me looking up at his retreating back.

'Do you think he'll be wanting these sketch pads?' she asked. 'Or all this equipment?'

I shrugged.

'He can always come back for anything if he needs it.'

We set off in pursuit, walking closely together. The rain had subsided, but the sky was still troubled, tumbles of dark shapes massing and threatening. It provided a dramatic backcloth for Melanie's first view of the Metropolitan, and I could tell she was taken with it. Her expression and the way her eyes ranged over it, from sharply slanting ribs to spiky crown on the corona, showed she was intrigued, despite herself.

'What do you think?' I said. 'It's great, isn't it?'

'Well, I think it's certainly…'

We reached the top of the steps and looked around for Gerard. I caught sight of him away to one side of the entrance, arms raised in curious fashion with both hands pressed against one of the struts, feeling, stroking, as if seeking comfort or communion. I walked over to him and looked into that strange, absorbed face.

'What is it telling you, Gerard?'

His hands continued to move along the rough surface of the rib, descending towards its base, his body arching over as if in semaphore.

'This is merely cladding,' he said.

'Yes. Yes, I see,' I said, and in fact at the base of the rib where the decorative cladding stopped you could see the reinforced concrete core.

'A small explosive charge, just here,' he said, pointing to the dark space in the acute angle created where the rib contacted the ground, 'would be sufficient, I believe, to fatally weaken it. The blast would have the tendency to push the strut outwards.'

He gestured with both arms to demonstrate the effect, like a football manager frantically urging his players upfield.

'Now, if a similar charge were placed at the base of say a third of the sixteen struts - let us say just five of them - then the cumulative effect would be to completely displace one side of the building. And with the weight of the corona, all two thousand five hundred tons of it…'

'I thought you said it was two thousand?'

He began wandering around the piazza, intent on examining the other ribs.

'The precise figure is unimportant. Suffice it to say that the vertical pull of that weight will be sufficient to fracture and rip apart the remaining struts.'

He glanced around, and his eyes were gleaming.

'Like a pack of cards, the whole grotesque structure will collapse in upon itself.'

'You've obviously done your homework, Gerard,' I said.

He stood still for a moment and smirked.

'The principles of physical science upon which this model of demolition is based are straightforward in themselves, and my application of those principles in this particular instance is, I believe, unexceptionable. Of course, certain approximations have had to be made where accurate data has been unavailable.'

'Like the weight of the corona, you mean?'

He gave me a cold glare.

'All that remains to be done now,' he continued, 'is to requisition sufficient dynamite for the purpose, and of course obtain the plans.'

'I hardly think explosives are going to be that easy to come by, Gerard.'

'Nonsense. Anything is obtainable via the internet - at a price, of course.'

I was startled out of complacency. Humouring someone, tongue in cheek, was one thing, but now I was forced to wonder just how far this lunatic would go, and I exchanged a worried look with Melanie.

'Well, let's talk about it later,' she responded, with a look of concern which I took as a rare tacit acknowledgement that Gerard might actually be insane. 'In fact I'd love to have a look inside. Do you think we've got time before the service?'

I looked at my watch.

'We've got just over ten minutes, so if we go now…'

I called over to Gerard.

'We're going to look inside quickly. Are you coming?'

He was continuing to stalk the piazza, examining each rib in turn as if visualising the blinding light of an explosive blast and the cracking of concrete, and then the slow, wreaking, shuddering descent of the structure into dust.

A figure appeared between Melanie and me, close to us both. Tall, unkempt and unshaven, carrying a bundle of newspapers, mumbling indistinctly.

'They'll not get it!' is what it sounded like. 'They'll not get it!'

Intrigued, I turned to follow for a few paces. He began saying something else, this time incomprehensibly, before beginning again with the refrain, 'They'll not get it! They'll not get it!'

He was quite intent, grasping the bundle tightly, and I wondered idly who they were, and what it was they'd not get - the bundle of newspapers, perhaps? - and why they wanted it in the first place.

'Robbie? Robbie, shall we go? I'd love to see inside.'

Her hand was on my arm and she was looking into my eyes with an ardent, eager expression. Surprised and delighted, my heart for once open to her eagerness, I slipped my hands into hers, drawing her to me and kissing her fiercely. So long, so long since I'd felt this close. The warmth of her body, her loving caresses. I knew for me at least it was simply the joy of release from the suffocating claustrophobia of Fairfax House. That close, edgy captivity, locked up with a madman.

Trapped, unable to escape. We kissed again, this time a slow lingering kiss.

'Come on,' I said softly. 'Let's go.'

I took her hand and we began to hurry back towards the entrance.

'What about Gerard?' she said, looking back as we walked.

I turned. The piazza seemed empty apart from Gerard, now some distance away and down on his hands and knees, his hair brushing the ground, closely examining the base of a rib. The shambling figure with the newspapers had disappeared.

'He'll be fine. I'm sure he'll find us before we go into the service.'

The entrance porch to the cathedral had various displays showing the history of the site and construction of the present building. We wandered over to one headed 'A litany of woes', which described in detail the structural and leakage problems of the cathedral from its earliest days. The piazza over the Crypt had leaked, the aluminium roof of the main cathedral begun to crack, the walls surrounding the podium begun to lean outwards, the resin holding the glass of the lantern tower had deteriorated, the glass mosaic cladding the concrete buttresses had begun to peel. 'Perhaps not surprisingly, the question was eventually raised whether to demolish and start again.' And of course then Gerard came to mind, and suddenly his notion of sweeping the place away seemed less outlandish given that the church authorities themselves were prepared to contemplate doing exactly the same thing.

The architect - Sir Frederick Gibberd (1908-1984). Designer of Heathrow Terminal 3 and Harlow New Town. And it seemed a fair question whether someone with a track record like that should really have been let loose on a cathedral.

'Look,' said Melanie, touching my arm. She pointed to another display showing a newspaper report from the 1940s headed, 'This boy is building cathedral by himself.' It went on to tell of 19 year-old Ronald Brady, a bricklayer's apprentice left alone to carry on building works as best he could when everybody else had been called up. Apparently he could lay up to 500 bricks per day in favourable weather. The piece had inevitable poignant overtones, given Gerard's obsession. The almost heroic yet futile attempt to construct something so vast single-handedly.

I thought of Gerard reading this and calculating how many bricks he could lay in a lifetime. 500 bricks a day for say 50 years. 500 times 365 = 182,500 bricks per year. Times 50 years - that's over 9 million bricks. Though in fact the Crypt alone contained over 6 million.

And then we were confronted by a glorious full colour representation of the Lutyens cathedral, and a portrait of the man 'regarded by many as the greatest architect of the British Empire'. And suddenly I found myself almost carried away by the breathtaking presumption of both the building itself, and of Gerard's crazed notions of constructing it.

'Come on, we'd better be quick,' said Melanie, breaking the unhealthy spell.

As soon as we entered the interior of the nave our eyes were drawn to the centre of the space and the canopy above the altar, and higher still the great lantern tower suspended high above our heads where light, of all colours and in great profusion, beat down.

'It's beautiful,' said Melanie looking around. 'Breathtaking.'

Her face was calm, happy and animated, and she seemed to have forgotten Gerard's antipathy towards the building.

The extraordinary acoustical effect of the cathedral's circular form was apparent from the moment we entered, the slightest sounds coalescing and persisting for seconds on end. And Melanie's softly murmured words became a shimmer that spread and merged, one syllable into another.

We walked a circular route past thin strips of coloured light, the tall windows which in rhythm with the side chapels defined the building's perimeter. A sign warned of some experimental sanctuary arrangement. I naturally began to wonder just how experimental such an arrangement could be, and by what criteria you would judge the success of the experiment. How would such things be measured? The analysis of experimental data should be rigorous and transparent and certainly not less so in respect of - and by the time I'd completed this line of thought we'd reached the entrance again and a quick glance at my watch found us hurrying outside, down more steps and along a pavement adjacent to the cathedral site, then down another short flight of steps to the Crypt.

We stood outside for a moment shivering in the cold air. It was a forlorn, decaying area, a sad entrance to the one realised fragment of Lutyens' dream. Crumbling, exposed brickwork showed almost to the brick where work had been abandoned fifty or more years before, now half hidden by the tangle of brambles and weeds. And I found the few architectural features of the Crypt visible from the outside heavy and ponderous. There was no sign of Gerard.

'We might as well go in,' I said. 'Maybe he's already inside.'

Melanie agreed, and so we passed inside, through an entrance vestibule where we were given service sheets and hymn books by an elderly, smiling man who nodded benevolently as he passed each item to us, and then through a passage into the main Crypt chapel. I quickly scanned the small scattering of people, maybe twenty or so gathered for the service. Our small friend was not among them.

'Where do you think he can be?' whispered Melanie as we took our places in a vacant pew. My mind ranged swiftly over a number of interesting options, but I managed to temper my reply.

'He's probably been sidetracked by some architectural delight, or travesty,' I whispered back. 'I expect he'll be along in a minute.'

Melanie seemed content and began to examine her service sheet. I looked around. My first impression was that we'd inadvertently wandered into a disused railway tunnel, or perhaps more charitably the interior of a Victorian underground station. But then as I absorbed the scale and proportions of the building, the swirling patterns of brickwork, concave spaces, tall, rhythmical archways, it became undeniably impressive.

And suddenly beyond the shabbiness of neglect I was aware of the power of Lutyens' vision - arising before my mind's eye great massing towers and pinnacles of brick surmounted by enormous shining dome, and...but then I rebuked myself for susceptibility to the effect of spending too much time in Gerard's company.

The organist, hidden from view, had been forced to manufacture a number of false closes within a rambling improvisation before the sudden appearance of a pretty, white-robed girl of about fifteen with dark hair and watchful brown eyes, holding a cross and leading in the officiating clergy. They passed us along the central aisle, then took their places behind a table displaying the usual tools of the trade - chalice, Bible, cross etc. - while the girl disposed of the processional cross and stood off to one side, fiddling with a bracelet.

The priest was a young, tough-looking Irishman with short, sandy hair, assisted by an elderly and rotund cleric, who when he came to speak his lines did so with startling deliberation and evident goodwill. Behind the clergy and within a large concave niche was the altar on which stood six candles. Four burned brightly, one guttered fitfully and the last, possibly symbolically, had already gone out.

We sang the entrance hymn. The priest greeted those present and proclaimed the presence of God.

'In the name of the Father, and of the Son, and of the Holy Spirit.'

'Amen.'

'The grace and peace of God our Father and the Lord Jesus Christ be with you all.'

'And also with you.'

'Let us kneel, and confess our sins to God in penitence and love.'

> *I confess to almighty God,*
> *and to you, my brothers and sisters,*
> *that I have sinned through my own fault*
> *in my thoughts and in my words,*
> *in what I have done,*
> *and in what I have failed to do.*

I glanced at Melanie kneeling to my left, eyes closed, intoning the words with an expression of extreme piety, her extraordinary profile captured in relief against the stark brickwork. Suddenly the warmth between us that had rekindled earlier up on the piazza transformed into an awareness, almost a vision of the fragility of our love, a love so profound and so pure, and yet so often compromised through nameless jealousy and harsh words, missed opportunities and careless put-downs when just a gentle touch or kindly glance would have been so easy. And it was then that I vowed to do all in my power to make recompense - simply everything possible that could make my wonderful, exquisite Melanie happy.

And from her in return? Just to engage with me and demonstrate enjoyment of my company. A simple desire to be with me - nothing more. Then with vivid clarity I saw again the heather-covered hills and hidden glens with sparkling streams dancing gaily down, and deserted sandy bays, and a weathered stone cottage with garden full of scents and colours, and the sound of children's voices playing and laughing. Realisation struck with the force of revelation, and with it all uncertainties dissolved. A conviction that if we only took this certain path then Melanie and I would be together for all the future in peace and happiness.

Thanks be to God.

My excitement at the prospect was impossible to contain. I put my arm around Melanie's waist and squeezed her gently. She looked at me in surprise, half pleased, half discomfited by such a secular gesture within God's sight. I managed to restrain impulses towards even more profoundly secular gestures, while crying inside with anticipatory joy.

Thanks be to God.

And the price to be paid for this heaven on earth? Only the absolute and final dissociation from the source of all the stresses between us.

Alleluia, alleluia, alleluia.

This is the Gospel of the Lord.

Praise to you, Lord Jesus Christ.

The priest began his address. Over to our right a baby cradled by a black guy cried and gurgled as he tried to sooth its tiny brow, while his white partner sitting by his side leaned over and ran her finger across the child's cheek. I slipped my hand into Melanie's. She looked round once more, this time with a questioning, wondering expression before smiling and squeezing my hand in return.

So where had the little master disappeared to? Had he found the plans? Was he even now working out the logistics of the building operation? Or had he somehow been sidetracked - perhaps by the shambling man? Perhaps they'd run into one another and agreed to go into business together. Maybe they'd agreed to launch The Shambling Man Revue - a fortnightly periodical dedicated to matters of pressing aesthetic concern in which learned academics would pen esoteric articles with titles such as 'A window is an infinitely subtle thing', and 'The place of the brick in the aesthetic consciousness of the national community'. And the shambling man would in all matters be Gerard's trusted lieutenant - blindly devoted, willing and eager to carry out his master's commands without hesitation. He would in fact be Gerard's de facto number two and heir apparent, with unrivalled access to the little master. Until Gerard, afraid of the shambling man's growing power and influence, and jealous of his common touch, has him terminated.

My God, that lying, dissembling little swine. It was all a charade - an elaborate hubristic fantasy. What his precise motives were I had yet to determine, but now all my intuition led to one conclusion. That the relationship between Melanie and myself, already in a state of uneasy equilibrium, was in danger of having that delicate balance destroyed by the random factor that was Gerard, setting in motion forces impossible to predict or moderate. Reasoning was out of the question - he was beyond rational argument. The only possible solution was to cast out the creature from our lives, once and for all.

Feelings of hatred and excitement vied within me for the remainder of the service, and consumed by these thoughts time passed largely unmarked. Then everyone around me was standing and I stood and began fumbling in my hymn book.

'...and join in singing Hymn 609 : Tell out my soul.'

The organ powered noisily into life as we sang the first two verses, and I glanced down to memorize the first few lines of the third verse. Then something drew my attention to my right. I turned and was confronted by Gerard's bright blue eyes staring into mine imploringly. Almost dropping the hymn book in shock, I took an involuntary sideways step, stumbling as my foot caught on a kneeler. The stark, almost deranged intensity of his look was new and frightening, despite my familiarity with his wide repertoire of moods.

And it wasn't just the eyes. The cheeks of his thin face were more sunken than ever. The hair, never carefully maintained, was wild and unkempt. Above the scruffy jeans was that curious black velvet jacket, reminiscent of a Victorian smoking jacket. The collar half turned up, paint of various colours streaked across it and what appeared to be grit or mud on the sleeves, presumably from lying on the ground examining the ribs.

'Where the hell have you been?' I whispered, shock turning to anger.

Instead of replying he began tugging on my sleeve like a distracted child.

'What do you want?' I said, trying to pull away from his grasp but then having to lean closer to make myself audible over the singing.

'We have to go,' said Gerard at last, with an insistent, hysterical edge to that chainsaw voice.

'Go where?'

'We have to go,' he repeated. 'Now!'

I looked round at Melanie. Completely oblivious, she was still singing piously and tunefully. The tugging on my sleeve began again.

'For fuck's sake!' I said, turning back to him. 'What the hell do you want?'

I looked around guiltily, afraid my voice might have carried.

'You need to take me to Toxteth. Now. I will not stand by and see my heritage spat upon by these vile criminals.'

The voice was rising in pitch and volume, and a few people sitting close by cast swift, enquiring glances. I touched Melanie's arm, and she turned to me with a questioning look.

'Come on,' I said, keeping my voice as low as possible. 'Our small friend requires our presence.'

She looked past me towards Gerard whose face was now a picture of pleading, puppy dog anguish. You could almost hear the whimpering. But before Melanie had a chance to react, the girl with the cross appeared stage left, and priest and friends duly recessed after her. I signalled Gerard to follow them out, and we all managed to skip out of the building briskly and pretty much unnoticed.

'What is it, then, Gerard?' I asked, standing outside in the welcome coolness. 'Why drag us out of the service just when it was getting exciting - and where have you been?'

'None of that is important. I repeat that we need to move now. What are we waiting for?'

Now, my car means a lot to me. I spent a long time searching out a low mileage Golf GTi 16V in black. Yet this was a chance to spend vital time with Melanie, alone and unimpeded, and in a building I found uniquely inspirational. Clearly a time to bury my fears and grasp the moment.

'Pick us up in a couple of hours from the Anglican.'

I threw the keys to Gerard. He caught them but looked nonplussed.

'I'm sure the Dean will be sorry to have missed you.'

'I thought you said it wasn't insured for Gerard!' exclaimed Melanie.

'I've changed my mind. And please, bring it back in one piece and undented.'

Forgetting his distress and astonishment for a moment, Gerard's emotions turned to anger.

'I could do things with that car you could only dream about!'

'No doubt. However, I require only that you return it to me in its present condition.'

With one last and not very friendly look, surprising in its intensity, he walked away without a further word. Shaking my head slightly at my impetuousness, I led Melanie down Mount Pleasant and across the road to Hope Street.

8

'It's strange, isn't it?' I said as we walked comfortably together past various university buildings and terraces of imposing townhouses.

'What is?' said Melanie.

'Well, everything really. Existence. Life. Stuff like that.'

She smiled. Suddenly I felt my decision to be the only right one. I was feeling euphoric simply being out in the open and away from Gerard. Just the two of us, alone together in a great city, breathing in the heady bouquet of salty urban air. And on top of that, the prospect of sharing my dream for the future with Melanie - though I'd decided to put off revealing the plan until we were actually inside the cathedral.

'Don't you sometimes wonder what it all means?' I said.

'What?'

'Oh, you know - life, existence, stuff like that.'

She hesitated for just a moment, marshalling her thoughts.

'I tend to accept the fact of sentient life in the universe without indulging in a great deal of introspecttion as to any possible philosophical significance.'

I kicked out at an empty milk carton lying on the pavement. It arced into the air and landed more or less in the centre of the road. A thin trickle of milk trailed from the open end.

'Oh sure. Sure. Yeah, I couldn't agree more. But you can't help but wonder why we do the things we do, what our motivations are and what the meaning of it all is.'

'I prefer specifics and practicalities to broad lines of philosophical inquiry.'

'Oh sure, yeah, I couldn't agree with you more. I think that's something we've certainly got in common.'

'And speaking of specifics why on earth did you say the car was only insured for you and me when you've just let Gerard drive off in it?'

'Well, that's an interesting question and brings us, appropriately enough, into the realm of meanings and motivations.'

'So what's the answer?'

'The answer is that my decision was based on the result of a balancing process involving a number of conflicting elements of both positive and negative value.'

A crumpled sheet of newspaper tumbled towards an empty bus shelter.

'Do you know what would really make me happy, Robbie?'

I have no way of knowing for sure, but I feel reasonably certain that my pupils dilated at the question.

'No, Melanie. Please tell me.'

'It would be for you to use your undoubted abilities in a positive and meaningful way.'

'Meaning what?'

'I just think you're wasted doing what you do and that you should be aiming for something much more challenging and rewarding.'

'Such as what?'

'What I'd really like would be to see you do an Open University degree in some subject which you find of interest for its own sake - philosophy, for example, or English literature or perhaps history.'

It's true that I had once expressed some interest in the Dark Ages.

'Something that would stretch your mind, and at the same time give you a degree. Which, whether we like it or not, is a precondition for entry into the professions and indeed senior posts in many areas. I just think it's such a waste that you never completed the degree you started.'

'Melanie, why does it matter to you so much that I'm degree-less, and that my job is so mundane?'

'It doesn't matter to me at all, Robbie.'

'Surely if you really do believe I'm moderately bright then I should be worthy of your respect, irrespective of qualifications or job status?'

'Of course I respect you. My respect for someone is not based on whether or not they have a degree.'

'In fact your concern seems to relate to precisely that quality of status.'

'That's absolutely not the case, Robbie. It doesn't matter to me what you do. My respect for you, for anyone, is based on their qualities as a person, on how they interact with people and on the strength and quality of their relationships. A person could be a road sweeper, yet I would still have absolute respect for them, provided that they were a person I could respect on a personal level and that their relationships were strong and mutually satisfying.'

'How unusually objective and impersonal. Yet I don't think you understand your own feelings or motivations. I think if you were honest with yourself or with your hypothetical inner self you'd admit that you or that inner self's perception of my worth - of both words and actions - was coloured by you or this hypothetical inner self's perception of my insignificant status and your view of me as a chronic underachiever.'

'That's nonsense.'

'I thought it might well be, which is why I decided against saying it in the end.'

'Oh, you are silly sometimes, Robbie.'

She took my arm, and after a while her hand slid down and clasped mine.

'But to return to the question of motivations,' I continued, 'why do you think he's doing it?'

'Who?'

'Who do you think?'

'You mean Gerard?'

'You have grasped my meaning with an uncanny lack of hesitation.'

'Doing what, anyway?'

'Well, I suppose doing all the strange, obsessive things that he does, all of which he takes so frighteningly seriously.'

I felt, through her hand, her body stiffen.

'Robbie, please, let's not get into all that again - not today.'

'You're quite right. I'm sorry.'

The tower of the cathedral began to loom before us, and Melanie began looking suitably awestruck.

'It's big, isn't it?' she said.

I agreed that it was big, and as we got even closer it got even bigger until as we actually stood beside it, it became very big indeed, and the scale of Melanie's astonishment as she looked up at the enormous tower was in harmony with the scale of the building itself, looming menacingly above us like some great pink sandstone monolith.

'Yes, it really is big, and especially the tower,' I said, as dark grey clouds drifted past its lofty pinnacles. Melanie nodded, still looking up and still open-mouthed.

'Do you think it possible,' I ventured, 'that it might have some kind of symbolic significance?'

She finally relaxed her neck muscles and cast me an inquiring glance.

'How do you mean?'

'Well, I...um...'

From her expression I judged the worth of the joke as hardly meriting the risk of pursuing it.

'Well, what I meant was...do you know, it's even bigger inside than outside.'

She looked questioningly.

'Not literally, of course.'

Mel smiled, and we passed through the unobtrusive entrance door into the cathedral.

At first we just walked around in silence. Melanie seemed overwhelmed by the cool, visionary beauty, surveying the vastness with an expression of wonderment. To me the interior always gave the impression of having been carved from solid stone somewhere deep underground, an impression hardly diminished by the light streaming in through huge areas of stained glass. Yet conversely there was also a strong sense of the building never actually having been created by human hands, but more of having existed forever, self-defining and eternal.

After a while, and with an almost proprietorial air, I showed Melanie the way down into the Lady Chapel, the first part of the building to be completed and the most overtly pretty and ornate. She was duly charmed and delighted, and we spent some time there absorbing its own special, intimate atmosphere, before climbing the stairs back into the cavernous world of the main building.

And found ourselves at length sitting in the central space under the great tower looking towards the east window and high altar. After thirty seconds or so of mutual silence and contemplation Melanie spoke.

'I was wondering about mum coming to stay next weekend, Robbie. I thought it might be rather nice if she was able to stay Saturday night, and possibly Friday night as well.'

It would be difficult to imagine a remark less in keeping with the mood created by our surroundings, and also less consonant to my taste.

'Oh,' she continued, 'and I was wondering as well about inviting some colleagues from work over some time. Perhaps a dinner party or something one evening, or possibly just drinks. It's so nice to meet people informally occasionally with no pressure of work or pressing deadlines. I was thinking of Keith, Eunice, Peter, Colin, maybe one or two others. What do you think, Robbie?'

It was strange to talk in this vast echoing temple where every word seemed charged with super-significance. As if in this His house He was overhearing every word and leaning an acute and terrifying ear down almost through the roof of the building to pick up every nuance of our conversation.

And it had an eroding effect on the reserves of courage I'd been trying to build towards my ultimate objective.

'Melanie, look I...yes, of course, whatever you want is fine. Look, do you think we could go and have a cup of coffee? There's something I particularly want to talk to you about. I can't talk in here. It's too big. Let's go into the café.'

9

At last we were seated. Biscuits had been broken and cups stirred. But even though the moment could be put off no longer, Melanie waiting expectantly, I felt an elliptical approach to be advisable. I cleared my throat nervously.

'Melanie, I... Melanie, where, in your opinion, are we going?'

Despite any initial hesitation I was yet confident that my facial expression and tone of voice would be sufficiently rich in import as to convey the depth of meaning possibly lacking in the words themselves. Melanie's confused expression, however, prepared me for disappointment.

'Well, we're going home, aren't we - once Gerard's brought the car back?'

And I was therefore less saddened by her reply and the concomitant failure of expectation than I might have been had the expectation been more deeply entrenched. Though given Melanie's level of intellect I did sometimes wonder whether this apparent obtuseness was a conscious ploy.

'That's not quite what I meant. Look Melanie, I've been thinking and I...I'm so sure now what I would like to happen. I know exactly where I'd like our lives to go.'

'What's this about, Robbie? What are you trying to say?'

'It's about us. I'm talking about where I want our lives to go.'

I shifted in my seat uncomfortably. This was more difficult than I'd anticipated. The adrenaline and excitement I'd felt down in the Crypt had subsided a little under the tension of trying to find suitable words to express my feelings. Or perhaps it was just the sight of Melanie staring levelly back across the table at me, a picture of wary neutrality.

'Look, I'm perhaps not managing to be very adept, and also at certain times in the past have also perhaps not always managed to be very adept at expressing my feelings. I know I can be a little turned-inwards emotionally sometimes. But I...I hope you know...you do know, don't you, that I really do love you?'

She smiled. A smile that managed to stretch her lips quite widely, almost violently in fact, thereby revealing a considerable number of shining white teeth. After a few moments she relaxed and took a sip of coffee. I tried to refocus on what I was saying.

'And...and what I want - what I would like - would be for our lives to be more than they are at present, very wonderful though that is. Because sometimes that very special thing that we have between us becomes somewhat obscured by all the trials of daily life.'

'What trials are you referring to specifically?'

Sometimes it was like wading through glutinous mud.

'Well, the trials to which I am referring to specifically, or specifically referring to, include such things as the paying of bills, the doing of housework, the daily grind of work, and possibly one or two other things.'

'What sort of things?'

'Well, things like...look, Melanie, this is a very difficult thing to say when it comes to the point, so I'm going to just come straight out and say it.'

In fact I was surprisingly nervous when it came to the point of actually saying those age-old, momentous words, notwithstanding that we'd lived together as a couple for some time.

'Melanie, I love you more than life itself, and I want to spend the rest of my life with you. So I'm asking you...well, the thing is...will you marry me?'

Her perfect eyebrows rose abruptly.

'You mean...marriage?'

'Your perception does you credit - once more you have interpreted my meaning precisely.'

'But...I thought you didn't believe in marriage. You've always said it was an outmoded and archaic institution.'

Melanie had a remarkable if selective memory for my past pronouncements - usually the more foolish ones.

'I don't believe in it - theoretically. But theory is one thing, and reality is another. And marriage is a third thing, with little to do with either of the others.'

'What are you talking about?'

'Look Mel,' I said, reaching out and taking both her hands in mine and gazing deeply into those exquisite cornflower eyes, 'I want you to come away with me. I want us to build a new life together. I want so much for us to be closer, and we can only do that if we build a life together.'

'We are together now, Robbie. We're a couple who live together in a house we jointly own. I don't understand what more you want.'

'I want you, for God's sake! I want all of you! Not just fragments fitted in and around some damned inexorable timetable. I seem to hardly see you, and when I do you're either working on some work you've brought home, or thinking about some work you've brought home, or doing something to that bloody house. Why can't you just do nothing sometimes? Why does there always have to be this goddamn ceaseless activity? It's like some sort of neurotic compulsion with you.'

Melanie withdrew her hands from mine, her expression stiff and inflexible.

'Look, I'm sorry…I didn't mean that.'

I tried to breathe deeply in an effort to relieve the tension in my chest and stomach.

'All I want,' I began slowly, 'is for us to go somewhere where we can be together all the time. Say we…just suppose we were to sell our house. We'd probably make enough profit to buy a little two bedroom cottage somewhere. That's what I want to do, Mel. I want us to move up to the Highlands together. Just the two of us. Property's cheap up there. We'd be able to buy somewhere outright with no burden of mortgage. Then we'd find some work we could do together. My God, Melanie, think how wonderful it would be! We'd be together all the time for the rest of our lives. We could bring up our children there. They'd have the space and security to grow up in the way we'd want them to.'

My ardour was met by uncertainty and perplexity.

'Robbie, I don't think I'm quite ready for children yet.'

'But we've already got names for them.'

Her expression immediately softened. There was even the hint of a smile.

'I know.'

'So?'

'Robbie, we can't have children just because we've thought up funny names for them.'

'Why not? Why does there always have to be a logical, sensible reason for everything? Why do we not just follow our instincts - do what our hearts tell us?'

'Robbie, I...I don't know what to say. There are so many reasons why I can't do what you're asking. For one thing, you talk about my career as if it doesn't matter. My work is important to me. I have a fairly important position at Lundy's - I'm directly responsible for a number of people who depend on my input. I can't just leave my job.'

'For God's sake, give your ego a rest. You're not performing some vital public service. You're a cog in the retail machine, just like me. A little higher up the scale, maybe, but of no greater social value.'

'Who are you to define what is and isn't of social value?'

'Christ, I couldn't care less whether a job has social value or not. All I'm saying is that retail doesn't exactly provide a basic public service like…well, like nursing or teaching or the fire service or whatever.'

'I see. And where do people working in those areas go when they need food or washing powder or a huge range of other goods and services?'

'I don't know. You'll have to give me a hint.'

'All I'm saying, Robbie, is that nothing is quite as clear cut as you're suggesting. Modern society is a complex of mutually dependent and symbiotic inter-relationships within a defining paradigm of…'

'Oh my God! Oh my God!'

I began making involuntary screeching noises which attracted some attention from nearby tables.

'For God's sake stop it, Robbie. You're embarrassing me.'

'Am I? Am I really? Then you are actually capable of emotion? This day has certainly been full of surprises.'

'Right. Shall we go?'

'No. I haven't finished saying everything I want to say.'

'Well, I think I've finished hearing everything I want to hear.'

'Does what I want really mean nothing to you?'

My evident pain for once breached those normally impenetrable defences, as her tone of voice and expression relented a little.

'Robbie, what would we do if we actually did what you're suggesting? How would we live - how would we pay the bills?'

'I don't know in detail. That's surely part of the adventure. Maybe we could start a business together - maybe we could run a shop or taxi service or something. And I'd like to start doing something creative - like, maybe writing music, for example.'

I said it tentatively, the idea having sprung unbidden to mind.

'But you don't know anything about music, Robbie.'

'Well, I'll learn. I could take lessons in composition from Gerard before we finally bid him farewell - I expect he taught Beethoven at some point or other. Please, just marry me, Melanie! Say you'll marry me and let's start a new life together and commit fully to each other.'

'Robbie, I don't know if...I'm just not completely ready for marriage yet.'

'Why not?'

Melanie was silent. A silence which filled my heart with a tight, gnawing bleakness. I looked across at a young, attractive couple sitting at a table. The woman was holding a baby boy of about six months, jiggling him while he looked around with wide eyes. You could tell he was a boy because he was dressed in blue. Between the parents sat a young girl, maybe three years old, with blond ringlets and a pink, hooded coat, playing with a Barbie on the table. You could tell she was a girl because her coat was pink. I felt a blend of loathing and vicious envy for their unthinking happiness as they chatted and cooed and pulled happy faces at each other.

'Anyway, what would happen to Gerard if we moved?'

I looked back at Melanie's face, trying to summon up surprise or any other neutral emotion at her apparent incomprehension, at the complete disregard for my feelings. A face so beautiful, like an idealised mask of innocence.

'You're quite right. That's certainly the important consideration. That little fuck-shit.'

The last comment made under my breath.

'What did you say?'

'I said the hell with it.'

She looked away for a moment, then back towards me.

'Going back to what we were discussing earlier, Robbie, is that okay, then, if I go ahead and arrange things?'

'Is what okay, then, if you go ahead and arrange what?'

'Is it okay if I invite some people from Lundy's over for drinks some time? Not next weekend, as Mum's coming then but maybe the weekend after?'

I closed my eyes for a few seconds, unsure as to which of many emotions raging within me was dominant.

'Oh sure. Why not? Certainly. It'll be something to look forward to. After all, everyone needs something to look forward to. To relieve the monotony as much as anything. Otherwise life would become an unending desert of loneliness, an emotional vacuum, in fact a complete symbolic paradigm of…whatever. And be sure to invite the key players. Don't waste your time with nonentities or deadwood. Life isn't short enough for that.'

'Okay, well shall I make it for around seven, then, on Saturday evening?'

'Sure. Why not? Certainly. It'll be something to look forward to. After all, we all need something to look forward to.'

'Well, shall I see if mum wants to come over in the morning next Saturday, then? Maybe fairly early so we've got the whole weekend? Or maybe even Friday night.'

'Oh sure. Sure. Why not? In fact the earlier the better. It'll be something to look forward to.'

'Robbie…Robbie, you're not angry with me, are you?'

'Angry? Me? God, no! I don't think I'm capable at this moment of feeling any emotion worthy of the name. Oh, I don't know though. Gluttony, maybe? Is that an emotion or just a character flaw?'

Melanie sighed and took a last sip of cold coffee. Her cup made a hollow clicking sound as she replaced it on the saucer.

'We really ought to think about looking out for Gerard now.'

'You certainly should. Unfortunately I won't be able to join you on this occasion. I've decided to take the train back to Leeds.'

'What?'

'I said I've decided to let the train take the strain, as I certainly can't take any more.'

'Don't be so silly, Robbie.'

'Was I using the wrong words? Oh well, perhaps you're right. But I liked the sound of them so much I decided to use them anyway.'

'You're not really taking the train back, are you?'

'Yes, I am. And in fact I'm going now,' I said, scraping my chair back abruptly.

'Robbie, please!'

When I reached the door of the café I turned and looked back. Melanie, still at our table but now standing, was looking at me with a pleading, tragic expression, the corners of her mouth pulled down alarmingly. And part of me wanted desperately to run back, take her in my arms and softly kiss those depressed lips. But the gulf was of her own making and it would have required superhuman generosity of spirit, beyond my capacity at that moment, to bridge the gulf. I walked out of the café, made my way out of the cathedral and without looking back set off towards the station. I took perverse comfort in the rain that was soaking my face and hair, and was now beginning to run down my neck.

10

Lydia. Such a musical and romantic name for such a small and ill-favoured woman. And Lydia's opinion of me was equally ill-favoured. Tending to range from average for the time of year to disappointing. From autumnal to wintry. From biting offshore northerly to positively cyclonic. In fact, I believe that she saw in me a light not necessarily more divine than her beautiful, clever daughter. Indeed, not to hedge around the issue, I knew she regarded me as a nothing, a nobody, a loser, someone with a nothing job and no ambition or prospects, and I think her great consolation was that we hadn't actually married, and therefore in her eyes the relationship was a merely temporary affair - a stopgap.

After returning from the bathroom Melanie walked around the room for a while, tidying up and putting things away. I experienced the familiar surge of desire watching her. That graceful, sinuous movement. The calm, exact beauty - the closeness of her, bending down in tight-fitting jeans to pick some item of clothing from the floor. Tumbles of golden hair flicked back over her shoulders as she stands up straight. Tossing her head like some eager thoroughbred with exquisite self-absorption. She glances towards me.
 'You know mum will be here in the morning, don't you?'

'Yes, I know.'
'It's a pity she wasn't able to come tonight.'
'Yes, it is a shame.'
'I'm sure we'll find some interesting things to do.'
'Yes, I hope so.'
'The garden's looking so pretty still.'
'Yes, it is.' A pause. 'What time is she coming, by the way?'
'Some time around ten o'clock, I would think - depending on the traffic.'

My mind wanders abstractedly, but I notice her give me a look accompanied, as our eyes meet, by a small smile. She finishes folding a tee-shirt, puts it in a drawer and slides the drawer shut. Then walks to the dressing table, sits down and studies her reflection for a few moments.

What was she thinking, seeing that extraordinary image looking back at her? I was never certain that she understood the value of what she possessed. To lack conscious, or at least evident, vanity would generally be accounted a positive characteristic, but surely in Melanie's case it implied either lack of aesthetic awareness, or else a freakish, almost disturbing level of self-control. For me there was an almost voyeuristic pleasure in observing Melanie and marvelling at her beauty, a beauty that remained a shining ideal, which nothing else came close to matching. Yet now I found myself desperately wanting also the closeness of a mutually responsive relationship. All that rubbish about the Open University - some damn degree or other, when she must have known I wasn't remotely interested. Of course, there is beauty even in self-absorption, in the dedicated realisation of self. But Melanie seemed self-immersed to a frightening degree.

She took a wipe from a box on the dressing table and began cleansing her face. I far preferred her without make-up, in fact had suggested on a number of occasions that she dispense with it entirely. Such beauty unadorned was such a rare gift. That she might one day actually require make-up, that such an icon of aesthetic perfection might be blemished and compromised by age was a repudiation of the concept of order and sense in a perplexing universe - I simply refused to accept it.

She threw the used wipe into the bin, then took another, dabbing some perfumed astringent on it before wiping around her eyes with delicate circular movements. There followed various other potions, the room now filling with that familiar combination of fragrances - warm, comforting and feminine.

Yes, you could interpret it simply as commendable lack of vanity. But surely even Melanie must struggle to accept the self-possessed vision staring back at her as normal - as an image one might reasonably expect to find returning one's gaze? That would require a superhuman lack of self-awareness.

She began rubbing cream into her face and hands, and as she did, and as the familiar perfume led to a wealth of happy associations, we were walking once more down a grassy path within the grounds of some ancient ruin. Warm, embracing light falling carelessly beneath a spreading tracery of green. A smiling, caressing breeze touching our faces. Hand in hand, gazing into an infinitely distant haze and a future without boundary or limitations. Experiencing beauty, tasting the eternal.

Dear, beautiful Melanie. I need you close beside me, always - I need to embrace your eternal beauty in a setting equally timeless.

Yet recently there were times when the future seemed to hold only the promise of dust. Immutable time had been a fleeting promise, and my mind was heavy with the transience of things.

'Gerard has promised to be around to meet mum.'

'That's good.'

'I can't understand how they haven't met before.'

'No, that is surprising.'

She glanced at me in the mirror, her look assuming an anxious quality.

'We will have a nice time this weekend, won't we Robbie.'

I find a smile.

'I hope so.'

'He's still very upset.'

This time I don't reply. I fix my eyes on her back. Still seated at the dressing table, she begins unbuttoning her shirt. She looks into the mirror again - I suspect a slight hardening of her previous glance, and quickly turn my eyes away. It was true that Gerard's behaviour had been yet more strange and unbalanced since our trip to

Liverpool. Things had begun to accelerate down an increasingly steep incline.

She stood and removed her shirt, placing it carefully over the back of the chair, then unhooked her bra.

'These things don't matter to him as such,' I said, watching her, my voice sounding colder and harder than I'd intended.

'What do you mean?'

She turned and stood before me - bare-breasted, impassive, self-assured. With difficulty I tried to focus on my argument.

'All this talk of terraces and warehouses and stone setts and all the rest of the rubbish he comes out with. I don't think they really matter to him in themselves.'

'Of course they matter. What do you mean?'

'Don't you see, these things are merely symbols of events which he can't control. It could have been anything - anything outside of his direct control, which of course includes practically everything. He's just latched onto one visible and recognisable phenomenon, that is housing regeneration, and with the sentimentality of distance has imbued housing of the past with a meaning and aesthetic significance far beyond its worth. It's a kind of madness - the utter pointlessness and depth of his obsessions.'

She reached for her pyjama top folded neatly at the foot of the bed, slipped it on and began buttoning it up. It irritated me intensely that I so rarely got to see her completely naked. She dressed and undressed in stages, following an unvarying routine.

'I don't agree with you. You only had to see how disturbed he was when we came back from Liverpool. That demolition scheme had really upset him.'

She undid the button of her jeans, and pulled down the zip.

'Disturbed. That's an interesting choice of expression.'

She pulled her jeans down, sat on the side of the bed for a moment to remove them, and then went over to the chair by the dressing table and placed them over it. Of course, theoretically there was nothing stopping me from gathering Melanie in my arms and assisting her into a state of complete undress - kissing her lips softly, whispering gentle, caressing words as our embraces became increasingly urgent and passionate. Somehow it never seemed to happen, in fact rarely even seemed appropriate.

She put on her pyjama bottoms, then pulled back the duvet cover.

'Aren't you coming to bed?'

By the time I slid in beside her, Melanie appeared to be asleep. Her back was turned to me, and her breathing was quiet and regular. Frustration condensed into anger, which by a process of transference became directed towards Lydia.

It was a mutual antipathy. I found it difficult, disliking Lydia so much, that she and Melanie were close, with a relationship from which I was necessarily excluded. Enmity towards one bled relentlessly to the other.

Mel's dad, Thomas, had been a builder. I'd never met the guy, or even seen a photo, but judging by the small, dark creature that was Lydia, Melanie must have inherited her Nordic beauty from him.

They'd built a detached red brick house in Mel's home town of Keighley. We'd driven past the house once, in our early days together - a large, paved forecourt where the vans had been parked, the upstairs window which had been her bedroom. I'd looked up and seen teddy bears in the window, stars in bright colours stuck to the pane and pretty pastel curtains. Presumably still some little girl's bedroom. I'd looked closely at Melanie's face as we passed, but whatever emotions she might have been feeling failed to register visibly.

The business had been a family-run venture employing around half a dozen people at its peak, with Lydia taking care of the accounts. After three or four years the after-work drinking sessions had become an everyday affair. The vans began to arrive back later and later. After one long session Thomas managed to put one of them through a hedge and onto its side, suffering cuts and concussion. But one of the lads sitting in the back had been badly injured and had taken several months to fully recover.

The negative publicity for the firm and subsequent loss of momentum signalled the end of the business. He lost his licence and became depressed and withdrawn, which he attempted to deflect by drinking heavily, while Lydia's anger settled into a deep resentment. When Melanie started school Lydia took various part-time jobs to try and keep the family together, but the marriage was effectively over. They divorced when Mel was six, the family house was sold, and Mel and her mother went to live in a small mid-terrace in another part of Keighley.

You couldn't really blame the woman for wanting someone substantial for her daughter. A doctor or barrister, maybe. Some kind of professional - perhaps an astrophysicist or motorcycle racer - somebody with serious career intentions. It wasn't difficult to understand why she resented my casual attitude to work. Melanie went back there sometimes, staying with her mum for a night or two. And she still kept up some kind of contact with her father.

That night I dreamed of rain, persistent and penetrating. Everywhere rivers overwhelmed their banks. I was driving down a narrow lane lined with stunted, withered trees. The road became a stream, and then a fierce torrent. Perched on top of a steep bank, as if deposited there by a sudden surge was a small blue hatchback, leaning sharply towards the swirling brown water. On the other side I caught sight of an elderly couple, bowed down as if by the weight of the downpour. Their heads were uncovered. They were forlorn and bedraggled, standing as if in silent tribute before some memorial. They had their backs to me, so I never got to see their faces.

Mum and dad were killed in a traffic accident when I was eight. I saw the police car drive up to school. I think I had some vague idea it was for a road safety talk. I was called through to the headmistress' room, where two police officers were waiting to speak to me. I stayed in her room until somebody came for me, presumably social services, and I ended up being fostered to a number of people. Lastly and for the longest period to a couple called Dave and Hilary.

11

Morning dawned bright and clear. I tried to greet it positively from behind a pressing, heavy headache. I turned slowly over in the bed, then reached out a hand to where I thought Melanie was lying. Meeting no resistance I raised myself on one elbow and peered at the empty space beside me before collapsing back into the sheets, shielding my eyes from the harsh light streaming through the curtains. My feelings were of inertia, sadness, regret, hopeless longing.

As a diversionary tactic I tried to calculate how long the journey from Keighley to Leeds would take, running through an inventory of all the potential dangers lurking along the route. It was not a generous or cheering line of thought, and I quickly abandoned it, closing my eyes, trying instead to think of nothing.

Sometime later I opened them again. Melanie was leaning over me, and for a moment my heart soared with joy and anticipation.

'Mum's here. We're just going to be out in the garden.'

And then it sank once more into the mattress.

'It's quite late,' she added, looking down at me with an indiscernible expression. 'Are you getting up?'

As far as looks were concerned it was difficult to see any resemblance at all between Melanie and her mother.

In fact, it seemed improbable that Lydia could have played any part in her creation. My stomach tensed as I approached them, sitting together at the camping table set up on the lawn, two pairs of eyes steadily following me as I approached. The tight, wiry hair, still dark but now flecked liberally with grey, seemed to press tightly on her skull, itself a size too large for her body. The hair and face together were like an expensive latex mask, hideously realistic.

'Good morning, Robert. You're a late riser.'

And you're an evil dwarf, but you don't hear me complain.

'Hello, Lydia. How nice to see you. An uneventful journey, I trust?'

'What are you having for breakfast, Robbie?'

'I'm not sure.'

'Well, do you want to get what you want and then you can come and join us.'

'Certainly. Nothing would give me greater pleasure.'

Nothing, that is, except sudden, violent and painful death. But as the possibility of that on such a fine, warm Saturday morning was remote, barring an unfortunate accident with the bread knife, it looked as if I was stuck with a throbbing headache and Lydia.

I wandered back into the kitchen to look for the knife. And find some bread, plus a packet of painkillers. I toasted the bread, made a coffee, found something for my head and took them outside. Lydia's quick eyes took in the tablets on the side of my plate.

'Have you got a headache, Robert?' she said, with a look of concern.

'Yes. It's difficult to say what might have caused it, although I did have some trouble getting to sleep.'

'Well, I hope you feel better soon.'

'Thanks, I hope so.'

'So,' she said, after a sip of coffee, 'are you still working in the retail sector, Robert?'

'Yes, I remain still firmly lodged in retail.'

'Melanie tells me you're thinking of doing an Open University degree.'

'Does she? That's interesting.'

The lines on the face were deep and unforgiving.

'Oh, I thought this was something definite.'

'No, I'm afraid there's nothing definite at present.'

'But what course were you thinking of doing?'

And no doubt there was another, unspoken side to her parents' break-up. It was all too easy, with the benefit of hindsight, to confuse cause and effect.

'We hadn't personally decided, I mean I hadn't personally decided. I mean Melanie had put forward a number of options, but I can't remember offhand which was the least unfavourable.'

'We'd discussed English and philosophy,' said Mel coldly.

'That's an interesting coincidence,' said Lydia, with a smile of recollection, 'as one of my neighbours, an elderly gentleman, has just completed a course in creative writing. Well, I say elderly, but in fact he's hardly older than me. Apparently his tutor was very impressed with his work. She suggested that he submit a couple of his short stories to a magazine. You know Mr. Smith, don't you Melanie - from over the street, almost directly opposite?'

'Probably. I don't know the name.'

'I'm sure you'll know him. He's a tall, very upright man with a white beard. A very courteous, correct gentleman. He was a petty officer in the merchant navy.'

'I've probably seen him.'

'Yes, I'm sure you will have done. He walks with a limp. He told me he fell down a ladder in the engine room and damaged a knee.'

I choked on a mouthful of coffee. After recovering my composure I asked which knee had been affected.

'The right knee, I believe. I think they're waiting for it to get a bit worse and then they'll give him a replacement.'

'That was pretty unlucky.'

'What was, Robert?'

'Falling down a ladder like that - especially in a...in a confined space like...'

I was momentarily unable to continue.

'Well, he told me they were caught in a storm, with very high winds, and the engine room had shipped quite a quantity of water. So I think the ladders were quite slippery.'

'I'll bet they were. Though I expect he's been in quite a number of storms, typhoons even.'

I glanced at Melanie, who was wearing a grim, fixed smile.

'I don't know if it was a typhoon as such. He doesn't speak much about his years at sea.'

'I'll bet it was a typhoon. In fact, I'll bet the majority of his stories are about typhoons. And shipwrecks, and mutiny on the high seas. With maybe the odd uninhabited tropical island thrown in for good measure - oh, and pirates as well, of course.'

Lydia laughed pleasantly, somewhat diminishing my enjoyment.

'So, are all his stories seafaring yarns, Lydia?'

'Not all,' she replied, still smiling disarmingly. 'He lent me the manuscript of an excellent short story about two Asian shopkeepers locked in a semi-friendly rivalry with each other. It was very amusing, and extremely well written. He's really very talented, and the most pleasant and entertaining man. In fact I'm very lucky altogether with my neighbours.'

She turned to Mel, who appeared to have adopted a state of Zenic calm by contemplating a slice of organic wholemeal toast.

'So when am I going to meet this lodger of yours?'

'I spoke to him this morning in passing,' said Melanie, taking a needlessly aggressive bite. 'I think he'll be coming out to join us shortly.'

'I can't quite remember his name, dear. Is it...'

'It's Gerard.'

'That's right. Gerard.' She mused for a few moments. 'So how do you get on with him, Robert?'

You might as well ask how one handles a snake.

'Absolutely fine. He's no trouble at all. Although I like to think of him more as a guest than a lodger. Or even a friend.'

'I'll go and see where he is,' said Melanie, rising abruptly. 'He can join us for breakfast.'

I watched Melanie disappear through the French windows. Lydia turned a concerned face to me.

'You know, Robert, I was just thinking that Melanie's looking very tired today. Has she been sleeping properly?'

'I hadn't noticed anything in particular. She seemed to sleep well enough last night.'

'I thought she was looking rather strained and anxious this morning. Perhaps it's just the pressure of work. I know she's particularly busy at the moment.'

I smiled.

'I have to tell you, Robert,' she continued, 'and I hope you don't think I'm interfering, but I'm quite concerned about this lodger situation.'

'In what way?'

'Well, I'm worried that having someone else living in the house with you, a relative stranger, could give rise to…well…tensions between you and Melanie.'

'Has Melanie been talking to you about Gerard?'

'I've heard one or two things about him which I find quite worrying. He seems a very strange young man. As far as I can make out he doesn't appear to have a proper job, or any job at all.'

'He's an artist, a writer, a politician in embryo and a whole host of other things. But none of these pay the rent.'

'Doesn't he pay any rent?'

'No, not a thing. He's supposed to, of course. It's just that he doesn't.'

'But surely that was the whole point of taking in a lodger?'

'Precisely.'

'And have you discussed this with Melanie?'

'Of course, repeatedly. He's given her the impression he's going to make a fortune by selling off his works of art. But any prospect of that is, believe me, remote.'

'This all seems so uncharacteristic of Melanie. She's usually so perceptive in her dealings with people.'

'Well, everybody has their blind spot. And Gerard does have a certain way with him. For the unwary, I think it can be quite beguiling.'

'I wouldn't put Melanie in that category.'

'Neither would I as a general rule. But there's no question that Gerard is very adept at manipulating people's emotions.'

'Do you like your lodger, Robert?'

I looked at her closely, wary of committing myself beyond a certain point, and aware that she in turn was observing me intently.

'Let's just say I prefer to maintain a certain distance in my dealings with him. I try to avoid being sucked into his schemes and preoccupations.'

Further discussion was shelved as Melanie returned. The contrast between mother and daughter, especially after several minutes exposure to Lydia, was extreme. As if stepping from some classical depiction of absolute beauty, Melanie's grace of movement seemed especially ethereal, her hair ebbing and flowing like some restless golden tide as she approached.

'Gerard will be out in a moment.'

Even as she spoke a small, dark shape emerged from the house. My insides tightened in a familiar grip as the shape came slowly closer to view. Unshaven and with dark smudges beneath the eyes, the little artist seemed barely capable of reaching the table as he stumbled dejectedly down the path. Melanie, on the point of sitting down, leapt to his side, guiding him with consoling words and steadying arm to a vacant chair, into which he collapsed dramatically. But instead of then remaining inactive, as one might have hoped and expected, after a few moments he suddenly sat rigidly upright, fists tightly clenched, staring intently in front of him.

'Vile criminals!'

The tormented scream erupted without warning and reverberated across the garden and over the walls of surrounding houses, seeming to hover in the air like some corporeal object, while everything in its path - every flower and shrub and tree and inanimate thing it encountered - seemed directly accused, or at least in some measure complicit.

'Evil lunatics and criminals! The destruction of beauty is tantamount to cold-blooded murder! The destruction of communities, with all their complex of interrelationships, is destruction of beauty equally profound, an action equally vile. Such ruthless acts of murderous intent directed against the national community must and shall be subject to the appropriate penalty!'

This was better than anything I could have hoped for, and compensated in some measure for having to endure his presence. Lydia's expression was one of disbelief, her face suddenly stiff with tension.

'Every fixture, every fitting, every lamppost, every house, every street, every community, every town and every city shall be rebuilt to their precise and original design. Everything shall be exactly as it was. But,' and here two imploring hands reached to the heavens as the insistent voice became yet more shrill, 'but - oh God! - but even then all history, all sense of continuity will be lost. Lost forever at the hands of moral degenerates and psychopaths! Insects that shall be crushed beneath my heel, with not a flicker of hesitation.'

If this performance was intended as some kind of ploy, the striking of a pose for some perverted purpose or other, it seemed to have seriously misfired. Lydia's face was taut, tight-lipped and silent. Melanie, aware of her mother's reaction and already twitching in acute discomfort, now jumped up and went over to Gerard, whispering something in his ear.

The transformation was extraordinary. Like turning a switch, Gerard rose, swept back his hair, and with a kind of precious and contrived gravity approached Lydia and extended a hand across the table, while bowing from the waist with preposterous formality. For a moment I thought he would kiss her reluctantly outstretched hand, but instead he was content to firmly grasp and shake it while intoning 'Lydia,' in a deep and vibrant tone. He then embarked on a series of enquiries as to the comfort of her journey, proposed length of stay and enjoyment of the weather, all of which received a curt response.

Undeterred, and with an initial jaunty enthusiasm Gerard began addressing Lydia at length. The subject of politics was introduced with a bold flourish and copious hand gestures. After a brief lecture on the preconditions for a sustainable society there followed a modulation to the aesthetic aspects of urban development, segueing through symbolism in art and the poetic beauty of motorcycle racing, to finally achieve a fitting coda in the familiar shape of Lutyens' cathedral.

Yet despite the artistry of the presentation, each topic received such a frozen-faced response from Lydia that even Gerard struggled to misinterpret the hostility. His confusion was palpable, the words faltering and dwindling until at last they ceased entirely, and he was left sitting silent and despondent, shoulders hunched and head bowed, for all the world like an abandoned waif.

My enjoyment of this scene, though considerable, was nevertheless seriously compromised by a number of hostile looks from Melanie, of an intensity which increased proportionately with each of Gerard's conversational miscues - as if it was my fault they hadn't hit it off. In the long silence that followed, Melanie, who'd been regarding Gerard earnestly and anxiously, turned to me and spoke crisply.

'Would you bring Gerard some toast please, Robbie?'

I looked at her and frowned.

'Can't he bring his own - '

'If you use the unsliced wholemeal loaf that's in the - '

'I know where the bread is.'

'You can slice it using the large knife with the serrated - '

'I know which knife to use.'

'If you could just toast two or three slices - do you want any more, mum?'

'What's that, dear?'

Melanie took a deep breath.

'Would you like any more toast? Robbie's going to bring some.'

'That's kind of you, Robbie.'

Was the smile that accompanied the words sincere? The deliberations of a well-hung jury on the matter might have been extensive yet inconclusive.

'I feel it's the least I can do, given the circumstances.'

'Well, perhaps just one slice. Thank you.'

'That's perfectly okay. Now, what about you, Melanie - would you like some more toast?'

'I don't want any toast.'

'Fine. Now what about drinks - would you like another drink, Lydia?'

'A coffee would be lovely if you're making one.'

'No problem at all. How about you, Gerard?'

The little artist was sunk in profound meditation.

'Just bring Gerard a cup of coffee, Robbie.'

'Fine. How does he take it?'

'You know how he takes it. Look - just go and get it will you, Robbie - or do you want me to go?'

'No, no, no. I shall go. I will go. I am just going.'

Melanie got up abruptly.

'I'll get the drinks. This will take forever otherwise.'

'Okay. It'll be nice to have your company.'

Once in the kitchen, Melanie turned on me with angry, accusing eyes.

'You're determined to ruin this weekend, aren't you? All I wanted was a quiet, relaxed time with mum, and you're trying to spoil it all with your usual clever comments.'

I stopped what I was doing in surprise and shock - as much at the bitterness of tone as the words themselves, the knife still clasped in my right hand, my left resting lightly on the uncut loaf.

'Why can't you just be pleasant and sincere for once, instead of always winding people up.'

'I haven't done anything. Why are you getting so angry with me?'

'It's so unnecessary. Why can't we just have a nice time together? Do you really think people don't notice?'

'There isn't anything to notice, for fuck's sake. Your mother doesn't like Gerard. Haven't you noticed that? For someone so supposedly intelligent you can be remarkably obtuse at times.'

She took a threatening step towards me, prompting me to take a step backwards, the knife still clutched tightly in my grasp.

'What have you been telling her about Gerard to prejudice her mind against him?'

'Oh, so you did notice that they didn't exactly hit it off, then? I didn't do anything prejudicial to our little friend. She asked me one or two questions, and I gave her one or two accurate answers.'

'Accurate answers!' she repeated in a cold, sarcastic tone. 'Yes, I can imagine what your version of accuracy might be like. Shall we say somewhat inaccurate.'

'Hey, that's pretty funny.'

'Oh…just get on with what you're doing.'

She switched the kettle on and started rattling some cups around. Why was she so hostile to me all of a sudden? Why always so quick to take that little fuck-shit's side in everything? I watched her for a moment as she picked up the coffee jar, surprised as ever to see something so exotically beautiful doing something so mundane. And her emotions and responses were just as enigmatic, as inexplicable as ever. I turned my attention reluctantly to what I was supposed to be doing. I began slicing the loaf, taking care to keep my fingers clear of the sharp, serrated edge. But after a few seconds my eyes were drawn irresistibly back towards her. She'd stopped fiddling with the cups, and was leaning back against a work surface, one hand covering her eyes, such that I couldn't see her expression.

After several seconds with both of us silent and still, I put down the knife and took a few tentative steps towards her. She was completely motionless apart from the hand gently rubbing her forehead and eyes. Now standing beside her I hesitated, then slowly reached out to touch her arm. She abruptly withdrew from the contact, but remained, for once exposed and vulnerable, her face still hidden. Without allowing time for pause or reflection I put my arm around her, leaning my head against hers, my face pressing into the sweet softness of her hair.

It was several long moments before her body relaxed and the stiffness and tension gave way to a compliance that quickly became a passionate embrace, and then she was clasping me tightly, her face against mine, and I could taste her tears as my lips pressed against her cheek. And then we kissed - fiercely, almost desperately, in a rare conjunction of physical and emotional longing. How long this embrace lasted I couldn't say, but at last Melanie pulled away and wiped some tears with the back of her hand.

'Look what you've made me do.'

Her tone was almost accusatory, as if I had betrayed her into weakness. She sniffed several times and again wiped the back of her hand across her face before grabbing a tissue from a box on a work surface. She wiped her nose and dried her tears, even as a blackbird's song came trilling with incongruous, careless vigour through the open window. Her features were drawn down and tragic. Yet perversely, for me the moment had greater meaning, a more profound sense of reality than anything in our everyday existence. Only in such rare moments were we fully alive to the myriad possibilities of emotion - each second filled with a heightened, almost sublime awareness, where emotion and reaction to beauty become the only true aesthetic, untainted by moribund considerations of style or structure. Pure feeling, awareness, emotion.

I put my hands on her breasts and gently caressed and squeezed them while whispering softly in her ear.

'Let's go upstairs. They won't miss us for ten minutes.'

Melanie sighed softly, opened her eyes and smiled agreement.

12

When we went outside again the sun was high in the heavens. A warm fragrance rose from the grass, now fading with the passing of summer. Melanie walked with a smiling, sensuous grace towards where Gerard and Lydia were engaged, remarkably, in what could easily have passed for rational conversation. Gerard was describing in animated style some recently published novel which seemed to him wholly derivative, in plotting if nothing else, of some traditional fable which he'd read in the original Icelandic. He waxed indignant that nowhere in the book had reference been made to its source, the author instead content to gather favourable reviews on the strength of the imaginative flight of fancy that underpinned the plot.

Preposterous! Wholly indefensible and unethical, tantamount in fact to blatant plagiarism! Fully intended to write to the publishers demanding an explanation. The creative process too precious a gift, creative insight too hard won to allow the false attribution of praise. An insult to all those genuine creative artists who strove in the face of near insurmountable difficulties to express original thoughts and emotions in as lucid and highly organised a form as possible.

It was lovely to see Gerard reinvigorated, discoursing with all his old fire and authority. I waited until he'd blown himself out on the subject before casually mentioning Captain Smith's tall tales. Gerard rose to the bait with spectacular predictability, claiming not one, but two completed novels which, even as he spoke, were under consideration by a number of major publishing houses. A bidding war seemed likely.

'That's great news,' I said, 'and unexpected. Still, it should solve all your financial problems, with any luck.'

'Money is hardly a consideration, though I do expect a level of financial remuneration consistent with the artistic value of the works.'

'Of course - and hopefully that should take care of the rent.'

'More important is the issue of artistic integrity - I mean in respect of their presentation - the typeface, layout, binding, and of course, most importantly, the cover of each work.'

'Yes, of course - the cover - I can see such things are important considerations, the cover in particular. Incidentally, do you have titles for your novels, Gerard?'

'The titles would mean nothing to you,' he replied with a dismissive wave of the hand.

'No, I'm sure they wouldn't. But just out of curiosity it would be interesting to know what they are.'

With just a touch of irritation, Gerard repeated that the titles would not in themselves shed light on the subject matter and that, therefore, for the present he preferred to keep them to himself. This curious reluctance prompted me to speculate that either the titles were ill-chosen, or that his claim to authorship was ill-founded. Lydia's dark, unwavering gaze turned suddenly back on Gerard.

'So how do you like your room here, Gerard?'

He looked blankly towards her.

'I was wondering how you liked your room,' she repeated. 'Do you find it comfortable?'

He appeared to contemplate deeply for a moment.

'Certainly the room is satisfactory in most respects - in terms of space, certainly. As an artist, in both the conventional and wider senses of the word, I find that having space to think, to contemplate, to work on a large canvas, in both the metaphysical and literal senses, is vital to the creative process, as is the opportunity to stand back sufficiently, both literally and figuratively, to gain perspective on a work in progress. As far as painting itself is concerned, an unfortunate limitation of my room is, of course, the lack of natural light. However, in a basement flat this is naturally unavoidable.'

The earlier look of dejection and lassitude had completely disappeared. The head was once more erect, the eyes animated.

'Perhaps you would be better advised to look for a top floor studio.'

'Financial constraints would make that impossible.'

'How much do you in fact pay in rent, if you don't mind me asking?'

Gerard shot a look at Melanie. The shoulders hunched a little.

'I don't recall the precise figure.'

'You must know roughly what you pay?'

'I think the rent Gerard pays,' said Melanie quietly, 'is appropriate to both the size of the room and the locality. What is more important is the quality of the art that Gerard produces. He's shortly going to very kindly allow us a viewing of a range of paintings which I believe I'm right in saying will form the basis of an exhibition. I haven't seen them yet, but I'm sure the sheer quality and range of styles of these works will be quite fantastic.'

'I do not paint in different styles,' said Gerard coldly.

'No, I didn't mean that - I meant...'

'The range of subject matter will naturally vary greatly, but the style of my maturity has not altered, nor will it do so. The technique I employ is one of realistic depiction which, by and through the context of the objects depicted, which may be fresh, surprising, perhaps sometimes shocking, and also by the use of symbolic attribution to these objects, assume meanings and hint at mysteries the significance of which we can only guess. This is both the sum and summation of my art - in transcending the obvious and the apparent I am able to lift the veil on the mysteries of matter and existence.'

The voice was low and emotional. The hands weaved a certain magic in their restless fluttering.

'The shadows themselves become an enigma, suggesting in their illimitable depths the mystery of the infinite, wherein every object is at once explicit yet unfathomable. This is the enigma of being, in which every aspect of life is at once explicable, yet beyond explanation or understanding.'

'And yet,' I said, 'in your political work you seek to explain the processes of human interaction, and create some perfect, ideal, rational society in which every aspect is defined by analysis of cause and effect. Surely, in the light of what you have just said, the attempt to do that is in itself something of an enigma?'

'Appearance and reality are very different things,' he replied, enigmatically. 'Our perception of events, and of our actions, is all that need concern us. The future will be determined by our interpretation of the past. And our reading of the present is informed through our understanding of the ambiguous, indefinable nature of matter. Herein lies the point of fusion, the crossover, the intersection between the discrete strands of my creative work, wherein the discoveries and insights of my art inform my political work, and vice versa.'

Melanie was rapt with wonder, all shining eyes and hair, her expression pliable and pure. Lydia's expression was somewhat less pure, and certainly less pliable - in fact rigid might be closer to the mark.

'Talking of art,' I said, 'is it true that you've sold one of your paintings for a five-figure sum?'

It was several seconds before Gerard was able to break free from his trance-like self-absorption sufficiently to turn his head and regard me uncomprehendingly.

'I was just saying that Melanie mentioned something about you selling a painting for quite a large sum of money.'

'I never said anything of the kind,' said Melanie.

'Oh, I thought you had.'

'No. What I said was that in my opinion any one of Gerard's major works should be worth at least a five-figure sum to a collector.'

'Oh, I see. Yes, I suppose that's certainly possible.'

She looked at me.

'And, of course,' I continued, 'an exhibition would be an ideal platform - a launching pad, one might say, for Gerard's reputation in the artistic world. And who knows how far into the stratosphere that reputation might rise? Who really knows how far - '

'I don't think it's necessary, or necessarily helpful, to look beyond the immediate objective, which is simply to make Gerard's work visible to a wider audience. It's the first step towards recognition by both the public and his peers. All the rest will follow.'

'So, Gerard,' put in Lydia, 'what's your background in painting - have you attended art college?'

'That was hardly necessary. My education in art, as in aesthetics, has been at the feet of the eternal masters. I have long worshipped at the altar of Beauty.'

I jumped up and threw myself to the ground behind Gerard's chair, pushing my face into the grass until I regained some control over my emotions. After a while I was able to get up again, and looked round self-consciously, taking care to avoid meeting Melanie's gaze. I began to brush bits of grass and dust from my knees and sleeves, then resumed my seat.

'Are you alright, Robbie?' said Lydia, with an expression of keen concern. 'I thought you must have been stung by an insect.'

'Yes, it was something like that, only worse.'

Lydia looked confused momentarily, a look so reminiscent of Melanie's expression of confusion that any doubts regarding direct lineage were firmly removed. Fortunately the look quickly passed as she switched her attention back to Gerard, resuming her close questioning concerning his art and background. And as the questions became more specific regarding his family and childhood, so the replies became more opaque and evasive, and Melanie more overtly uncomfortable. In the event her intervention was not required. Demonstrating commendable presence of mind, Gerard deftly steered the conversation back to his novels, with claims of a letter from a literary agent praising his work in extravagant terms - 'innovative submission, enjoying it immensely, delighted to read more of his work' etc. etc.

'I'd love to see the letter, Gerard,' I said, 'if you've got it to hand.'

This harmless remark silenced Gerard for a moment. He cast another quick look towards Melanie before turning back to me.

'I'll go and look for it,' he said, slowly rising to his feet. 'However, I can't guarantee finding the letter. In fact I have no recollection of retaining it. Such praise is of little significance to the creative artist for whom the only arbiters are faith in his own judgement and the sublime sanction of posterity itself.'

I watched the retreating form with some sympathy. Despite the defiant speech, the shoulders had drooped a little and the head was less firmly erect.

'Well,' I said in a light-hearted and encouraging voice, leaning comfortably back in my chair, 'what shall we do for the rest of the day? Any plans, Melanie?'

Neither her tone nor expression exuded friendliness as she replied.

'What I'd like to do, in due course, would be for the four of us to go out for lunch together. We could perhaps go into Harrogate, or just find some nice little pub in the country. And then a country walk - into the Dales if the weather holds, which it looks as if it's going to do.'

'Four?' I said.

'What?'

'Did you say the four of us?'

'Yes, I'd like you to invite Gerard. I'm quite concerned about him, and also I'm sure he doesn't eat as well as he might.'

'Why don't you invite him? Or even better, why don't you not invite him.'

Melanie took a deep breath.

'It would be an opportunity for mum to spend some time with him, so that she could understand why it's so necessary to support him. You only have to listen to Gerard speak, about art and politics in particular, to appreciate the originality, the innovative grandeur of his mind.'

I regarded her with a renewed sense of wonder.

'Melanie, he's supposed to be supporting us with rent for his room.'

'Are you going to ask him or not?'

'No, I'm not.'

There was an uncomfortable pause, broken at last by Lydia speaking slowly and hesitantly, looking anxiously at her daughter.

'Melanie, I'd really be quite happy not to go out to lunch with Gerard, if it's going to cause problems.'

'It need not have caused any problems.'

Melanie stood, then paused, looking perplexed and uncertain. Her hair caught the bright sunlight. She didn't attempt to change her mother's mind or remonstrate in any way, but instead turned to me with a decided expression.

'You'll have to stay here with him then, Robbie.'

'Stay with him? Does he really need someone to babysit him, for God's sake?'

'All I'm asking you to do is stay and look after him.'

'Oh, what the hell, why not - what time will he want feeding? Do you think he might need changing as well?'

She just looked at me for a moment, then shook her head.

'Is it really necessary to use such pejorative expressions? Gerard needs our company and our support just now because he's still in a fragile emotional state. That is why I'm asking you to stay here with him, as it's apparently unacceptable for him to come to lunch with us.'

'Oh for God's sake, this is just crazy. I'm bloody sick of this whole situation. You really ought to listen to yourself sometimes.'

I stalked off towards the house, feeling at once ridiculous and self-conscious, and aware that every step was being monitored by hostile eyes. Even as I began mechanically shoving some plates under the kitchen tap I saw Melanie walking grimly towards the house. I braced myself, but to my surprise she was calm and quietly spoken, in itself somewhat ominous.

'We're going to leave shortly. Mum's feeling a bit upset. I don't know when we'll be back.'

'What's she upset about?'

She looked coldly at me.

'What do you think?'

'How the hell should I know?'

She took one of her patient deep breaths.

'I'm not discussing this any further at the moment, Robbie. But I think we need to have a talk later.'

13

I spent some time staring out of the kitchen window, watching leaves of trees and bushes moving languidly in the afternoon sunshine, while plaintive sounds of birdsong, an occasional distant car horn, a child's cry drifted through the open window. Another day dissolving slowly into emptiness. The silence in my heart was not of solitude, but of psychological isolation. Despite myself I'd felt a slight, perverse interest in Lydia's visit. Any contest of wits and exchange of pleasantries was better than the empty silence of one's own thoughts.

I didn't hear him approach. He was just suddenly there - and striking a pose, as ever, for emotional effect. There was, of course, no sign of any letter. I determined to ignore all the melodramatic droopings and stumblings.

'They've gone out,' I said sourly.

I'd turned from the window to speak to him, and now watched as he collapsed into a chair at the kitchen table and buried his head in his hands, elbows propped on the table. I regarded the diminutive figure, and especially the lank hair, with distaste. It was a continuing mystery as to why he persisted in inflicting his personality on me.

'Sometimes I despair,' he said, lifting his head, the voice vibrating with emotion. My eyes widened hopefully.

'I...I don't know that I can carry on much longer. It all seems so hopeless...hopeless. I am surrounded on all sides by the destruction of all that I hold most dear. Which of us could carry such pain, and yet carry the fight forwards. I stand alone in this battle, Robbie, and I sometimes doubt how much greater pain I can absorb, and how much longer I can lift the standard, alone and unaided, and march into battle once again. I grow weary.'

The voice was hoarse and low, the hands subdued. My amusement was tempered with genuine compasssion.

'Why don't you give it up, Gerard?' I said, speaking gently and softly. 'Why don't you give up your quest and just live a normal life, taking pleasure from everyday things? Get a job - you're a clever, intelligent guy, you wouldn't have any trouble. Get yourself somewhere to live. Have a social life and I'm sure in time you'd meet someone nice that you could share your life with. I really think you'd find life so much more fulfilling than setting yourself impossible targets and getting yourself worked up over events you can't control.'

I expected an explosive reaction, but his response was calm and considered.

'You have no idea how much I crave a normal life, Robbie. It would be so easy to do what you're suggesting, and a part of me yearns deeply to do just that.'

'Well, why not do it then?'

'Who then would carry the fight forward? Who among us is equipped with both the philosophical insight and political knowledge to lead this fight? Rare indeed is the conjunction of philosopher and natural leader. For many years I have looked in vain for the appearance of just such a one. Yet almost against my will I have been forced to the inescapable conclusion that, despite my many failings and inadequacies, of which I, more than anyone, am all too aware, it is I, and I alone, who must lead this crusade towards enlightenment, purity and truth. But these qualities alone would prove as elusive as a baby's dream without the exercise of an iron resolve - the imposition of a dominant will upon the susceptible feminine psyche of the masses.'

The bright blue eyes were reignited and the head was thrown well back. Again as though a switch had been thrown, he seemed quite abruptly to have regained the full glory of his self-belief.

'The masses have an outlook typically feminine - emotional, irrational, easily swayed by force of personality and emotional appeal rather than logic or rational argument. They respond rather to feelings than ideas. A large mass of people is simply not capable of following any complex argument or train of logic. Therefore, anyone wishing to carry the masses with them must have the ability to condense their ideas to a single, unified, elemental form, comprehensible to even the biggest dimwit, and then with tireless energy and force of will repeat this single idea endlessly, yet with endless creative energy in its presentation.

'This message will strike a resonance with their instincts, their inner voice, so that with constant repetition a sympathetic vibration, an harmonic resonance is created which becomes a great unstoppable force. There is a clear analogy here with the effect of the rhythmic impact of movement on a structure when that movement synchronises with its natural period of oscillation. I mean that if even a small force is applied to a structure, and the period of movement of that force happens to coincide with the natural period of oscillation of that structure, then the amplitude of the oscillations becomes greater and greater until it assumes unstoppable momentum. It is because of this phenomenon that soldiers marching are ordered to break step when crossing a bridge, particularly a suspension bridge. And in the same way, it is by the steady, hypnotic repetition of an idea, presented with passion and an absolute, unswerving consistency, no matter that the idea may contain a number of elements, and provided that this idea fires an arrow directly into the hearts of the susceptible masses, yearning as they are for the strong man capable of leading them to enlightenment and truth - then, I say, a sympathetic vibration is created of extraordinary proportions, out of all scale with the lone individual sounding this clarion call.'

'These are interesting ideas, Gerard,' I said, weathering the onslaught, 'but with the best will in the world I still don't see how one person, no matter how talented, can make a difference on the scale you're aiming for.'

He gathered himself in his seat with all the glorious inflation of his self-conceit, and swept back his hair.

'It is true,' he said, 'that there are those that see me as a dreamer - a man of wild, extravagant ideas. I am aware that there have been some that laugh at my ambition.'

The hands swooped, then soared once more like swifts.

'I have often been a prophet crying out in a wilderness of apathy and material obsession. You ask me how one man can challenge destiny. Yet it is a fact that only the highly gifted individual, the lone genius - ignored, derided, despised by those with whom he must share his daily crust, apparently insignificant in everyday life - it is this man, I say, part prophet, part philosopher, part political genius, who shall rise like the dawning sun when time of need and crisis is upon the land.'

'Yes, the trouble is, we seem to be in a period of sustained prosperity at the moment. Inflation is low, unemployment is low, earnings are high, growth is…'

He shook his head impatiently and raised an imperious, peremptory hand.

'The illusion of stability is purely ephemeral. A time of reckoning is at hand. The enemy of civilized society is everywhere, within us all, like a tumour draining and corrupting the body. They are animals, Robbie - creatures of base instincts - aggressive and territorial.'

A strange, intense light was burning in his eyes.

'Violence is an aberration! Such instincts shall and must be neutralized! All low instincts of vengeance and aggression will be sublimated into a system of peaceful, harmonious co-operation - something refined, something beautiful, something pure. If you only knew how I hunger for the purity of pure existence. This,' he said, indicating his physical body by striking it hard with both hands, 'this is merely an encumbrance. How I yearn to be free of its constraints. To enjoy the absolute freedom of mind and imagination. For the obliteration of personality, the loss of identity itself. To be part of something greater than myself, something in which my very identity shall be subsumed within the greater identity of a society that is pure and beautiful and free from aggression. The power of my will fused with the beauty of this conception. A New Society shall become my identity, and the only identity I have shall inhabit this glorious conception. And these ideas shall spread beyond the narrow span of this world. The truth and purity of A New Society shall spread across the galaxy, and then to every corner of the universe. Dominion shall, in time, be mine.'

Then, like a fierce summer thunderstorm it was over, as swiftly as it had begun. After a while he rose and left the room, head held high as if the eyes of the world were fixed upon him. It was a strange and disturbing episode.

As the evening wore on, there was still no sign of Melanie and Lydia. I wandered out into the garden, the light now fading quickly. There were no shadows, only an enveloping gloom. I knelt down on a patch of brownish grass in a hidden corner of the garden. I looked at the shapes created by lumps of the dry, crumbly soil. Strange sculptural forms. I looked in wonder at the extraordinary simplicity and beauty of a flower, its petals, leaves and stem. A movement close by caused me to look up.

'I didn't see you out here,' said Melanie, standing almost beside me. I couldn't discern her expression in the thick dusk. Rising, I turned to face her.

'And yet I was here,' I replied. 'When did you get back?'

'Just now.'

'Where's your mother?'

'She's gone home.'

'Already? I thought she was staying the night.'

'She decided against it.'

There was a coolness in the autumn air.

'I'm very worried about Gerard,' I said.

'Oh, don't start that again,' she snapped.

'Start what? You were worried about him earlier, so why can't I be worried now?'

'If I could take anything you say seriously Robbie, it...oh, it doesn't matter.'

We stood in silence for a while as the soft scents of autumn gathered round us with the darkness.

'Are you coming in now?'

'I'll be in shortly. I like being out here at this time. It's so quiet and peaceful.'

She may or may not have smiled - I couldn't make out her expression.

'I'll see you when you come in, then,' she said quietly.

I watched her walking towards the house, her body becoming gradually indistinguishable. Only the gleam of her hair remained until that, too, disappeared.

14

'Robbie, what are you thinking?'

Melanie was regarding me with a wistful, almost hopeful expression. An unaccustomed softness in her eyes.

'I...I was just thinking about things. Why are you looking at me like that?'

'Sometimes, Robbie...sometimes I think I catch a glimpse of the person I used to know, and it makes me very sad.'

'I'm still the same person I've always been. Nothing's changed.'

'Well, perhaps it's me that's changed then. We just don't seem to be able to meet on the same wavelength these days. I just don't seem to be able to reach you.'

Maybe if you looked at me once in a while, stopped burying your head in your work.

'I don't know what you're bothered about. Everything's fine as far as I'm concerned.'

Melanie's expression withdrew into her usual strained, noncommittal mask.

'Look, Mel, if anything puts a dampener on our relationship it's this damned Gerard business. As long as I'm writing this thing it means we can never move on and leave all those events behind us. In fact...look, why don't I just abandon this book? Why don't we put the past into a little box somewhere with a tight lid on it and start afresh, just the two of us - just like it used to be?'

In a moment of weakness I had agreed to write an account of Gerard's life and works, tentatively entitled *Portrait of Gerard*, and this so far largely non-existent biography had become an obsession with Melanie.

'Robbie, it's very important to me that Gerard's achievement and the extraordinary scope of his vision is more widely recognised. We know what Gerard was capable of, but it's so important that the rest of the world knows it too. Both to preserve Gerard's legacy for posterity…'

Oh, please.

'…and also to bring publicity to bear on his art. If we could only throw a spotlight on Gerard's wonderful paintings…'

I'd like to throw something on them. Preferably a lighted match.

'…then his standing and status as an artist would be raised immeasurably. Besides, after all the work you've put into the book it would be very unfulfilling for you just to stop and never complete it. You need…no, I don't mean you need, I mean, I think it would be a big boost to your confidence and self-esteem to complete a project, especially one as important as this.'

'What gives you the right to patronise me like that?'

'I'm not patronising you, Robbie. I was just…'

'Yes, you were patronising and demeaning me. Why should you infer that my self-esteem is, or maybe should be, low? Because I've never achieved anything in your eyes? Even though I'm perfectly satisfied with my role in life myself. The trouble with you is you're obsessed with status. With tangible, measurable success - by your own conventional criteria.'

'That isn't true.'

'Of course it isn't. That would, of course, be my only reason for saying it. Or would it? Am I making that up as well?'

'Stop being so silly, Robbie,' said Melanie with a flash of anger.

'Look, I like what I do. It may not mean anything in the grand scheme of things. It might not impress anybody when you tell them what I do for a living. I know it doesn't impress you. But I'm perfectly content doing it. Why do you have to feel such contempt for me simply because I don't have the rat race mentality, or the overweening ambition of a Gerard?'

'It always comes back to that, doesn't it? You're always so defensive in any situation where you think I might be comparing you to Gerard. Look Robbie, I admit I admired him. He was that rare individual with the courage to dream, the intellectual power to bring substance and depth to those dreams, and the drive to try and make them a practical reality. But that doesn't mean I think any less of you.'

'It's difficult to imagine how much less you could think of me.'

'Robbie, it's only because I think you're capable of so much more that I sometimes feel a little disappointed that you don't make more of your abilities.'

'Whatever I did would never compare in your eyes to the genius that was Gerard. How can anyone match up to an icon?'

'You must stop doing this to yourself. It's absurd to measure yourself against someone who's dead. Look Robbie, you're alive and Gerard's dead. Isn't that enough?'

'Not for you, I suspect. I'm sure you wish it was the other way round.'

'You're being ridiculous. Don't say such things.'

15

It had started in a fairly civilized fashion. Melanie was entertaining the rabble from Lundy's by extolling Gerard's extraordinary abilities - the artistic gifts, the utopian vision, the political genius - even the old standby of Lutyens' cathedral received an airing, provoking the exchange of one or two wondering looks. They appeared to me a most random assortment of unappetising no-goers, shuffling their feet aimlessly amidst the grotesque splendour of Fairfax House. The curtains were drawn back to reveal the tall, elegant windows performing their intended aesthetic function, while the chandelier sparkled merrily.

They'd all arrived more or less together, and Melanie introduced me to each in turn. Each subsequent conversation had been brief, and followed a similar course. What do you do, Robbie? Do? You know, career-wise. Oh, you mean work-wise? Quizzical look. Yes, what line of business are you in? I work in retail. Management? No, sales assistant. Oh. End of conversation. Defined by my status as being of no further interest, which suited me fine, as I was then at liberty to observe the Lundy's cream at play.

Alpha male of this group was Keith, sales director at the Grayson Street head office. A grey-bearded, plummy-voiced, bespectacled bore. Receding head overflowing with planning strategies, sales projections and product lines - and the sales curves of a certain young, attractive, ethnic female.

'In fact I was chatting with Rushani the other day. She's under Mark, of course, my opposite number at McCormack's. You've met Mark?...lovely girl. From Sri Lanka originally. Seemed very bright. Certainly an asset to Mark. It's such an important opportunity for both companies. I didn't go into details with her, of course. She set up the meeting with Mark for next week...yes, we're discussing the whole impact of the joint marketing strategy...perfect features and such a wonderful olive complexion...we're expecting something in the region of a 15% reduction in costs over the whole sector and improved penetration in market areas which haven't traditionally been our forte up to this point.'

Keith's number two, Peter, was a thin, wan individual, a captive of diminishing returns, ineffectual to the point of self-atrophy, appearing on this occasion with his slack-jawed, timorous girlfriend whose name, like her personality, was so unmemorable I've completely forgotten it. Let's call her Alice, for the sake of calling her anything. I remember her large, frightened eyes and floral print dress. Harmless enough if you ignored the aesthetic aspect. And after all, chinless Peter, black stubble compensating desperately but ineffectually, was hardly catch of the week.

Eunice, Keith's personal assistant, was a medium to small, plumpish middle-aged woman, with a small round face that appeared to have been over-painted once too often. The several rings she wore on plump, stubby fingers were misleading, as she'd never married. It was an open secret, however, and in some quarters a standing joke, that she held a quiet, unobtrusive torch for Keith.

Filling a considerable part of the room with his formless bulk and fetid voice was Colin. I'm not quite sure what Colin's position in the Lundy's hierarchy was, but even now the thought of that charmless lump of dough makes my skin crawl. I realise it's remarkably hard to like anyone called Colin, but this specimen was the worst of its kind. Big, rugby player's body, large loud head and multilayered chins. All overbearing manner, cold eyes and dirty jokes. Sweaty hand grabbing at Melanie with contrived mateyness whenever he had the chance.

Melanie. My own dear, beautiful Melanie. Statuesque and beautiful beyond imagining. All shimmering loveliness and glowing intellect. A crime against the natural order of things for you to be mixing with this human flotsam. All I want, all I have ever wanted, is to hold you close, to have a life with you that would shut out all this ugliness.

Colin becoming playful. Already onto a third glass of wine, still stuffing himself with nuts and crisps. The butcher's slab of a face glowing with malicious intent while Melanie chatted quietly with Keith and Eunice.

'Where's this lodger of yours, then? Eh? You know what they say about lodgers - I wouldn't have a lodger in the house with my bloody girlfriend. I'd throw the bugger out the window. Oi, whatsyourname!'

This directed at me.

'D'you reckon she's slept wi' 'im yet? Eh?'

The fat head went back and he laughed - a noise similar to the barking of a seal. A few nervous glances strayed in my direction. Melanie pretended she hadn't heard.

'If you and whatshisname were married it might be different, but some people think singles are fair game. Mind you, some buggers think marrieds are fair game, too. What do you think Eunice, eh? D'you reckon married men are fair game?'

A loud snigger. Eunice followed Melanie's lead in pretending she hadn't heard. She turned hurriedly away, edging clear of the men, drawing Alice with her.

'It's nice to have a chance to meet you, dear. I've heard so much about you from Peter. How long have you two known each other?'

Alice looked startled and uncomfortable at the question. Her lips worked slightly, but nothing audible emerged.

'What was that, dear? I'm sorry, you'll have to speak up.'

She pushed her ear close to Alice's mouth, trying to catch the words.

'I'm sorry, dear, I still can't...'

'Oi, Keith. Oi, you'd better watch it mate. She'll have you by...'

'More wine, anyone?' said Melanie loudly.

'…if you're not careful.'

Peter's stubble turned a delicate shade of pink, and he shifted uneasily behind his drink as Melanie stepped in.

'You were having problems, Keith, with McCormack's on the figures, weren't you? Wasn't there some dispute as to whether they accepted our figures?'

'They have to accept our figures - I don't see there's any doubt about that. There's no reason they should have any problem with them, anyway. You did the figures yourself didn't you, Peter?'

'Well, I…'

'You did prepare the initial report?'

'Well…'

'Was that the one I used in the meeting, the first report, the one that landed on my desk, or the one that came from Eunice? Eunice,' - calling over to Eunice - 'did I use the report from you about the joint marketing strategy?'

'You certainly got the second one, Keith. I think it incorporated all the main points and all the figures from the first report. It was based on Peter's notes in any case. Now the first report, whether that reached you independently, and whether it played any primary role in the initial meeting, or whether it played any secondary part in any subsequent meetings, I don't know.'

'Nice one, Eunice,' put in Colin. 'Trust you to clarify the situation. That's a shitload of help.'

He chortled happily, spraying partly-chewed peanuts, then poked an exploratory finger at a plate of sandwiches lying helplessly on a side table. Eunice gave a better impression this time of not having heard him.

In the middle of this interesting debate, and probably to Peter's relief, the living room door sprang open. The company hushed as the object of considerable curiosity came bounding in amongst them. The little artist silently surveyed the gathering, which in turn, and with some wonderment, contemplated him.

Gerard gave every appearance of having recently fallen headfirst into one of his masterpieces. The dark, dank hair drifting carelessly over his eyes was streaked with ultramarine, vermilion, in fact just about every colour you could imagine, and the effect continued down his tee-shirt and jeans. The thin, hollow cheeks were unshaven. There were dark creases beneath his eyes. He looked as though both sunlight and sleep eluded him on a regular basis.

With a cursory nod to the men, Gerard proceeded to where Eunice and Alice were huddled in awed contemplation, Melanie taking the opportunity to make the introductions.

'Eunice, this is Gerard. Gerard, Eunice. Gerard, Alice. Alice, Gerard.'

'Gerard,' began Eunice, 'I've heard so much…'

Eunice' voice trailed off as Gerard, taking her hand, focused his gaze directly into her eyes. Her mouth fell open and her body began to tremble. She felt as if every recess, every nook, every cranny of her soul was being explored by deft and experienced fingers. It was all she could do to keep her knees from giving way. She felt dizzy. The room swam before her eyes. The merrily sparkling chandelier swam. The functional curtains swam. In fact even the aesthetically pleasing windows swam. The effect on Alice was similar, if less noticeable, her jaw already being apparently only tenuously connected to the rest of her head.

I'd seen the Gerard phenomenon before, of course, so it was no great surprise. Still, once again I experienced irritation that a scruffy, nondescript little jerk should have such power. It was clearly a conscious act of seduction - presumably some hypnotic technique. A sensible, mature woman would be reduced to a quivering heap within seconds by one blast from those eyes. As far as I could judge it had something to do with the way he kept them trained unflinchingly for just a moment or two longer than most would judge polite or comfortable. And on this occasion he wasted no time in pressing home his attack.

'What is your position on windows, Eunice?'

Eunice looked blank, confused and generally incapable of forming an opinion on anything at all. An understandable reaction, perhaps, given the question. Gerard instead turned his fire on Alice.

'Alice, you have presumably considered the pivotal aesthetic role performed through and by window design?'

Alice's lower jaw was suddenly in freefall - in grave danger, indeed, of terminal disconnection. I stepped forward in the hope of retrieving the situation.

'Gerard, not everyone appreciates as you do, as indeed I now do, as we do, the central role played by window frames in the cultural life of this country. How highly, in fact, would you rate the importance of window design as a social and cultural reference point?'

Gerard threw back his head and with an impressive gesture swept the hair from his brow. The small, feminine hands became extraordinarily expressive as he spoke.

'Window design as such is but a part, a component of the wider picture. There are many elements which make an urban landscape an artistic and aesthetically satisfying whole, and it is difficult to state with absolute conviction that any one of these components is any more important, or carries any more weight in aesthetic terms in the overall composition than any other. What is beyond doubt, however, is the absolute impossibility of overstating the importance of aesthetic integrity, of homogeneity, in any artistic undertaking. Certainly that which we can state with conviction with reference to window design can be applied with almost equal force to, for example, roofing materials - to slates, tiles, thatching, copper sheeting, even corrugated iron. And we ignore at our peril the aesthetic merits of ashlar, of all the harmonious yet contrasting brick bonds, of modes of decoration, of street furniture - telephone boxes, street lamps, stone setts. But the vital point, and it is difficult to stress this with sufficient force, is context. Context is all. It is, in fact, quite literally, everything.'

For a moment Gerard paused, though the afterglow of his abrasive voice still lingered in dark corners of the room. The eyes of Melanie's guests were already taking on a hunted, defeated look.

'The architect does not have the right to impose his vision upon an urban landscape, without regard to the context of the setting, no matter the quality of that vision. And yet why should we attach such importance to context? Why is this of such absolute and pivotal importance?'

Keith, as befitted his position of seniority, was the first to rally.

'Of course, there's little question that Rushani would undoubtedly be a huge asset to any company.'

'Well, I…um.'

'Yeah, I'll bet her assets are bloody huge, eh?'

'This should, must and will forever underpin every aspect of society, for if our actions are not driven by aesthetics, by the primary consideration of what enhances our lives and gives them beauty, then human existence will forever be a hollow and superficial experience. The integration of aesthetics into every aspect of our lives must and shall be, above all else…'

'What was that dear? You'll have to speak up.'

'Certainly I have no doubts at all about Rushani's potential. Given the sort of opportunities which we could provide at Lundy's she could most certainly go all the way.'

'Yes, er…Keith, but…um…would that mean…'

'You fancy going all the way with her, eh, Keith me old mate?'

Colin cackled loudly.

'It's not her potential you want to get your hands on, is it me old mucker? It's her bloody tits!'

'Yes, we can say with absolute certainty that a landscape defaced by, for example, electricity pylons, quarry or motorway, may well be 95% intact. However...'

'I'm not sure, dear. I thought he was talking to you, but on the other hand he's not exactly looking at either you or me.'

'It's just that I...um...the...er...'

'I don't know what you think, Eunice,' said Melanie quietly, 'but I believe the new system is already paying dividends in terms of the level and quality of presentation of information in particular.'

'And yet 95% of the aesthetic integrity is lost, destroying the artistic and emotional impact of the whole irrevocably.'

'...such a wonderful olive complexion, such exquisite almond eyes...'

'I think the new system has been a big success, Melanie. You should be very...'

'Oi, Keith, you randy...'

'This must be our glorious crusade, for through the ages it is clear that History will favour those who...'

'What did he mean by 95%?'

'You see it's just that...not that I'm worried, er...Keith...I wouldn't want you to think that...'

'I'll bet she's got an arse on 'er, eh, me old mate?'
'What dear? No, I think it's just paint. At least I hope it's just paint.'

Melanie? Was she aware of the strange dynamics of this party? Was she aware of the general sense of discomfiture? Was she conscious of Gerard orating apparently to himself? She appeared as serene and exquisite and imperturbable as ever. Though perhaps there was just a trace of tightness around the mouth and eyes. Nevertheless she was able to be holding a rational conversation with Eunice and Alice - as rational at any rate as their present overwhelmed and confused mental states would allow - while still paying rapt attention to Gerard's interminable posturings, a feat of mental dexterity of which possibly only Melanie would have been capable. Aware also, apparently, of the division of the company into two distinct camps. Three if one regarded Gerard as a separate sentient entity. Certainly she soon suggested to Eunice and Alice that they reconnect with the men.

'That's a wonderful idea, Melanie. Are you coming, dear? He's such a wonderful man to work for, you know.'

'...a wonderful soft voice, quite exotic...'

'It's just that...erm...you see I'm just...um...not exactly worried...'

'I do like my men to be real men. I'm not keen on these modern ideas where men are trying to be...'

'Oi, you talking about my old mucker here, Eunice? Real man - him!?'

Crude, raucous laughter rang out in counterpoint to Gerard's harsh, metallic speech. Keith's eyes glinted behind his glasses, the mouth a thin line.

'...several important consultancy projects on behalf of the Brick Research Council. It is clear from my work in this field that the future of bricks is assured. Indeed, the position of bricks in the future aesthetic, artistic and commercial development of this nation is without question. I state this unequivocally, notwithstanding that many of the findings of my report were challenged by the Prestressed Concrete Society. This was only to be expected. However, whether in the great strides made towards European Brick Harmonisation, in which I was involved in a possibly pivotal capacity, or in new developments in the field of vertically restrained brickwork cladding, it is clear that the age of prestressed concrete is over. And that whether in the areas of prefabrication, prestressing or in the more traditional uses and varieties of courses and bonds - the stretchers and stacks and quarters and headers - the glory of the brick in all its infinite variety, from Yellow Stock to Tudor Red to Staffordshire Blue to Accrington Blood, from Fletton to Brindle to Gault, from dry to brown dry to cream dry pressed facer, from double bullnose to clay paver to interlocking clay paver, the brick is and will remain pre-eminent within the built environment. And for this reason...'

'Who the fuck's that bugger talking to?'

Involuntarily, inasmuch as everyone would have preferred to ignore everything he said, we all turned to follow the direction of Colin's glare. Gerard in full flow was a sight to behold, but it was indeed unclear as to whom the torrent was directed. I looked at Melanie, and detected an increasing unease at this exposure of her protégé. She attempted, unsuccessfully at first, to draw Gerard's attention, while Colin began lavishing his charm on Alice.

'Now then, Alice, fancy a bit of red meat?'

Alice leapt as far as the large, damp hand clutching her waist allowed, but was powerless to prevent herself being drawn into Colin's bulk. She squeaked perceptibly.

'What'd she say?'

'She said they're both vegetarian,' replied Eunice coldly.

'That wasn't the kind of meat I had in mind.'

Eunice shuddered while Alice squirmed and implored. Peter coloured and shuffled, eventually directing anxious and ineffectual looks towards Keith, but hopes of a positive response from that quarter were dashed. Keith was too preoccupied with Rushani's wonderful olive complexion, almond eyes, exquisite features, long legs and perfect body, much to Eunice's discomfort.

'Extraordinary jet black hair, such a wonderfully soft voice...'

'Gerard,' began Melanie, 'I was wondering...'

'Oi, Keith mate. Where's yer better half tonight, then?'

'Keith,' said Eunice plaintively, 'can I get you something? Melanie's made some delicious savoury vol-au-vents.'

'...extraordinary potential...'

'Gerard,' repeated Melanie, increasing the volume, 'I believe you have some interesting ideas on the place of business in the national life?'

Gerard seemed to wake abruptly from his subterranean trance, bricks temporarily sidelined as he looked over, as if noticing everyone for the first time.

'What? What was that?'

'Y'alright mate? Still building yer frigging cathedral?'

Melanie gave Colin an exasperated look, taking in at the same time the Alice, Colin and Peter situation.

'Colin,' she said. 'Would you get me a lemonade with a slice of lemon.'

Even Colin was unable to ignore such a direct request when it came from Melanie, and releasing Alice sidled off to get the drink, which allowed Alice to scuttle for protection behind Peter and Eunice. Melanie turned back to Gerard.

'I was just wondering, Gerard, if you agreed with Keith on the importance of business in the development of a nation.'

'I was making the point, Gerard,' put in Keith, 'that business is the prime mover - the catalyst - in the economy.'

'Met his wife have you, Eunice?'

Alice made herself practically invisible in Peter's shadow, while Eunice with grim determination failed to respond to Colin.

'The strength of the building industry in particular,' continued Keith, 'is always, of course, the true measure of the buoyancy of an economy.'

There was fire dancing in the bright blue eyes as Gerard replied.

'Nations and states are created not by business or the desire to create wealth, but by the imperishable force of self-preservation, the inextinguishable will of a people to express their national identity. As far as the national psyche is concerned business is never more than a means to an end. Yet does this mean that such jealous preservation of the essential characteristics of nationhood militates against the coming together of nations, the fight for international brotherhood and cooperation? No, and again no! This is the position of misguided or malicious knaves who would strive for strength from the shackles and bonds of weakness. The guiding hand of History makes clear that…'

'Keith mate, get your women together, give 'em a party!'

'…and for this reason the scale of buildings must and shall always reflect their relative importance in the spiritual development of the state. It is an act of profound symbolic significance that the monumental buildings of both church and state should exceed both in terms of scale and of architectural embellishment the creations of capitalist business - the office blocks, hotels, department stores and so on. And in this relationship of scale and grandeur shall be enshrined our overriding belief that business shall and must always be the servant of the state. The alternative is to believe that the state is an institution which exists merely for business reasons, and therefore to be governed from this point of view.'

'I wouldn't say exactly that, Gerard, nor can I agree with you. If we consider - '

'I would say precisely that! And what is more...'

'Ever tried three in a bed, mate?'

'...the organisation of a community of human beings working within a common moral and philosophical framework, united in and by their...'

'I bet Rushani'd be up for it! The dirty bitch!'

'...and dedicated to the...'

'How dare you!'

Keith's beard was bristling, his body stiff with anger.

'How dare you speak of Rushani in that way!'

There was a shocked silence, in which even Gerard stopped ranting and watched the unfolding of events with apparent interest.

'Keith, please!' said Melanie. 'It's not worth reacting. Just forget it - please!'

'I don't have to stand for that kind of thing.'

Colin, standing a little way off, had a leering half-smile on his face. Still popping peanuts in his mouth and chewing contentedly.

'I'm sorry, Melanie,' said Keith, putting down his glass and making a show of looking at his watch. 'I'm leaving. Karen will be expecting me.'

He walked with great deliberation to the door, while a flicker of pain rippled over Eunice's face.

'Don't worry, Melanie. I'll see myself out.'

'See yer, mate!'

A few seconds passed, then the front door could be heard being firmly closed. I was enjoying Melanie's party far more than I could ever have anticipated. Melanie, though, was looking unmistakeably crestfallen, while Eunice, Peter and Alice had the appearance of lost souls wondering just how long eternity could possibly last.

'In business, as in politics, as in any effective military organisation, only one system of command is possible.'

You had to admire it - that wonderful detachment. The way he could slip with perfect ease back into his rhythm, as if nothing had happened.

'Responsibility proceeding upwards and authority proceeding downwards. There can never be a system based on any other principle where there are clear, defined objectives to be achieved. That much is absolutely clear.'

'Hang on a minute, Gerard.'

I felt the time had come to up the ante a notch or two.

'I thought this wonderful new society of yours - what's it called - A New Society? - I thought this new society was all about direct democracy and self-determination, where ordinary people control for themselves the factors which affect their lives.'

Gerard in reply managed to convey both irritation and imperious condescension.

'Of course that is my ultimate objective, and will remain so. However, it should be clearly understood that this perfect condition of society cannot be approached in a single step. The consensus required to do so represents an impossible objective. It is necessarily a two-stage process. Furthermore, it is necessary for this to be recognised, and for power to be gathered into a single point of focus, into the hands of a single individual with the vision, the strength, and the will to harness and direct the thoughts, emotions and desires of a people, themselves crying out for the strong man to lead them, to mould them, to direct their thoughts and emotions towards the desired objective. Who will lead if not the strong man? No one! Who will follow if not the emotionally susceptible masses? No one! Who will…'

'What the fuck does it take to shut this bugger up?'

'…if not the inviolable…'

'God knows. I've tried for long enough and I've never yet found a way to…'

'No one! The proof of History is that the strong man has the right, indeed the sacred duty, to carry through what he wills. It matters not one whit that well-doers pontificate about moral superiority. Absolute right is and always shall be subservient to absolute strength. Only the strength which can withstand the storm is truly strong. Only the leader who can demonstrate an iron will and the capacity for strength of steel can demand the absolute loyalty of a people. Only - '

'Only fucking well belt up, will you!'

Colin's face had turned an interesting shade of brick red.

'Give it a rest for fuck's sake.'

A frightened silence descended once more upon the room. Colin's earlier boorish amiability had vanished, replaced by hard-eyed anger.

Like sheep caught in a thunderstorm Eunice and Alice huddled closer than ever. Eunice's face was now close to cracking with tension, while Alice's jaw was close to - well, let's just say it was a critical situation. For the first time that evening I experienced a degree of warmth towards Colin, an embryonic feeling of fellowship, as if two souls had at last found a common stamping ground.

Gerard started towards Colin with wild eyes and clenched fists. Only the near instantaneous reactions of Melanie prevented a collision as she practically threw herself into the rapidly closing gap.

'Gerard,' she said, breathing heavily, her graceful form separating the two antagonists, 'there was something I particularly wanted to ask you.'

Her face was tense and drawn, the hint of a tragic Madonna in her aspect. Gerard stopped abruptly, curiosity momentarily overriding the desire for retribution. The assembled company - what was left of it - released a collective breath.

'You mentioned the other day this remarkable theory you've developed.'

Melanie's voice for once betrayed real emotion, though whether this was due to Gerard's theory, or the general tension of the evening, was a matter for debate.

'I admit I didn't quite understand the principles of it, but I'm sure that's due to a lack of scientific knowledge on my part. Do you remember, Gerard? I believe it involved the theoretical possibility of becoming invisible.'

With a combination glare and sneer Colin turned heavily away, like a bull from whom the cape has been suddenly withdrawn.

'Of course I remember,' snapped Gerard. 'I'm hardly likely to forget one of my foremost scientific discoveries.'

A derisive snort resounded across the room.

'Tell us about it, Gerard.'

'Yes, do tell us about it Gerard,' I echoed. 'It should be so very interesting.'

'It's much more than interesting,' said Melanie coldly.

'Well, perhaps interesting's the wrong word.'

'How would it work, Gerard - how would this theory work?'

'It is more than merely a theory. There is no question of its feasibility and eventual practical application. The key lies in superconductivity. I take it you are all familiar with the term?'

Nobody moved or spoke.

'Very well. Superconductivity is the term used to describe the property of certain substances that have no electrical resistance. It, that is superconductivity, occurs in some ceramic materials, but in metals, which is what concerns us here, it occurs at very low temperatures. Imagine a chilled, superconducting disc. Let it be levitated over powerful magnets - it is an inherent property of superconductors that they repel magnetic fields. This, that is the superconducting disc, is then set revolving, rather like a compact disc. Now, any object placed above the disc appears to lose a percentage of its weight. Of course in reality the mass of the object has not changed, but the effect of gravity on it has decreased. The device is, in fact, shielding the object from gravity.'

'Gerard, Gerard!' I cried. 'I'm sorry to have to compromise the originality of your ideas, but didn't I read somewhere that a Russian physicist - Podkletnov, I think it was - came up with the idea of 'gravitational force shielding' by exactly the same principles that you're expounding here?'

'That may be so,' responded Gerard loftily, and with startling footwork. 'Many of my more profound discoveries have inevitably become common currency in scientific circles. However, this particular theory goes far beyond anything that Podkletnov may have derived from my ideas. The key to the application of my theory as regards invisibility lies in the speed of rotation of the discs. I envisage two chilled superconducting discs, levitated over magnets, revolving at approximately

50 million rpm. They would be implanted within the human body at right angles to the vertical axis. Anti-gravity of such power would thereby be generated that light itself would bend in both planes around the person, giving an onlooker the impression that the person is not there. Of course, a side effect would be that the person would be capable of flight, which raises a number of both problems and possibilities.'

'I've never heard such total and utter cock in my life!' shouted Colin. 'You're frigging bonkers, mate. You and your bloody theories and your great new society and your fucking cathedral - you're completely bloody barmy!'

At this Gerard transformed into a twitching, screaming demon. The veins in his forehead and neck became dangerously distended, the eyes bloodshot and popping from their sockets. He embarked upon a detailed analysis of Colin's parentage, intellectual gifts, physical appearance and powers of logical reasoning which would have been both comprehensive and illuminating had it not been interrupted by a bellow of anger from Colin, now moving heavily across the carpet towards Gerard.

'Why, you little runt, I'll…'

What the outcome would have been had Melanie not reacted immediately and decisively doesn't bear thinking about. Once again she moved with lithesome grace and speed, this time confronting Colin directly.

'How dare you!'

'Yes, how dare you,' I repeated softly from behind Eunice.

They were standing face to face, eyeball to eyeball. It might have been a trick of the light from the still merrily sparkling chandelier, but Colin's face appeared to be melting by the second under the intensity of Melanie's gaze.

'What do you mean, me? It was him saying all those things, and - '

'Get out, Colin. Now!'

They continued to stare into each other's eyes for what seemed quite a long time, and then just as Colin's chins were starting to quiver uncontrollably he dropped his eyes, turned and slammed out of the house.

'What did he call him?' asked Eunice.

'I think he said runt,' whispered Alice, her voice for once audible and almost animated.

'Oh. I thought he said - '

'That's it!' cried Melanie suddenly. 'I'm sorry but I've got a splitting headache and I'm going to have to ask you all to leave.'

The three remaining guests quietly put down their drinks, then filed sombrely past Melanie.

'Thank you for a lovely evening,' said Eunice, her voice trembling and uncertain. Alice said something, but nobody was quite certain what it was. Peter, the last guest to say his farewells, brought up the rear.

'Melanie…I…um…that is…er…'

'It wasn't your doing, Peter. Good night.'

16

After the Indian summer of mid-September, towards the end of the month the weather turned much colder. A raw east wind began to blow in from Whitby, then across the open expanses of the North York Moors. The weather reflected my mood as the month progressed, a mood increasingly bleak and despondent, as periods of intimacy and happiness with Melanie became increasingly rare. There seemed to have occurred a drawing apart either side of some intangible divide, though on the face of it our daily routines continued much as before. The change had come abruptly, yet without either of us being truly aware of it at first, or knowing exactly when or why. Like some heavy lever falling into place within some massive lock - some action, some event, some thought even, had secured a bulkhead between us. Something had changed forever.

Melanie was out, attending one of her weekly Taekwondo and Shotokan training sessions, so I was quietly minding my own business watching mindless hokum on TV. Some American soap with some fat, crumpled-raincoat-wearing, lollipop-sucking, Mustang-driving retired medic/cop/FBI agent/private investigator solving a number of baffling, mysterious murders, while doing no more than any average, got-lucky television actor could reasonably be expected to do.

Suddenly, above the grinding of predictable acting came the more ominous noise of footsteps ascending. Ah, my inconsequential friend. Congenitally unable to leave me in peace. Coming, doubtless, to torment me with yet more ingenious plans involving dominion over the universe, or the most aesthetic arrangement of street lamps for any given urban setting.

Why pick on me, for God's sake? What have I ever done to you, apart from allow you to live rent free, by default, in my basement while you pursue insane, impossible dreams, and occasionally paint something so incompetent or repulsive that even Melanie would be hard pushed to mount one of her nauseating eulogies?

The footsteps suddenly ceased. I fully expected to hear the front door slam shut, but instead there was silence. I sat still, listening intently for any sign or sound of movement. Half a minute passed. My nerves were just starting to jangle, and I was thinking about jumping up and surprising Gerard at whatever he was up to when I heard the slight clink of two glass objects coming together. Then a soft knocking at the door. I leaned forward, mystified.

'Come in,' I called.

Gerard usually burst into the room without warning, launching himself onto one of the settees before dazzling Melanie with the breadth of his intellect. This time a few more seconds passed, then the door opened and Gerard's head appeared, an almost apologetic expression on the thin, pinched features.

'Can you spare a few minutes, Robbie?'

'Gerard! Do come in. What can I do for you? I'm afraid you've just missed Melanie - she's out learning how to hurt people.'

'No, it wasn't Melanie - it was you I was hoping to see.'

With that he walked into the room carrying a bottle of wine and two glasses, put them on a small table in front of a settee and sat down. He poured each of us a glass, then sat back, for once curiously passive and hesitant.

'I know what you think of me, Robbie,' he said at last.

I felt a cold thrill, instantly wondering how much of my private and as I thought confidential musings on Gerard had been generously shared with him by Melanie.

'What on earth do you mean?' I managed to say.

'I know you think I pay Melanie too much attention.'

He looked at me, perhaps trying to gauge my reaction. I returned his gaze blankly.

'You know, I'm a very emotional person, Robbie. I tend to feel things more intensely than most people. It's the engine of my creativity - it's what drives me. And Melanie has such natural empathy. She's so open with her emotions, so warm and generous that it's impossible not to respond to her.'

Are we really talking about the same person here? That cold, blank, work-obsessed automaton? My Melanie? A case of mistaken personality, surely.

'But I assure you, I'm not trying to appropriate her affections in any way. That's something I would never do. As you know, I am dedicated to my artistic and political goals, and destiny demands that I remain single-minded in pursuit of those objectives. In any case, my heart is already given to another.'

He paused for a moment and I looked at him in surprise, and with a degree of scepticism.

'I had no idea you're in a relationship. I've never heard you mention anyone before.'

Gerard reached forward, refilled his glass, then with a deep sigh sank back into the settee.

'I still love someone more than anyone or anything in this world. But I have no contact with her any more. None at all.'

His voice wavered slightly.

'I haven't seen her for many years. I don't even know if...'

The words trailed off. He silently handed me a letter, still in its envelope, carefully opened at the top with a knife. I took out the letter, which was crisp and clean, lovingly preserved.

Dearest Gerard,

I very much regret that it won't be possible for me to see you or communicate with you again, either now or at any time in the future. I know this will be difficult for you to accept, but I also know that in time you will find the strength to do so, and to achieve all those great objectives of which you are so capable. In different circumstances all things might have been possible. However, we must accept the workings of fate. Some things are at once too difficult to overcome, and yet too painful to accept. There was a time once, it seems long ago, when I believed in a spirit that sometimes came and dwelt within me, a wanderer that would transport me from this world of care and suffering and allow me glimpses of the boundless love and joy that is Eternity. While the messenger came, winter had no bitterness for me, and the heavens were thick with stars. There was no doubt, no fear, only the assurance of eternal liberty. However, I was mistaken. My faith has been disproved. I wish you well, always.

Your friend,

Sarah

I sat in silence for a while, trying to visualise the kind of person who could write such an extraordinary letter. Yet there were things in it that had a familiarity which at first I was unable to pinpoint. Taking the letter at face value I felt a surge of compassion towards Gerard.

'You must have been devastated.'

Gerard nodded, staring at his glass.

'How close were you...I mean, tell me about her. What was she like, this Sarah?'

He turned to me, eyes lit by that familiar flickering light of fanaticism, leaning close, his voice low and emotional.

'She was the most extraordinary, wonderful human being that ever walked the Earth. There has never been anyone like her. If you ever need a reason for existence, for human consciousness, for all the accumulation of human suffering, she alone provides justification.'

The thought crossed my mind that watching darts on TV, beer in one hand, packet of crisps in the other, was actually quite sufficient reason to exist as far as I was concerned. But generously kept such musings to myself.

'So how did you meet her, Gerard?'

'You know Otley, I suppose?'

I nodded.

'I lived there for a year, just renting a room. Painting and sketching, developing my political theories. You see, Robbie, the whole area, the mill towns, the chimneys, the warehouses - in a small radius you've got the Wharfe valley, Worth, Calder and Aire. A hugely rich resource for my art in terms of the dramatic character of the landscape. Great stone mills, lines of stone terraces. I draw on it even now in my art, though of course I prefer brick for its visual texture. Anyway, I don't remember exactly when I first saw her. I just remember gradually becoming aware of her presence. As you know, Otley's a small place anyway, and as it turned out I lived just a couple of streets away from Sarah. Once I became aware of her existence I'd sometimes see her walking into town, or in one of the shops, always alone. In fact that was the thing that struck me about her straight away - she seemed to be…slightly aloof from what was going on around her. As if none of it really had anything to do with her. Even from a distance she seemed to be somehow separate, existing within herself. She was so different from anyone else I'd ever encountered. I was - still am - overwhelmed.'

The eyes shone again, head and hands shaking with emotion, his lips trembling.

'Oh, you can't imagine such beauty, Robbie. Not conventional beauty perhaps, but…physically she's tall, slim, lithe, graceful. She wears her hair shoulder length, reddish brown, darkish. And her face…oh, how exquisite! Pale, grave, sometimes sad, but her look so expressive, such a depth of soul and feeling. You can't possibly imagine! Her eyes are so beautiful - sometimes a dark storm-cloud grey, sometimes the deep intense blue of the ocean. Yet she doesn't often look at you, not directly. In fact, anyone who didn't know her would believe that Sarah is simply shy. But that would suggest that she would invite human contact if she were able. No, it's a barrier thrown up by choice, a defence mechanism to safeguard herself.'

'Safeguard from what?'

'Her inner life is more important to Sarah than any outward human contact. She lives for this inner, spiritual life. Her disgust for humanity is reinforced by any form of contact. I believe I can say truthfully that I was her only meaningful human contact outside of her family. But generally her material life falls so far short of the extraordinary force and beauty of her spiritual experience that she simply rejects it as meaning nothing to her. She withdraws as far as possible into herself. She refuses to compromise that vital link with the spirit within, the messenger of hope she talks about that promises eternal liberty and union with the universe. It is her life force.'

'Surely this 'messenger' suggests some kind of outside agency?'

'Well, that is the whole point, isn't it. Is it some outside force, perhaps some form of supernatural experience. Or is it a self-induced state brought on by certain specific circumstances, which she may or may not be able to control.'

'So what's the answer?'

'I don't have any answers.'

A long, contemplative silence followed. Gerard sat, head bowed, absorbed within his thoughts. In this welcome break from self-indulgent ramblings about some unlikely heroine, the first glimmerings of a connection began to form in my mind. I could just begin to see what Gerard's game was and which side of play he was coming from. But the idea was barely taking shape when he jerked back to life, and remembered that he had a captive audience.

'Anyway, Robbie, as I was saying, I became gradually aware of Sarah, though I still didn't know her name at this point, of course. And I noticed that she often took the same route down into town, to do the family shopping presumably, every couple of days or so.'

'You seem to have been observing her quite closely, Gerard.'

'I happened to be making some preliminary sketches of a row of terraces in the area,' he replied, only partially masking irritation at the interruption. 'Therefore I came to know fairly well when she would be walking back up to her house, usually weighed down with a couple of bags of shopping. And I would make sure that I happened to be walking the opposite way along the same route at the appropriate time. After a while, gradually, almost imperceptibly, she began to recognise me. A slight glance of recognition I received - no more than that. It was hard work and took a deal of effort, as she would rarely make eye contact, her gaze usually fixed on the ground. This pattern continued for weeks, and I became increasingly frustrated by my lack of progress. I decided I had to engineer some kind of conversation, even though I knew this strategy had its risks. So one day when she was again burdened with heavy-looking bags, I spoke to her, though my heart was almost jumping out of my chest, as you can imagine.

'Could I help you to carry those? They look rather heavy.'

She paused, and a slight pink tinge crept into her complexion as she glanced, though briefly, directly at me, and for the first time I experienced the wonder and depth of her expression. Without replying, she put down the bags, leaning them against a wall, then flexed her hands which had been tightly clasping the bags. At last she shook her head. Preparing to carry on, she paused again as a thought appeared to cross her mind.

'I thought you were walking in the opposite direction, in any case?'

Her voice, though soft, was clear and musical, and altogether delightful.

'I…I was,' I replied, 'but I'd just decided I'd gone far enough today when I saw you with those bags and wondered if I could be of any help.'

The look she gave seemed to mingle amusement with incredulity.

'Thank you,' she said softly, 'that won't be necessary.'

And with that she picked up the bags and was gone. Yet when I next met her several days later she gave me a smile of such beauty and serenity, her face seemingly lit with a divine light. I'm sure in retrospect it had nothing to do with seeing me. Yet it gave me sufficient encouragement that a few days later, and despite my extreme anxiety, I stopped and somehow found courage to ask if I could meet her some time, maybe go for a drink together. Her face became grave and troubled, and only after what seemed like an eternity of silence did she reply, saying she never drank, but that she would be willing to go for a walk with me some time.

My excitement and exhilaration at this response was so intense that I could hardly reply coherently. I felt as if all the most beautiful music in the world had begun swirling simultaneously around inside my head in an infinitely complex harmony. No harsh or loud or sudden sounds, no drums or other percussive effects, no blaring horns or trumpets - just the shimmering euphony of strings and woodwind, a delicate, decorous and perfect euphony.'

Ah, Gerard, my dear friend.

'Well, after that we began to meet, perhaps once a week at first. For me there was such pleasure in doing the simplest of things. Wandering among the streets and shops, exploring hidden alleyways. Maybe taking in a café. Sitting close to her, gazing at that unique, calm beauty. Until, raising her eyes to mine, and knowing her aversion to eye contact, I'd look down instead into my cup, or across at those who would never know the joy of Sarah's company.

'After a few months together we'd sometimes hire a car. A bright summer's day, watching the river at Bolton Abbey catching the sun in a series of infinite, dancing reflections. Making its endless, melodic way towards Leeds. Then in the cool of the evening, coming across some lonely country church. Sarah happily exploring the churchyard, standing among the gravestones reading the inscriptions, oblivious to everything but her own thoughts and sensibilities.

'Sometimes we'd visit Rievaulx. Even though Sarah had been there before, each time we went she never ceased to be delighted to be there once more. She practically ran around the grounds of the abbey, jumping with glee from stone banks down onto grassy aisles. Running her hands along the stonework, feeling the texture, tracing lines and patterns cut hundreds of years before when the place had a roof, before the weathering of wind, rain and ice. Finding in the choir arches and pillars a haunting, delicate beauty. The pathos of its ruin both moving and enchanting her. She seemed so happy then, so content.'

Gerard paused, overcome by the emotion of his recollection. I took the opportunity to stand up and stretch, wandering over to look out on the fast-fading evening. Prelude to a cool and moonless night. Street lamps were already lit, casting a menacing glare over the parked cars. I wondered if Melanie had finished yet, and at this very moment was making her way home, in all her sublime and frightening beauty.

Of course I knew now, knew for sure. Earlier suspicions had crystallised into a definite form. I'd still play along with friend Gerard, but I knew. In fact I decided to drop one or two hints. Just to let him know that I knew. See his reaction.

'I suppose she has a brother, this Sarah?'
'What?'

'Sarah - she has a brother?'
'Yes. Why do you ask?'
'And two sisters?'
'No, just one - Anne. What are you on about?'
'Anne. Yes, of course.' I laughed inwardly. 'I should have guessed. And their father - a widower, no doubt?'

Gerard was eyeing me suspiciously.

'How on earth would you know that?'

'Let's just call it a lucky guess, shall we Gerard? Now tell me about the dynamics of this family. Did you ever meet them all together in a normal family setting?'

'I went round to Sarah's house once, and once only, at her invitation, to have tea with her and her family. It was not an experience I ever wanted to repeat.'

'So you met all of them on that occasion?'

'Yes. We all sat round a table. Sarah had cooked the meal, and she served it while we sat in silence. Dominating this table, sitting at its head, was Sarah's father.'

'What was he like?'

Gerard paused, staring directly ahead, as if at some deathly vision.

'I can still see that great white-topped head. Its grim face presiding over the table. Tiny, darting eyes directing baleful menace from under bushy white eyebrows. These malicious glances seemingly fairly equally divided between me, the intruder into this pleasant family gathering, and his unfortunate son, Patrick. Poor Anne was ignored by all, except Sarah, throughout the meal.'

'Tell me about him, Gerard. Can you remember any details of conversations you might have had with him?'

'I can remember every single word that was said at that meal. Every word. It's not the sort of occasion you could easily forget.'

Especially, no doubt, when you've rehearsed every detail a thousand times. This was becoming a consummate performance - every detail seemed to lock together perfectly.

'Mr. Nicholls was a civil servant, working at some Ministry department in Harrogate. From what little Sarah said about him I think it was in quite a lowly capacity considering his age - clerical assistant, I believe. And as a result he carried this massive chip on his shoulder at being still on the lowest rung of the ladder. And I believe he compensated for this by domineering over his family.'

'Especially Patrick?'

'Poor Anne was too young and timid to stand up to him, and Sarah was never the target of his anger and bullying - in fact she held the family, such as it was, together. She lived so much within herself, in any case, that she would never have allowed outward oppression to affect her inner being, her soul. She suffered on behalf of the other two, though.

'But it was Patrick who was the target of most of Mr. Nicholls' bile. Patrick was much like any other seventeen year old. Rebellious, contemptuous of authority, pushing the limits. Quite normal for his age, and in any normal circumstances I'm sure he'd have matured and settled into a pleasant young man. But he never stood a chance. Now, one of Mr. Nicholls' compensations for his stunted career was, as I've said, in tormenting his family. But the other great mainspring of his malign drive was his faith - supposedly faith in a just, merciful and forgiving God. So his spare time was taken up with spreading his message at any of the churches in the area who'd have him - Methodists, Baptists, United Reformed.

'And like all evangelicals, the message was about the importance of personal conversion, of living a spiritual life inwardly as well as outwardly, the necessity of baptism affirming personal faith, and so on. In fact, he even founded his own ridiculous sect, the Evangelical Church of the Divine Forgiveness, of which he was not only founder, prophet and preacher, but sole member, Sarah having refused to join.

'Now, you'd perhaps expect such a devout individual to practice what he preached. To be tolerant, benign, forgiving. In fact he was a closet Calvinist, and I believe this is why Patrick hated him so much. It wasn't just that he was on his back all the time, but the fact that he was such a hypocrite - preaching redemption through conversion and commitment to faith on the one hand, while secretly believing, and not troubling to hide his views at home, in predestination on the other.

'Patrick understood all this perfectly well. He loathed the whole idea of Calvinism, and reckoned that in setting up this ludicrous sect his father was appointing himself God's mouthpiece on who was heading for salvation, and conversely which poor bastards were predestined for Hell. This was Mr. Nicholls' revenge on anyone who'd slighted or demeaned him, including everyone who'd ever gained promotion over him, and now in his eyes looked down on him. It was straight into Hell's fire for them - no questions asked. And Patrick always felt he'd been put in the same category, and no matter what he did or how hard he tried, Mr. Nicholls had his number and his future neatly mapped out.

'So, as I say, on this particular occasion we were sitting around the table in the cold, austere dining room. There were no pictures on the walls, no ornaments, just a threadbare carpet, table and chairs. And placed high on the wall behind Mr. Nicholls' back a large wooden cross. The chairs were hard and rigid, with practically vertical backs. We sat there in uncomfortable silence while Sarah brought through the serving dishes. Meanwhile, waves of displeasure were washing over both me and especially Patrick.

'Sarah sat down, and after she'd been passed all the plates to serve out the main part of the meal, put her hands in her lap and stared straight ahead. There was an air of unhappy anticipation around the table as we waited. Finally, the unpleasant, ponderous tones of Mr. Nicholls began to fill the room, heavily underlined and somehow made more sinister by the thick Yorkshire accent.

'By t' grace o' t' Loord Jesus Christ, und by t' power invested in me, ahr bless this meal.'

An audible, but undefined grunt came from Patrick. He reached for his knife and fork, then paused as his father started up again.

'We beg thee, Loord, fur furgiveness fur arl t' worldly sins, an' especially t' sins o' blasphemy…'

The voice rose in volume by several increments on the final word. Patrick seemed to grip his knife and fork a little tighter.

'…intemperance…'

Again a pointed, stabbing glare.

'…und, most heinous of arl i' t' Loord's eyes, lack o' feeth in t' Loord's furgiveness, un' lack o' respect fur t' agents o' t' Loord's work. Furgive them, O Loord, fur they know not what they do!'

As the roar subsided, and as if to signal that she'd heard enough, Sarah reached forward, took the lid off a serving dish, and put some vegetables on her plate. The others followed her lead, while Mr. Nicholls lapsed into welcome silence, breathing heavily.

The meal continued for a few minutes in peace, bar the clink of cutlery on plates. Then Patrick happened to murmur something softly to Sarah sitting alongside him, obviously intended for her ears alone. Something innocuous - whether she was planning to be in or out that evening, I think, from the odd word I caught.

'What?' cried his father. 'What's that ye're saying?'

'It's got nowt t' do wi' you. I were saying something private to Sarah - a'reet?'

'Thare'll be no secrets at this table oor i' this 'ouse. There are no secrets i' t' eyes o' t' Loord. We are revealed in arl oor nekedness i' t' eyes o' t' Loord, un' there is no redemption fur them what are set i' t' ways o' sin - only t' Loord's wrath un' anger, und everlasting torment.'

'Fur God's sake, why don't yur jus' mind yur own friggin' business.'

A fist came down on the table, shaking the plates and rattling the loose cutlery.

'Never tek t' Loord's name i' vain, or abuse t' agents o' t' Loord. T' Loord 'as marked them what tek 'is name i' vain, un' them what shoo no faith, un' them are marked by God fur etarnity fur etarnal torment un' damnation. Thems every action fur etarnity is preordained by God, un' there will be no salvation fur them sools marked by t' Loord!'

'If it's all preordained then God knows every word I'm ever goin' to say. So if I don't say what I were goin' to say 'e might get confused and upset, and yur wouldn't like that, would yur? Yur 'ole friggin' system'd fall to pieces. Except God would already know I only weren't sayin' what I were goin' to say to try an' confuse 'im, because 'e'd already preordained that an' all - reet?'

'What kind o' nonsense is this?'

'Look, Dad, just leave it, will yur? Just leave it, fur Christ's sake.'

"ow dare ye, ye yoong puppy! 'ow dare ye blaspheme un agent o' t' Loord! 'ave ye no pride, no respect? 'ave ye no manners? Ye're a disgrace! Do ye 'ear me, a disgrace! T' me, t' Loord, an' t' memory o' yur moother. When ahr think of arl that yur moother did fur ye, un' when ahr look at t' way ye choose t' repay 'er, with yur drinkin', yur leet 'ours, yur blasphemy, yur…'

'What 'appened t' mercy and compassion, Dad? An' t' Church o' t' Divine Pissin' Hypocrisy?'

With a roar of rage Mr. Nicholls leapt to his feet, grabbing across the table at Patrick, sending the water jug flying, its contents cascading over the table. Patrick, agile and fleet of foot jumped up, managing to dodge the outstretched arms. Red hair flying wildly, he bolted out of the room and the house.'

I shifted in my chair.

'Nice quiet meal, then?'

Gerard seemed not to hear, continuing as if from a prepared script.

'Poor little Anne had been sobbing quietly to herself, while Sarah had just sat there quite still, staring ahead, not reacting at all. Now, though, she ran out of the house after Patrick. I got up, and going to the window saw that she'd caught up with him and was talking intently, one hand on his shoulder. I looked around at Anne, still in tears, and wondered if I should try to comfort her. Mr. Nicholls meanwhile had subsided heavily back into his chair, still agitated, his face red and blotchy, mumbling and muttering darkly into the wet tablecloth.

'I decided at this point that, on the whole, the charms of tea with the Nicholls family had perhaps been greater in the anticipation than the event, and on this basis escaped thankfully from the house and approached

Sarah. On seeing me, young Patrick shrugged off Sarah's hand and ran away down a backstreet.

'Sarah looked at his retreating back for a few seconds, then turning to me glanced briefly and unhappily at my face. I felt such overwhelming love and compassion for her, yet 'Is Patrick okay?' was all I could think to say. She sighed and shook her head in wearied resignation.

'As okay as he'll ever be, given the circumstances.'

'How often does this sort of thing happen?'

'How often? I've given up counting. What possible chance does he have? I try to keep things together, keep some semblance of normality, for Anne's sake as much as anybody.'

'She was really upset when I left the house.'

'I must go back.'

She paused.

'Are you coming?'

I hesitated for a few moments.

'I'm sorry, Sarah, but I don't think I...I mean, thanks for dinner and everything...'

She half smiled.

'When will I see you again?'

She looked into my face once more, such conflicting emotions revealed through the deep, expressive power of her look.

'I don't know.'

I longed so much then to reach out and touch her. To take her hand and feel its warmth. To take her in my arms and press her body to mine - to feel her heart beating against my chest. To push back stray hairs from her forehead and caress her face. To press my lips softly against hers. Never had Sarah seemed so frail and human, yet so full of moral power and spirit.'

'So why didn't you?'

Gerard looked up. He'd become so engrossed in his story that I think he'd forgotten I was there. He became a little embarrassed and defensive.

'Do you think I don't spend every day wishing that I had? Sarah simply didn't like being touched. She couldn't entertain the idea of physical contact. The only time we ever touched in all the time I knew her was when she took my hand briefly after giving me that letter.'

'That's crazy. What kind of a relationship is that?'

Gerard gave me a strange look and shook his head slowly.

'Just to be with Sarah for a few minutes was worth more than a lifetime of any other kind of love with anybody else. She simply couldn't accept anyone, even me, intruding on her inner self, her spirituality. I was always happy to accept those limitations.'

'But surely you wanted the relationship to develop? Surely a full relationship between two people isn't possible unless the barriers come down, at least to some extent?'

Gerard was silent for some time.

'Of course I wanted her to accept me fully,' he replied at last, 'to allow our souls to come together and meet on equal terms. Maybe, given time…she did enjoy our friendship - she must have done, otherwise she wouldn't have continued with it. But still she always remained remote, almost aloof sometimes. And she was uncommunicative to the point of barely saying a word for long periods of time. Even when she was pleased about something, a small gift or a trip out, she would acknowledge it with a smile rather than words. But such a smile! A smile that you remember for the rest of your life!'

He paused, apparently reflecting.

'Apart from Rievaulx, the only place where she would really lose her reserve was in the emptiness of the open moors. We'd walk high on the fells in the Dales. She knew all their names. In fact she seemed to know all the hills we could see, near and distant. Every tiny stream, wending its way below, she knew like an old friend.

'Sometimes she'd lie on her back in a grassy clearing among the heather and bracken, shielding her eyes, watching the clouds take shape, drift on, dissolve, take on new forms. We'd see a bird of prey hovering in the silent vastness, then drop lethally upon its victim. Prompting Sarah to moralise on the strong and the weak, the uncertainty and brevity of existence. The unconscious cruelty of animals, and the knowing, conscious depravity of humankind.

'She talked freely and openly, lying on the warm earth, playing with a piece of grass, her mind roaming widely and diversely. From theories on the density of matter in the universe and the nature of black holes, to her favourite authors, or the beauty of blackthorn blossom in spring. She was interested in and moved by anything and everything around her. She loved especially all wild creatures, feeling an affinity with their freedom, their 'power of wing' and communion with the earth she loved so much. And this love of animals was evident in everything she did.

'I remember once we were walking along a road by a wide stretch of river. It was dusk. The silence was almost overpowering. The great bulk of the fells a dark, forbidding presence either side of us. Suddenly, appearing out of the gloom like a familiar came a woebegone, tattered cur, a sheepdog perhaps formerly - though it was difficult to tell from its filthy, bedraggled look. Limping sadly, its tongue lolling from its jaws.

'With a cry of joy, and disregarding its appearance, Sarah bent down and began caressing the animal, talking softly as she stroked its head and sides. After half a minute or so of this attention, and without warning, the dog repaid Sarah by sinking its teeth into her leg before disappearing as swiftly as it had come into the gathering darkness.

'I started forward in alarm to help her, but without a word or cry of pain Sarah took a few steps, then jumped from the roadside into a pool of the river, rolling her jeans up from the bottom of her leg to bathe the wound. I could see the blood running down, discolouring the water as she stood in the freezing pool. I tried to sympathise, to commiserate with her for the pain she must be feeling, but she impatiently brushed away my concerns. The bite was of no consequence.

She was concerned only about the dog, wandering the night unloved and uncared for.

'Then there was the time she rescued an injured bird we found on the moors. It was incapable of flight - one wing was badly torn. Sarah carried the poor creature all the way back to the car, a mile at least, calming it with soft words. Then nursed it as I drove back to Otley. She was devastated when the vet told us the injury was too severe to treat. She became voluble about the evil of mankind that could cause such suffering to a beautiful creature, though there was no proof I was aware of, or that the vet mentioned, to show that the injury had been caused intentionally.'

'What happened, Gerard? Tell me what happened to split up you and Sarah. She sounds quite a remarkable woman.'

Of course I was asking only out of academic interest, to see in what creative manner Gerard would conclude this tragic little tale. But I was also aware of the time, and that Melanie might be back at any moment. Gerard appeared for a few moments to be collecting his thoughts.

'After the dinner incident I told you about, Patrick soon went from bad to worse. The oppression of his home life seemed to make him lose all self-restraint.

'He took to spending every night in the pub, drinking heavily. I don't know where the money came from. I know drugs were involved as well, but to what extent I'm not sure. He was forever getting into fights, often through pointlessly goading and taunting lads equally tanked up. Sometimes the fight would spill out, or they'd get thrown out and continue in the street.

'Sarah and I came across this once coming back from a late night walk around the town. There was a crowd of people shouting just outside the Black Swan, and Sarah spotted Patrick in the middle of it, face covered in blood, being held and thumped by some lad towering over him. She ran over, grabbed this character by the hair and dragged him to the side of the street, where his face appeared to make sudden contact with a wall. She left him there on the ground holding his head and went back to Patrick, supporting him back home where she bathed his face. This took place about a month or so after that dinner, when Patrick's decline had already set in. In fact it was the first time I'd seen Sarah since then, and almost the last time I ever did. She didn't look well even then, but it was nothing to what followed.'

'At least you did get to see her again,' I said quietly and encouragingly.

'A couple of weeks later Patrick somehow got hold of a huge, powerful motorbike - a Kawasaki Z900 if I remember rightly. Of course, he was riding it illegally. He'd never passed any test to ride that size of bike. And a few weeks later, high on drink and drugs, he crashed it into a stone wall on the road between Otley and Harrogate. It was in all the local papers. The police estimated that the bike had been doing over a hundred when it hit the wall. Patrick had no chance at all. You know, if only he'd come to me I could have taught him so much about lines and lean angles and throttle control.'

Gerard sighed deeply.

'I sent flowers, of course. I sent a card of condolence. I subsequently wrote letter after letter to Sarah begging her to get in touch. I was beginning to despair of ever seeing her again when out of the blue I received a brief note saying that she needed to see me. All this time I'd respected her privacy, her need to be alone after Patrick's death. I could only imagine how much her grief would have affected her. So I was overjoyed, believing that she wanted to resume our relationship. I wrote back in great excitement suggesting that we meet at our usual place in the middle of town.

'When the day came I got there in good time and sat on a wall, waiting, scanning the faces of passers-by on that crowded Saturday morning. And when I did at last see Sarah, at first I didn't recognise her. I looked away, then looked back with feelings of mounting shock and disbelief. She'd always been slim, but now her frame was emaciated. How she'd even managed to make it down into town I have no idea. She could walk only slowly, and each few steps seemed to leave her breathless. I jumped up in fear and alarm and went to her, but she refused my offers of help and support. She made her way painstakingly by her own efforts to where I'd been waiting, sat down and closed her eyes for a few moments. Her breathing was rapid and shallow.

'At last she opened her eyes, turned slowly to me, and reached out an unbearably thin hand to mine, clasping it tightly for a few brief seconds. When she spoke her voice was a whisper, barely audible.

'Gerard, I can't stay. I have to get back. I just wanted to give you this in person. It seemed the least you deserved.'

She held out the letter, her arm and hand trembling, her eyes sunken, faded and disinterested. For the last time I looked into her face, now pale and wasted, a piteous shadow.

I read the letter, shielding my eyes and face as its meaning hit me. At last I turned back to Sarah. But she was gone. I leapt to my feet and began searching frantically, trying to spy her in the crowded streets, tracing any route she might have taken. But she'd simply disappeared. It was as if none of it had ever happened, and her appearance had been merely a vision, a trick of the mind.'

Gerard turned to me, his eyes glistening.

'She gave Patrick everything she had to give, not just because he was her brother, but because he was a human being and he was suffering greatly. With the loss of his mother, Patrick needed his father's love more than ever. Sarah could see how anguished Patrick was by his father's constant rejection, however he tried to conceal it. Even before he died, Sarah was grieved by the injustice of Patrick's treatment, which in her mind led directly to his death.

'And I think it was this inconsolable pity for Patrick after he died which left her completely unreceptive to the messenger of Hope. And without those visitations her faith was destroyed, her credo disproven. Don't you see, Robbie, Sarah was more than just a beautiful, compassionate woman - she was a visionary, a mystic. And her visions had simply ceased to come.

'So Sarah withdrew more completely than ever into herself, isolating herself in almost total silence and refusal to respond to outside contacts. She became imprisoned within a cell of her own making, and without her messenger the way out was lost.'

From the front door came the sound of a key being inserted into the latch, and the door opening. Gerard at once scampered off into the hallway and down into his lair, and moments later Melanie came into the room wearing tight black leggings and white tee-shirt, both of which followed the contours of her body with unnerving precision.

Despite the coolness of the evening her hair, tied back for practical reasons, was sleek and shiny with perspiration, glistening also on her forehead and above her lips. She didn't immediately acknowledge my presence, firstly looking at her watch to check the time of her run back from the gym. Then, sitting down on a settee, she looked towards me, unsmiling, but not overtly unfriendly.

'What have you been doing with yourself - watching TV?'

'No, I've just had a hilarious evening with Gerard, who was spinning some outrageous tale, presumably with the intention of diverting me from his attentions to you.'

'How many times do I have to tell you that Gerard is simply a friend, on a purely and strictly platonic basis. You're suffering from a completely irrational jealousy. You hate it that I might actually enjoy having a friendship with another man.'

'Tell me something. Have you ever told Gerard about my suspicions regarding his obsession with you?'

Melanie jumped up, her eyes hard and cold. I jumped as well, but dextrously managed to keep a settee between us.

'If you don't drop this you're going to make me very angry. Just stop it - now!'

'Okay, okay. I was just floating an idea. There's no need to jump off the deep end. Look, I wasn't asking completely randomly - there's a very good reason. And if you stop looking at me like that I'll explain it to you. Please,' I said, indicating the settee, 'sit down for a minute.'

Melanie looked deeply into my eyes for a few moments, then reluctantly sat down. I sat down opposite her, before relating Gerard's story, down to every last quiver of emotion, trying my best to be faithful to the artistic pretensions of the original. When I'd finished, Melanie, who'd listened intently, turned to me, her eyes shining in a manner uncomfortably reminiscent of Gerard.

'Oh God, how he's suffered!'

Oh God preserve me from unvarnished, wide-eyed naivety.

'Melanie, you don't really believe all that nonsense, do you?'

'Why shouldn't I believe it? You've just told me that's exactly how Gerard told it to you.'

'Yes, but that doesn't make it true, for God's sake. Does nothing strike you about this story? Does it not ring any bells?'

'What do you mean?'

'I mean he made the whole thing up, yet again. Really, it's blindingly obvious. This Sarah he claims to have had a relationship with - it's Emily Brontë! Can't you see that?'

Melanie looked stupefied for a few moments, toyed briefly with amusement, then settled on anger mingled with synthetic concern.

'Robbie, I honestly don't know whether what you do is deliberate or in fact whether you have no control over your delusions, but this crusade to discredit and belittle Gerard is becoming obsessional. I think we must try and get some kind of help for you.'

'Do you know anything about the Brontës?'

'Of course I do. Don't forget I come from Keighley. I probably know far more about them than you do.'

'So you'll be well aware that every event in Gerard's story was lifted straight from Emily Brontë's life.'

'Robbie, you're making connections where there aren't any. Emily Brontë was hardly the first or last person to be bitten by a dog. And she certainly wasn't walking with her boyfriend in the Yorkshire Dales at the time. In fact, I think that's the key thing you need to remember, which undermines your entire thesis. Emily Brontë never had a boyfriend, and all that we know about her character suggests that she was incapable of forming or sustaining that level of relationship. Sarah cannot be Emily Brontë for that very reason.'

'Okay. I'm not saying there aren't inconsistencies and flaws in Gerard's story. But it's absolutely consistent with Gerard's matchless vanity that he should consider himself the only person in the world capable of getting close to Emily Brontë. Therefore it's beside the point that in real life she never had a boyfriend. We're not talking real life here, we're in the world of Gerard's tortured imagination - a world of phantoms and shadows.'

'I despair, I really do.'

'Well, so do I. But Gerard needs our help, and maybe we should try to be there for him.'

'I don't know what to say to you any more, Robbie. It's like living with a stranger.'

'Look, why don't we just ask him to leave, for God's sake. And then maybe we could go back to how it used to be. Just the two of us, just ourselves. You know, we could still make this work.'

Melanie didn't reply, and a cold silence settled over the room. I felt a pervading sense of hopeless dislocation. Of being able to see someone in every detail, but unable to reach, touch or communicate with them. Like seeing a face that you love aboard an ocean liner, and you're trying to catch their eye, but then the ship begins slowly, inexorably, to move away from the dock. And still she doesn't see you, and now the ship is gathering momentum and still, desperately, you try to catch her attention, to somehow indicate how much you love her, how much she means to you. But the ship is steaming steadily into the distance now, and it's difficult to make out her face among the strangers crowding the rails, waving, blowing last kisses to family, friends, loved ones. And then it's a dot on the horizon, and the echo of its passage on the sea's surface has settled, and everything is calm once more.

'Did you make this story up, Robbie?'
 'What?'
 'Are you sure you're not just making up this story about Sarah?'
 'Of course I'm not making it up.'
 'Robbie, the story as you've told it doesn't make sense, even on its own terms. If Sarah is as he describes, or as you say he describes, she would never have made friends with someone outside of her family at all, never mind someone who randomly approaches her in the street. The story as you've related it to me lacks inner logic.'
 'What do you mean - as I've related it to you? I've told you the story of Sarah exactly as Gerard told it to me. If the story doesn't make - '

'Just a minute, I haven't finished. As for your suggestion that Gerard made all this up, but based the character on Emily Brontë, there are numerous instances where the characters, names and events are radically different from the well-documented, historical facts concerning the lives of the Brontës.'

'I'm not denying that there are certain - '

'Just a moment, Robbie, let me finish. Emily had two sisters who survived childhood, for example. In your version there is only one.'

'Yes, but - '

'And Branwell Brontë was driven to self-destruction by the treachery and double-dealing of the woman he loved.'

'Yes that's true, but - '

'Not by the oppression of his father. Mr. Brontë was apparently a supportive, even indulgent parent to his children, certainly by the standards of the time.'

'Okay, so Mr. Nicholls isn't at all like Patrick Brontë except in appearance. But that's just to put me off the trail, because he knew that otherwise I'd know what his game was.'

'In that case, why didn't he change the names completely if he wanted to cover his tracks?'

'Look, I think it's fairly clear he was taunting me, daring me to make the connection and challenge him about it.'

'Why should he want to do that? Even if we grant the premise of your argument, ludicrous as it is, what would be the point?'

'It was a form of test - a trial to see how much he could get away with, how far he could push me. And now, of course, he's pre-empted any accusation I might have made against him by flagging up this bogus explanation. It's brilliant, it really is! He's a genius! In fact I now believe in his genius as strongly as he does himself.'

'I think quite genuinely you're in the process of losing your mind. Look - either what Gerard told you was completely true. Or the story is basically true but you have changed and embellished certain parts to make Gerard look ridiculous. Or else you have simply made up this whole episode for the express purpose of assigning to Gerard motives he doesn't have, and to make him look yet more ridiculous.'

'So you admit the story is ridiculous?'

'It would be ridiculous if you just made it up.'

'But if Gerard made it up it would be a tender, moving love story?'

'If Gerard really did tell you that story, which I doubt, then I'm sure it is true, and therefore he couldn't and wouldn't have made it up.'

'Well, why don't you ask him whether he made it up or not?'

'I have no reason to doubt Gerard's word, so if he did tell that story, as you say, then it would be true, and if he didn't it would only serve to underline your rather fragile mental state. I don't think my asking him would be productive either way.'

'It just comes down to a question of trust in the end, Melanie, doesn't it?'

'Yes, Robbie, I'm afraid it does. And I think you need to take a long, hard look at yourself and your increasingly hysterical jealous delusions.'

By a huge effort of will I managed to contain the hatred and resentment raging within me.

What would it take to turn our relationship around - to prevent it from sliding, apparently inevitably, into absolute indifference, or worse? That we were being pulled apart was indisputable. Yet despite my present feelings and past differences, my passion for Melanie remained as deeply rooted as ever, as was my conviction that all we needed was time together. Time to reconnect, to be ourselves and do all those little things we used to do, away from the pressures which circumstances had brought to bear.

17

Returning to Fairfax House one evening from a meal out at Burgers - U - Like, I was reminded once more of how Melanie's driving was every bit as sensuous and aesthetically satisfying as her physical form. The turn-in to corners so smooth and perfectly judged that the point of entry became practically imperceptible. Braking and acceleration appearing to seamlessly overlap. Her slim, sensitive hands delicately caressing the top of the gear knob in executing swift and flawless changes.

My eyes involuntarily followed a path from her left hand, up her arm to the nape of her long, delicate neck. Passing streetlights cast a rhythmical glow of illumination on the profile of her face, on the perfectly rounded forehead and classically straight nose. My gaze then descending once more, past the strong yet feminine shoulders, wonderfully firm breasts, down to those long, strong legs, with their warm promise of...

Melanie glanced briefly over at me.

'What are you looking at?'

'Nothing, nothing. Nothing at all. Nothing...I was just admiring your driving.'

The mere sight of Fairfax House tended to reduce my good intentions by several increments. And on seeing the living room lit up through the curtains, my heart sank further still. Please let not the little master still be up. Let him not be in our living room, waiting, as a spider crouches at the centre of its web - motionless, infinitely patient, poised for the first slight tremble of movement before springing into pitiless action.

'I do hope Gerard has disappeared for the night. Do you think we left the living room light on by mistake? I'm fairly sure we did. Yes, we must have done. Look, it's almost ten o'clock. Gerard will have gone to bed by now. That's it, of course, we must have left it on by mistake. By the way, I think there's some snooker starting in a few minutes.'

'Really.'

Melanie sounded surprisingly disinterested.

'Yes, really. Do you doubt my word? I'm not given to lying about these things. Just think, Mel, we could sit down and watch it together.'

Melanie, meanwhile, had deftly inserted the car into a space and was now waiting with only a hint of impatience.

'Come on, Robbie. I don't want to stand here forever.'

Moments later we were walking side by side towards the front door.

'Wouldn't that be wonderful?'

'What?'

'Watching the snooker together. Weren't you listening?'

'You know I don't particularly like snooker, Robbie.'

'Well, you ought to. All those handsome men in well-cut evening dress leaning provocatively all over the table.'

'That sort of thing doesn't interest me at all.'

She put the key in the lock.

'Well, it ought to. Snooker is supposed to appeal to women in particular. Why do you think so many women watch it for hours on end?'

'So why do you watch it, Robbie?'

She threw the car keys onto a silver plate bowl and opened the living room door.

'Well, I...what the...'

A nightmare vision greeted us. The gruesome daubs which passed as Gerard's art were everywhere - floor, settees, sideboard - any available surface was simply littered with the things. As I glanced around with mounting horror, image after grotesque image entered my brain, searing and burning into my senses, which reeled and faltered - desperately I clutched the door jamb for support. And there, there in the centre of it all was the little artist, still busily arranging his...artwork.

'Gerard!'

Melanie, standing in the centre of the room with hands clasped together, was looking at the pictures with the eager, rapt expression of a little girl surveying her Christmas presents.

'Gerard!' she repeated. 'This is wonderful.'

'Which one in particular?' I asked hoarsely, still feeling faint, yet genuinely curious to know if there was even one that could be regarded as adequate. Melanie gave me a cold look.

'All of them,' she replied tersely, turning her back. 'Gerard, I had no idea you'd done so many wonderful paintings, or that the standard...well, they're just so good.'

The little artist paused in his distribution of the paintings to give a modest, self-satisfied smirk. From a pile of half a dozen canvases stacked casually against one of our almost new, off-white settees, he drew one, then with an awkward gesture held it out towards Melanie.

'This is for you,' he said, pausing before adding, 'in grateful appreciation for everything you've done for me.'

What the fuck was that supposed to mean? She hadn't done any more for him than I had, and I obviously wasn't getting a free picture - not that I wanted one of the bloody things. Unless of course she had done more for him than I had, which knowing and therefore not trusting the pair of them, was always possible.

'Oh Gerard,' she said, 'I don't know what to say. Thank you. Thank you so much.'

She held it at arm's length and gazed at it for a moment. Gerard stepped forward with an irritated gesture, snatched the picture and turned it through ninety degrees.

'It goes this way round.'

Melanie smiled apologetically.

'I'm so sorry, Gerard. Yes, of course.'

She held it out again for a few moments.

'I think...I need to see it from a greater distance to really appreciate it.'

'How about Jupiter?' I asked.

Melanie managed to prop the picture on top of the television. Then, carefully avoiding the odd stray canvas lying on our freshly-fitted carpet, she stepped back to gain the full effect.

'It's wonderful, Gerard,' she said, after half a minute's silence. 'It's really beautiful. What...I mean, is it meant to be representational?'

'What on earth are you talking about?' exploded the little master. 'It's you. It's a portrait of you. Can't you see that?'

Just for once Melanie was on the ropes, and it was going to be instructive to see how she'd get out of the situation. That she would I had no doubts, though she was reeling a little at this point. From where I was standing, the top of the picture was just a yellow blob, which might or might not be taken as representing Melanie's hair. Under this was a daub of blue, a jumper perhaps, or a coat or jacket. Then two white lines to the bottom of the picture, the whole set off against a pink background. To be honest it could have been anyone - or anything for that matter.

'I've never seen anything quite like it,' I said truthfully. From the corner of my eye I could see Melanie looking on suspiciously.

'It's quite remarkable,' I continued, shaking my head as if in awe. Gerard grunted, perhaps slightly mollified, and began shuffling yet more canvases.

'You've captured the inner beauty of your subject with rare skill. I particularly like the striking juxtaposition of colours, and the symbolic symmetry of the work.'

'It's not symbolic at all,' snapped Melanie. 'You heard what Gerard said, it's a portrait, and an extremely flattering one too. And what could possibly be symbolic about symmetry, even supposing the portrait was symmetrical, which it clearly isn't.'

She was good. Say what you like about her but you have to admit she really was good. Speed of reaction, footwork - she had the lot.

'Well,' I said, trying to launch a small counter-offensive, 'you could argue that symmetry in art is the perfect realisation of order and balance, and that the symmetry in Gerard's very wonderful portrait is intended to symbolise his subject's exquisite mental and psychological equilibrium.'

Melanie opened her mouth to offer a riposte, then rather comically closed it again and frowned. Obviously trying to decide whether I had insulted, or alternatively complimented either her, or Gerard, or both. Or whether I was just taking the piss, which of course was in fact the case.

Our discussion was interrupted by the clatter of flying canvases. With what seemed unnecessary violence Gerard was collecting his works and stacking them in apparently random piles around the floor. I always found something hilarious about Gerard's anger, like seeing a small child stomping around pulling angry faces.

'Be careful you don't damage any of those pictures, Gerard,' I called.

He wheeled on us, his face red and hot, eyes boring angrily. Running a hand through the lank, ebony hair with an impatient gesture.

'One day my work will be appreciated by those who are not complete imbeciles!'

Almost screaming the words.

'You're not talking about us, Gerard, surely?'

'If you knew anything you would know that representational art is not about producing some quasi-photographic image.'

'I'm sure it isn't,' I replied, somewhat mystified.

'Neither of you have the faintest idea about the meaning of art. So I would appreciate it if you didn't venture any more uninformed and ignorant opinions.'

And with that he grabbed a handful of canvases, went out into the hall, kicked open the door to the cellar and disappeared from view. Followed by a prolonged series of bangs, perhaps of something falling down the basement steps, and a steady stream of high-pitched cursing. I turned away, hoping to hide my amusement, as Melanie stepped quickly to the cellar door.

'Are you alright, Gerard?'

She waited anxiously until the sounds of more muffled banging and muttering were heard, then came and sat back on the settee with a sigh. I hurriedly composed my features.

'Why,' I asked, 'do you suppose our little friend had put all those paintings around the room? Surely not just to impress us.'

Melanie glared.

'Gerard told us several weeks ago that he was going to stage an exhibition of his work.'

'Not here, surely?'

'Of course not. He was giving us an exclusive preview and, I expect, hoping to receive some words of praise and encouragement. And all you could do was mock and deride his work.'

'Me? What on earth are you talking about? I quite specifically and fulsomely lavished praise on his portrait of you, or whatever it was meant to be.'

'That's always your way, isn't it. Insincere praise, followed by some insidious snide remark. You can't even offer straightforward, upfront criticism. Instead it's always mocking, weaselly words followed by some sly comment, like a stiletto in the ribs.'

'Look, you didn't even know what the fucking picture was meant to be until he told you. You didn't even know which way round the bloody thing went.'

'That is not true.'

'It is so true, as you well know. And stop encouraging the little pervert - he's got enough problems as it is.'

'How dare you call him that.'

Melanie had risen from the settee and was now standing menacingly a couple of feet from me.

'Well he is little.'

'Don't be clever. Don't call him...'

She paused as Gerard's footsteps returning from the cellar grew louder.

'Don't call him that word,' she hissed.

'What? You mean pervert?'

Melanie took a step towards me, and I took one hurriedly backwards.

'Look,' I whispered, 'I want to help him as much as you do. I'm going to put him in touch with Mike Fraulent.'

'Don't you dare even suggest it.'

We paused and took up neutral positions as Gerard entered the room and began gathering another armful of masterpieces.

'Gerard,' I called, beginning to pick my way carefully through the debris.

'Robbie, I'm warning you,' said Melanie quietly to my back.

I turned briefly towards her.

'Melanie, trust me - I'm not a doctor...Gerard, you know sometimes our concerns and worries seem bigger and more important to us, more threatening even, when seen in isolation. Sometimes, if they can be viewed in a wider context, they appear relatively trivial, unimportant even.'

A canvas slipped from Gerard's grasp and rolled, corner over corner, for several yards before toppling, paint-side first, onto a vacant piece of carpet. I winced, more at this than at the inspired stream of invective that followed.

'And there are people very skilled and experienced in helping us to understand and come to terms with these...worries. Very kind, understanding people with, as I say, a lot of experience in helping people who might have certain concerns and little problems. I wonder if you've ever - '

'What the hell are you talking about?'

Gerard dropped the artworks in a pile and strutted over, confronting me face to face - in my own living room - my own home.

'Perhaps you'd like to explain yourself.'

'Well, Gerard,' I said, hesitating for a moment while struggling to select the best form of words. 'I'd like to think that my meaning, like my intentions, was completely transparent.'

'What exactly were you insinuating with that little speech? And how dare you use that tone with me - speaking to me as if I were a retarded child! Counselling? Is that what you were driving at? Counselling?'

He spat the word like some vicious and obscene oath.

'You are like every other philistine in this world! You, with no concept of beauty, of form, proportion, balance, style - in short, any basic grasp of aesthetics. You, with no understanding of the central role that aesthetics should play in our consciousness, in the national consciousness, in human consciousness itself, without which we are little better than animals! Competing without pity or compassion for survival. Nothing more!

'Any fool or knave could understand that a world without aesthetic passion is an arid wilderness of base desires and empty gestures! Devoid of finer sensibilities, those very sensibilities which set the human race apart and proclaim our unique position among living beings. And because I dare, dare to strive in my art to express our unconscious desires in works of conscious and transcendental beauty, dare to reach for the heights of achievement, to grasp that eternal, burning flame of aesthetic revelation, dare to care about my art with an intensity of passion which you and your kind can only dream of, you dare to mock this great artistic quest and cast insinuations upon my emotional stability! Of course, this is no surprise. This is the fate of the great man throughout history, of every great artist, every great political leader - to be mocked and derided by those who do not deserve to breathe the same air or stand on the same piece of ground.'

I'd never been on the receiving end of such a hefty dose of the hairdryer treatment before. The impassioned face was inches from my own, contorted with fury and emotion, eyes popping, and each successive point punctuated with melodramatic arm and hand gestures. I turned to Melanie for support. She was standing impassively, arms folded, her expression suggesting that I was getting exactly what I deserved. Clearly little prospect of help from that quarter. And although I could fully appreciate the humour of the situation, there nevertheless seemed a danger of it all getting out of hand. Taking on Melanie alone the odds were unpromising. Melanie coupled with a raving psychopath was a distinctly unrewarding prospect. It was up to me, as a mature and responsible individual, to try to defuse the situation.

'Gerard, Gerard, my dear friend, you're taking this all far too seriously. All I meant was - '

'Some might be astonished that at the very time when I am creating the foundations for a world revolution through A New Society and my political activity, something which I can honestly describe as an heroic struggle for the existence of any meaningful human society, I should nevertheless at this time be dedicating my will to the revival and resurrection of Art. That beside my great struggle to lay the foundations of a new and sustainable society offering humanity a fresh opportunity, a chance of rebirth, I yet find time also to lay the foundations for a temple to the goddess of Art. I will not be drawn into debate with those who, to judge from their non-achievements, are lunatics in the world of culture, destroyers of Art. I will not be drawn into personal dispute with such as belong in either prison, or possibly some secure accommodation.

'There are, nevertheless, some well-intentioned folk who might object that my efforts in the name of Art are neither necessary nor of pressing urgency. Are not practical considerations more important? Is not the satisfaction of the material needs of life more important than the erection of great buildings, the composition of beautiful music, the creation of visual works of power and emotional impact? No, no and a thousand times no!

'Art is not an activity of human life which can be summoned at will and then dismissed as mere frippery. When the human spirit, oppressed by suffering and anxiety, falters in its faith in the future, then is the moment for Art, for the purity of aesthetic ideals, to become more than merely palliative and balm to the tortured soul, but to be its regenerator, its lifeblood! The great cultural attainments of artists throughout the ages stand as the highest achievements...'

Stranded amid the verbiage I stole a glance at my watch. Damn! I'd probably already missed the first couple of frames. And it was the best of the semis tonight, the match which, in my opinion, should have been the final. I decided to begin an experimental edging process towards the TV.

'...of the great civilizations of the past without the visible, physical manifestations of their...'

If I could just very cautiously and without anybody really noticing...

'...great lines of Kings and Emperors without their palaces and cathedrals? What of the Romans without their temples and underfloor heating? What of the Egyptians...'

'Yes, John, I agree with you. I don't think Ronnie looks settled yet. Nobody doubts he's the most naturally talented player the game has ever seen. But he's up against a young man full of confidence in himself and his game.'

Come on, just give us the score. Must be two nil. They can't have had time for more than a couple of frames.

'...and it has been suggested that in devoting my energies towards the realisation of Lutyens' masterpiece that I am diverting my attention unnecessarily from my political...'

Three nil. Bloody hell!

'It's important for Ronnie to settle down and try and win this one before the break. If 'e can win this one 'e'll only be two be'ind, and there's a big psychological difference if 'e can put one on the scoreboard and go for 'is cup of tea two be'ind rather than four be'ind.'

'Well, John, a Hurricane or a Whirlwind at their peak might have been able to blow out this amazing conflagration we're witnessing, perhaps even an in-form Wizard. So let's see what the Rocket can do. Breaking off now for the fourth frame.'

'...and it must always be remembered that the erection of public buildings on the scale of a great cathedral provides a timeless significance, an eternal value...'

I wish the little prick would pipe down - I can hardly make out what John and Ted are saying half the time.

'I agree with you, Ted. This young man, once 'e's in the balls, 'e's practically unstoppable.'

'...in doing homage to his eternal genius, we may one day look and wonder, that men may...'

'...talk about his long potting, John. It's quite remarkable how...'

'…such as will grow to the stature demanded by these higher tasks, and we have no right to doubt that if the Almighty gives us…'

'…tremendous tactical ability, Ted. It's true 'e doesn't often 'ave to use it. But it's there when 'e…'

'…will gain the consciousness of a higher destiny!'

I tore my ears from the absorbing commentary and turned to take in a surreal and disturbing scene. Either unaware or unmoved by the fact that I was now watching TV Gerard was continuing to declaim to the empty air in front of him. The eyes were glassy and staring. The voice soaring to shrill climaxes, with many high-pitched rasping notes, and then dropping through an emotional, vibrating glissando. There was a strange bounce to his shoulders as emotion gripped him, an arching of the neck, a kind of self-absorbed defiance. By turns threatening and pleading - the hands imploring and beseeching, then as suddenly chopping and dismissing in cold fury.

He was undoubtedly totally unaware of me now, and though Melanie was all rapt attention across the other side of the room he appeared equally oblivious of her. I looked on in horrified fascination at what seemed incontrovertible proof of the poor creature's mental unravelling. It was like watching a fly on a window sill in the height of summer, buzzing around aimlessly on its back as the last moments of its life ebb away. Helpless, out of control. Does it know? Does it have any idea of the brutal reality of its situation? Does

Gerard on any level have self-knowledge or insight into the reality beyond his outrageous outbursts? Watching him now it seemed very evident that he hadn't.

Again I felt a real outpouring of compassion, a determination to do something positive to help him. And also a degree of shame. Melanie was right in one sense - my mockery of Gerard was cruel and unworthy. He needed help, not calculated derision. But I still felt she was terribly mistaken in playing up to his delusions, reinforcing his psychosis. We had to get professional, independent help.

I sidled over to Mel and sat down beside her, speaking quietly, my head close to hers.

'Well, are you convinced now?'

'Shh!' she said, holding up a hand and leaning forwards. 'I want to hear this.'

I glared at her in disbelief and exasperation.

'Melanie,' I said, raising my voice, 'do you realise what we're witnessing here?'

'Of course I do,' she whispered. 'It's a demonstration of Gerard's extraordinary capacity to speak extempore with remarkable command over his message and material.'

'No, no, no, no no! Are you really as stupid as you pretend to be, or are you not pretending? Look, for God's sake - look at him! He's not aware we're here. He's talking disjointed gibberish to some imaginary audience, who presumably are all cheering wildly and chanting his name. Listen, listen. Ger-ard! Ger-ard! Ger-ard! Ger-ard! Then he'll hold up his hand - look, he's doing it now - and the crowd quieten to an awed, expectant hush, and then in a low voice, throbbing with emotion, he'll start to wring their hearts, particularly the women - look, there he goes, look at their faces. Look at the hungry, shining eyes, the arms outstretched towards him as he plays like a virtuoso on their susceptible female emotions. Look, look as he manipulates their responses, building and building their emotional excitement - they can hardly breath now, the tension so expertly held and controlled, mesmerised by the vehemence and passion. And now the climax can't be far away, tears of ecstasy running down their faces, somewhere a stifled sob, an emotional flood tide that can't be held in check much longer, a frenzy of sexual excitement...'

I gasped in pain and surprise from a sharp blow to the side of my face. Melanie had risen and struck me with an open hand in one swift movement. I involuntarily put a hand to my stinging cheek.

'How dare you! Get out!'

'Melanie...'

'Your mind is disgusting. Now get out.'

I stumbled to the door, more shocked than hurt, casting a hurried glance behind me. At least my humiliation hadn't been witnessed by the little prick, still oblivious to everything but the swirling, emotionally charged atmosphere he'd created in his head, and still clearly possessed by his ecstatic, trance-like state. Oh, I'm going, Melanie - don't you worry about that! Slamming the door behind me. This is personal now.

Mike? It's Robbie.

Sorry Mike, it's a bad line. I said it's Robbie.

Yeah, long time no hear.

It's never been that long, surely.

How's things then, Mike - how's the practice?

Well, I guess there's never any shortage, is there.

Yeah, yeah, she's fine.

I know.

Well, she is, yeah. I'm very lucky.

I know.

Oh, she remembers you, Mike. She often talks about you. I think you made quite an impression.

Not quite what I meant, Mike. You bugger, you haven't changed.

Really. I'm sorry to hear that, Mike, I really am.

So you didn't know anything about it?

Always the way, isn't it.

Yeah, I know. It's a bitter irony, Mike.

No, I meant you being a psychiatrist, with all your knowledge of human emotion and behaviour, being caught so unawares.

I know. Undoubtedly. So why did she...

Sure.

Yeah.

Oh, I know.

Yes, I'd really like that, Mike. In fact I did have an ulterior motive in calling you. I wondered if I could draw on your expertise - informally.

No, no, it's someone who lodges with us. Lives down in the basement. Guy called Gerard.

No, nothing like that, thank God. Well, as far as I know. Although I do have some worries regarding him and Melanie. But that's a private thing. No, it's all to do with having a basic hold on reality, or lack of that, that worries me.

Well, yes, I am seriously concerned.

Well, I know nothing about psychiatry, Mike, as you know. But even as a layman I'm pretty certain the poor guy is seriously disturbed.

No, I don't really think that's possible.

Look, maybe if I came along and described his behaviour to you?

Sure. I understand that.

Sure.

Yeah.

Oh, I know.

Okay, fine. Well, let's do that, then.

Look forward to it, Mike.

Okay, fine. Well, see you soon, then.

18

Somerset Drive. A wide, leafy, sleepy road in one of the many prosperous parts of Harrogate. Along its length monstrous stone villas, like vast, friendless mausoleums, standing back in haughty grandeur from the heavily cambered, tree-lined avenue. A hansom clatters past. In the distance a chaise approaches, while beneath the branches of tall sycamores a party of young, elegant ladies in long dresses, parasols in hand, stroll in the perfumed air, leaning close in conversation and the exchange of precious confidences.

I lock the car and look again along the empty street, oppressed by the autumnal, dying feel of the place. Yet surely once young, vibrant spirits must have spent their childhood here, played games with eager eyes and merry faces. And later hoped, and planned and dreamed. And loved, and saw the turning of love and the passing of dreams. And over time and the passing of long years found resignation of spirit, quiet endurance, the coming of peace.

If it was left to me I'd sweep away all symbols of the past, all monuments, private and public. I'd get the bulldozer to dingy, memory-encrusted piles like this. But in its way musing on the future is just as morbid. Both past and future admit the passage of time, change and decay, advancing age, and death.

So instead why don't we dispense with them altogether. In fact, why don't we agree that there should be no time. Or at the very least let time enjoy a well-earned retirement. Let it kick off its boots and warm its feet before a blazing fire, glass of port in hand, gazing reverently at the willow-pattern plates upon the picture rail and Constable's Haywain, forever marooned in river silt, hanging eternally above the fireplace. Let there be only an infinite present where Melanie, my own dear, radiant, perfect Melanie, can exist forever in all the glory of her matchless beauty.

The porch door sprang open, breaking my reverie. And there was my old friend, dressed in blue shirt, off-white slacks and sandals, coming towards me with hand outstretched, eyes crinkling and beard twisting into something resembling a smile.
'Robbie - how are you? Good to see you!'
Mike Fraulent wasn't such a bad bloke. Tall, with a pleasant, longish, intelligent face and cultured, well-modulated voice.
'Mike. Nice to see you again.'
His handshake was aggressively firm - unfortunately, in my experience, often indicative of a defensively inadequate personality. The transformation in Mike since I first knew him was striking. The mischievous long-haired rebel had shrunk with precipitate haste into bearded middle age.
We walked back along the path, and as Mike indicated particular points of interest among the shrubs and

flower beds I looked up at the house. Semi-detached, similar in general appearance to Fairfax House, but possibly even more epic in scale. Somehow, though, managing to be less blatantly offensive. The stone facing and stuccoed gable, though grey and depressing, were less of an aesthetic slap in the face than red brick.

'Come in, Robbie. Come in and welcome.'

We proceeded through an elegant hall into what appeared to be Mike's consulting room, spacious but sparely furnished, with two large windows overlooking an unkempt garden.

'We'd just had the windows replaced when Susan...'

Mike trailed off, hiding his emotions by going over to the windows, opening and closing one pointlessly several times.

'It was very expensive, of course, but it's worth it in the long run, and means the place will be easier to sell, which is what things will probably come to. And one of the first things potential buyers look for is modern, high-quality double glazing.'

He sighed and wandered back towards me.

'And there's no doubt it looks so much better, so much cleaner and neater than the old windows. And of course they don't need painting every couple of years.'

My heart leapt for joy. The wonderfully sanitary high-quality benefits of aesthetically superior plastic windows! What a joy for the occupants they must be - hygienic, tasteful, and of course they never need painting, not even every couple of years. Gerard, my dear friend, if only you were here to share this moment!

Which thought reminded me of the purpose of my visit.

'I hate to trouble you, Mike, at a time like this when you've got problems of your own.'

'Not at all, not at all. Life goes on, Robbie. I'll be more than happy to help, if I can. By the way, I'm sorry Melanie didn't come with you. She would have been more than welcome, you know, more than welcome.'

His face had assumed an intense expression.

'Well, she was kind of busy, Mike. Planning another offensive, I think - I mean planning some more decorating.'

'That's a shame. What a remarkable woman! She's someone whose beauty, once experienced, remains fixed in one's consciousness. I find myself thinking about her quite often. It seems impossible to quite put her out of mind.'

You're just not trying hard enough.

'Well, she's certainly thought-provoking,' I replied.

'A remarkably beautiful woman. Remarkably beautiful. I'm sure you realise how lucky you are, Robbie.'

'Well, Mike, good fortune comes in many shapes and sizes, and in fact often strikes when you're least expecting it.'

'Remarkable, quite remarkable!'

Oh God, I'm surrounded by perverts and lunatics.

'Now Robbie, please - sit down, sit down.'

He waved a hand towards a large black leather armchair - the equivalent, by its appearance, of the traditional psychiatrist's couch. Why were we in the consulting room? Why the doctor/patient set up?

And why the two large, eye-catching, undeniably pornographic and certainly wildly inappropriate paintings on the walls of a professional consulting room? One depicting a male figure displaying an erection of extravagant, one might say heroically unrealistic proportions. The other portraying a naked female whose legs were so far apart that I was reminded unaccountably of one of the many vehicular tunnels through the Swiss/Austrian Alps.

'Make yourself comfortable, Robbie, just try and relax completely.'

I managed with difficulty to divert my attention from the paintings.

'Mike, you do realise I'm not here on my own behalf?'

'Of course, of course...now Robbie, tell me a little about these worries, these concerns of yours. When do you think they first started?'

'They started the day this guy came to live in our home. No, in fact they started the moment he first knocked at the door to look at the room. It was obvious to me from the start that he was an obsessive crank. Instead of making normal conversation, like any rational person, the first thing he did on setting foot in the place was start a diatribe against plastic window frames. And he'd arrived on the doorstep carrying four paintings with him. I ask you, Mike, who on earth goes to the house of a prospective landlord with the intention of displaying so-called artwork. It just makes no sense at all.'

'Hmm,' said Mike, the bearded features nodding slowly while he tapped a biro against the pad on his lap. 'Hmm. This friend of yours - what do you call him?'

'It's not what I call him - it's what he's called.'

'Hmm. Jeremy? Geraint? Gavin? Gary?'

'Gerard.'

'Hmm. This friend of yours, this Gavin...'

'Gerard.'

'I see. So you call him Gerard...'

'I keep telling you, it's not a question of what I call him, it's what he's called, or that's what he's always told us he's called. Look, it doesn't matter what his name is, for Christ's sake...'

'Robbie, Robbie, I can only help you if you have an open and positive attitude. Try to put to one side these defensive feelings that - '

'I am not being defensive.'

A pause.

'Now, what was Melanie's initial reaction to Gerard? I take it she was there when he called carrying these paintings.'

'Oh yes, she was there alright. She thought the sun shone out...she thought he was wonderful, and still does. He can do no wrong in her eyes. She said at the time that he'd make the perfect lodger, and everything's been pretty much downhill ever since.'

'Hmm...hmm...so...perhaps if we look a little more closely at what we know of your friend's background, personal history, family life and so on.'

'We know next to nothing about him. This is another disturbing thing. He's never told us anything about his family, or parents, siblings or anything. It's as if the guy's come from nowhere, just tumbled off another planet. It's another thing I find strange and unsettling about him.'

'Hmm...interesting...hmm...'

The beard was pivoting with slow, rhythmical strokes.

'So you know nothing about his childhood? I'm sure you're aware, Robbie, that the key to understanding the man lies in knowing the child.'

'Well, I'm afraid I can't help you there, Mike. The only biographical information I have on Gerard's past life is a story he told me quite recently. And I have every reason to believe that the whole thing was a fabrication.'

'Ah! Now...whether your friend was telling the truth or not, there may be much to be gained from examining this story in the absence of more concrete information.'

Mike rather theatrically outstretched his palms, inviting me to begin. So I told him the whole sad tale of Sarah/Emily, much as I'd told it to Melanie, including my suspicions of Gerard's motives for doing so.

'Hmm...hmm...interesting...this may well give us something to work with. You're convinced that your friend was making up this story?'

'Well, I think it's fairly obvious. His tale is littered with references to the Brontë family, and Emily in particular, even to the use of names, though they've been switched around a bit.'

'Sarah?'

'For some period a housemaid or kitchen maid to the Brontë family.'

'Hmm…hmm…if you're correct, and I say if, that this story is largely an invention, then that raises some interesting possibilities. If we look at the young man in the story - this…'

'Patrick.'

'Patrick, then there are clear indications of a disturbed childhood. And if Patrick is partly or wholly a vessel for the transference, the substitution, of events from Gerard's own life, then it may be a way of dealing with certain childhood traumas, bringing them to the surface, which Gerard would otherwise try to repress - indeed conceal, possibly even from himself. From what you've told me there was clearly an abusive relationship on the paternal side. And I think we can infer from the father's character some level of corporal punishment in earlier childhood. The physical abuse of this period may then have metamorphosed into the emotional and mental abuse which you've described.

'This raises the question of why Patrick's, or as we are speculating, Gerard's father should feel such antipathy towards him. And a number of possibilities come to mind. Now the mother has clearly died at some point in the child's life, obviously a traumatic event in itself. If, and I must stress again - if the mother died during childbirth then this might well account for the father's hostility, blaming his son for the loss of his wife. And any feelings of guilt and possible self-reproach and self-hatred which the child might develop upon discovering this event, that his mother effectively sacrificed her life for his, would simply be reinforced by the father's attitude towards him.'

'Gerard's story doesn't point in that direction, Mike. It was certainly my understanding that Patrick's mother was around for at least part of his childhood. That was the inference.'

'Hmm...hmm...well, we can put that idea to one side for the moment.'

Fraulent sounded put out that his theory should be discredited, but quickly rallied.

'Very well. Now, from what you've told me there is clearly an obsessive side to Gerard's character.'

'Obsessive? Christ, the guy's one great mass of obsessions. It's difficult to know where to start. Well, for example, what prompted me finally to call you was his behaviour the other evening, so bizarre it almost defies belief.'

'Does Melanie share your view on Gerard's behaviour?'

'Melanie? He can literally do no wrong in her eyes. He could dance naked through the streets of Birmingham and she'd still manufacture a rational explanation.'

'That's an interesting figure of speech.'

'You know what I mean. He could do something so extreme and bizarre that in anybody else I'm sure she'd be able to see the behaviour for what it was. But Gerard - well, let's just say she has something of a blind spot.'

'How does this make you feel, Robbie?'

'What do you mean?'

'Well, what are your real feelings about Gerard? Do you feel he's undermining you in your own home?'

'Well, of course he is.'

'And are you jealous of his effect on Melanie? Do you feel she's giving him the attention and respect that she should be giving you?'

'Well, yes of course, it's a ridiculous situation, yet she seems totally oblivious to the impropriety of her behaviour.'

'Do you have feelings of persecution, Robbie? Do you feel that Gerard is plotting against you? Perhaps actually working in conjunction with Melanie, and that you're being deliberately victimized, perhaps even spied upon?'

'What the hell are you driving at? It's not me or my problems that we're supposed to be talking about here. I resent the insinuation behind those questions.'

'Robbie, Robbie, you really mustn't be defensive about these matters when all I'm trying to do is establish your real feelings concerning this friend of yours.'

'He's no friend of mine, so let's concentrate on his problems, not mine.'

There was a pause, during which the beard pondered deeply.

'You indicated on the phone, Robbie, that your friend had a particular problem in relating to reality. What did you mean by that?'

'It's a question of where to begin. The evening I called you, for example, he'd presented Melanie with a painting - he's one of our foremost artists, by the way, among his many accomplishments. Melanie and I then had an interesting discussion concerning the symbolic aspects of the work, which unfortunately resulted in Gerard becoming quite agitated. Then he was in my face ranting about me being a philistine, his mission to revive Art, the importance of art in a social and political context and so on.

'I should point out, by the way, that not only is Gerard a great artist, but also a political genius, social reformer and creator of a new utopia which is going to transform the future of mankind. His ambitions encompass starting a new political party, establishing political control over this country, then by some master plan or other taking over the entire world in preparation for unleashing his utopian vision. And when you factor in an emerging musical genius, and I use the word advisedly, it gives you some idea of what we're dealing with here.'

'Hmm...hmm...interesting.'

'And then to top it all there's what I personally consider Gerard's crowning ambition, his masterpiece - even though it may not be significant historically or politically compared with his other goals. But to me this symbolises the pathos, the hopelessness of all his dreams. Gerard intends building a cathedral. Not just any cathedral, mind you, but the Lutyens design intended as Liverpool's Roman Catholic cathedral. And he actually believes this will happen. He believes that he can single-handedly mastermind the construction of this enormous building. I don't know how you view it from a psychiatric perspective, but to me such detachment from reality is very disturbing.'

'Hmm...hmm...interesting.'

I became aware of Fraulent watching me with a thoughtful expression, the fingers of his hands pressed lightly together in a pyramidal shape.

'I'm not saying the guy doesn't have some talent, Mike - I'm sure he does. It's just that everything is so over the top, so divorced from the practical realities of what is actually possible.'

'Hmm...hmm...there are a number of indicators from what you've told me. Of course, normally I would say that a definitive diagnosis is impossible without meeting your friend, and there being an opportunity for quite extensive analysis. However, perhaps that isn't absolutely necessary, after all,' he added quietly and reflectively. 'I think there is little question that we are dealing with a pathology here. It remains only to define the precise nature of that pathology...now, if we look at the symptoms you've described, would it be fair to say, Robbie, that there's been a deterioration in Gerard's personality during the time that you've known him?'

'That's a tricky one, but yes, I suppose if you think that the worst he did when we first knew him was obsess about window frames, imagine himself as the 'heir of de Chirico' and threaten to build an enormous cathedral with his bare hands then, yes, you could say he was pretty normal back then. He's certainly become increasingly strange since then and what's more appears to be completely unaware of the effect of his behaviour on other people.

'A while ago, for example, Melanie threw a drinks party for some work colleagues - a kind of informal bonding session is how she imagined it. The whole thing descended into farce as soon as Gerard appeared. To begin with, his appearance was bizarre. He looked as if he hadn't washed for days. His hair was lank, unbrushed, falling down into his eyes. His clothes were spattered with paint. Everyone else was smartly dressed, and there was Gerard like a scarecrow who'd seen one winter too many.'

Fraulent's features creased into a smile.

'Hmm...hmm...'

'But then he came out with this theory, which he obviously believed in one hundred percent. Some ludicrous thing about how you could become invisible if you had discs rotating at enormous speed implanted into your body. Completely off-your-trolley stuff, but when someone started making fun of it Gerard went stir-fry crazy, hurling abuse, ranting - like the incident with me the other night only worse. It almost developed into a fist fight with this other guy, who was about five times Gerard's size, incidentally, until Melanie intervened and - '

'Melanie?'

'Yeah, she kind of jumped between them - to protect Gerard, no doubt - and ordered this big lump out of the house. Of course when confronted he deflated like a pricked balloon. Nobody's capable of withstanding the force of Melanie's personality - except for the mighty Gerard himself, naturally enough.'

'Remarkable woman, quite remarkable.'

Is there anyone sane out there - anyone at all? Speak to me! Fraulent paused, adjusting his beard slightly with a little waggle or two.

'Very well. So we have an apparent progressive deterioration of personality, a withdrawal from reality - you've told me Gerard spends most of his time in his room working on plans which, as you've described, show little grounding in reality.'

'That's about the size of it.'

'And then we have the delusions of grandeur, seeing himself as a great artist, a great musician. In a political context, clearly regarding himself as some kind of Messiah with a mission to change or recreate the world. And you have documented quite clearly the pronounced emotional instability.'

A pure, warm beam of sunlight suddenly appeared. Slanting at an acute angle through the window and throwing an orange glow on a small patch of floor. Specks of dust drifted languidly in its path like tiny lost souls.

'I don't want to delve too deeply into technicalities here, Robbie. Strictly speaking, various tests would be necessary to rule out several other psychiatric illnesses presenting similar psychotic symptoms. However, I think I should make it clear to you at this point that the symptoms which we have been discussing all point to one particular psychiatric condition - a condition known as schizophrenia.'

Bingo! Gotcha! I knew the little bastard was mad and now we had it from the Fraulent's mouth!

'However, Robbie,' continued the beard, apparently reading my thoughts, 'you must not equate the use of this term with madness. I must emphasise to you most emphatically that what I am quite specifically not saying is that Gerard is mad. Schizophrenia is a complex condition, in fact effectively an umbrella term encompassing a number of disparate symptoms which may or may not be disabling, depending on their severity. It might in fact be helpful, Robbie, if I run through these symptoms very briefly, outlining how they are classified. Then we could take a look at the various possible explanations of schizophrenia, and try to interpret these as best as we are able in relation to what we know about Gerard.'

'Fine.'

'Now, the most recent and widely accepted system of classification has grouped the symptoms of schizophrenia into three main sub-types: paranoid, disorganized and catatonic. For our purposes it may be more helpful to focus on the traditional distinction between two main symptom categories, the first of which is termed acute schizophrenia and which is characterised by what are known as positive symptoms - delusions of grandeur, delusions of persecution, both visual and auditory hallucinations, the first two of which are quite clearly evident in what we know of Gerard's behaviour.'

My mind furrowed in perplexity as I quickly reviewed our conversation. The only time we'd touched on feelings of persecution was when Fraulent had made impertinent insinuations about my feelings towards...

'...other major symptom category is termed chronic schizophrenia, characterised by what are known as negative symptoms. These can include loss of drive, apathy, cataleptic stupor - the adopting of strange postures such as standing motionless like a statue - excessive motor activity - odd, sudden movements, gestures, facial grimaces. Echolalia - the repetitive echoing, in a mechanical fashion, of words just spoken by other people. As far as I am able to judge, Gerard's behaviour doesn't present symptoms within this category, as yet.

'But, as it were, shading between these two categories, in the model recognising three main sub-types we see symptoms such as disorganised thought and speech - the kind of rambling, illogical statements which Gerard often displays. Disorganised behaviour - the inability to perform basic daily activities such as keeping oneself clean, dressing appropriately and so on - again we can recognise this. Behaviour which demonstrates a lack of awareness of the effect on others - inappropriate silliness or laughter - the orating to thin air which you've described. It's clear to me that aspects of Gerard's behaviour up to this point fall within, but not beyond, this particular spectrum of symptoms.'

'So what you're saying is that schizophrenia is progressive and moves from one extreme of delusory obsessions to start with, to eventually a state of complete apathy?'

'Well, certainly recent studies, and by recent I mean within the last twenty years or so, appear to confirm the view of schizophrenia as a progressive disorder. Magnetic resonance imaging has allowed researchers to examine live brains, enabling an enormous breakthrough in our understanding of schizophrenia. And studies using this technology show definite structural abnormalities in the brains of many patients with schizophrenia.

'One difficulty lies in establishing whether pre-existing structural abnormalities make a person susceptible to schizophrenia, or whether the onset of clinical symptoms cause structural changes. In other words, establishing the causal direction. But it certainly appears that abnormalities are found more often in those with negative/chronic symptoms, rather than positive/acute symptoms. And many who do demonstrate acute symptoms go on later to develop chronic symptoms, suggesting a further degeneration of the brain. To me this clearly indicates the progressive, deteriorative nature of schizophrenia.'

'So whatever the trigger for the disease in the first place, you see schizophrenia as a progressive illness where the patient degenerates from a deluded or manic condition to a passive, apathetic state?'

'Not always, Robbie, not always. Yes, that can be and in severe cases is the course of the illness, but it would be premature to take that as an assumption in Gerard's case. A proportion, perhaps somewhere between 15-30% of schizophrenic patients have a single episode, or a few brief acute episodes, and then make a full recovery. A larger proportion of patients will suffer an episodic pattern of acute symptoms throughout life, yet still manage to maintain a reasonable level of functioning whilst in remission, often while still presenting negative symptoms. Only in fact for the remaining proportion of patients is there an unremitting course of deterioration from acute to chronic symptoms, with the patient left unable to function normally in society. Robbie, do we have any evidence of drug use by Gerard?'

'Well, I…no, not that I'm aware of.'

'Hmm…hmm…the symptoms of amphetamine psychosis, for example, are similar to paranoid schizophrenia. But you see, Robbie, trying to pinpoint a single cause, or combination of causes in the development of schizophrenia is a highly complex area. There's convincing evidence for both structural and neurochemical abnormalities in the brains of people with the condition. Almost certainly a range of factors will play a part, singly and in combination. Genetic factors, disruptions to the normal processes of brain development, emotional stress, trauma to the brain, birth or prenatal complications leading to brain damage. Pre-eclampsia, for instance, is seen as a significant risk factor. Yet even though it's a common prenatal complication, not all infants affected go on to develop schizophrenia. Possibly sometimes *in utero* complications interact in some way with a genetic predisposition, and certainly all recent research seems to indicate a strong genetic link for schizophrenia. As I say, it's a very complex picture.

'But if Gerard's mother - and here we're looking also at Patrick as a substitution figure - if she died at the time of Gerard's birth as a result of pre-eclampsia, and it is a potentially fatal condition, then this would tie in well as a causal link with the schizophrenia, and as a possible explanation for the early death of Gerard/Patrick's mother, and therefore for his father's subsequent antipathy and persecution. And it's worth remembering that there is a strong correlation to relapse rates among discharged patients in families with a high level of expressed emotion. Overstimulation through high EE, that is expressed emotion - precisely the kind of criticism and hostility expressed by Patrick's father - is believed to precipitate positive symptoms in schizophrenia. Hallucinations, delusions, restlessness, the last two certainly displayed by Gerard. I think it's evident, Robbie, that a clear pattern is emerging here.'

There was a wild, excited light in Fraulent's eyes and an unusual level of animation in his voice. The pad and pen had dropped to the floor beside his chair. His hands, which till now had been still and calm, now moved restlessly.

'Well, Mike, you may or may not be right concerning Gerard and his relationship with his father. But to me we seem to be in the realm of pure speculation in drawing a direct parallel with this Patrick character. As I said earlier, I simply don't have any knowledge of his background or childhood. But in any case, in respect of the pre-eclampsia theory, as I've told you before, if the story as Gerard told it to me is true, then I don't think Patrick's mother did die during childbirth. The inference was clearly that she was around for some of his childhood.'

'Robbie,' a hint of cranky impatience entering Fraulent's voice, the beard wobbling dangerously, 'we have to be wary of the extent to which we identify Gerard, and Gerard's life experiences, with Patrick. Patrick may indeed be a substitution, but that doesn't necessarily imply that every event described directly parallels Gerard's own experiences. We must be prepared to give credit to a creative mind. There may well be elements of variation and invention in Gerard's relation of past events. You yourself have cast doubts on the veracity of his account.'

'I think the little bastard's a congenital liar.'

Fraulent regarded me thoughtfully.

'You certainly have very strong, indeed very strongly negative feelings towards Gerard, don't you Robbie?'

'Not at all. I have no feelings towards him whatsoever beyond a wish to help him as far as I can, which is why I'm here. And then a wish that he would go out of my life forever and I'd never have to see or think of him ever again. But you yourself seem to be acknowledging that Gerard's story is pretty slender evidence on which to draw any firm conclusions.'

'Of course it is. I told you quite clearly at the start of our discussion that a definitive diagnosis would be impossible. I've made the best attempt I can, and given what you've told me I'm reasonably confident that Gerard is a schizophrenic. To go further than this in an attempt to provide a possible explanation for the condition, and on the basis of such slight evidence, will necessarily involve speculation. But I emphasise once again that that is all it is - pure speculation. If you're not satisfied with this process, Robbie, then I suggest we close our discussion.'

'I'm not criticising you, Mike. I'm just trying to establish the parameters. This isn't my field of expertise, don't forget.'

'I realise that. Very well. If we put to one side the theory of the mother dying during childbirth, then another equally valid explanation is possible. It's quite common in obsessive, driven individuals to find an excessive attachment to one or other parent, the drive to succeed being fuelled by an extreme desire to please or satisfy the parent. And sometimes this derives from a desire for vicarious wish-fulfilment on the parent's part. Feelings of frustration at their own failures transferring to the child and transforming into an obsessive drive for success. If this is the case with Gerard then the degree of attachment to his mother may well have been of a brooding, malignant, incestuous intensity, perhaps even to the extent of physical desire.'

I stared at Fraulent in horror. In his excitement sweat was standing out on his brow. The beard was twitching wildly.

'Perhaps Gerard despised his mother for prompting these desires, and harboured a deep, subconscious and long-repressed desire to destroy her for this reason. So when she dies he's racked with guilt, and the resulting self-hatred pushes him into acute, that is paranoid, schizophrenia.'

'This is ridiculous. Where the hell have you come up with this theory?'

'Not at all, not at all, Robbie. It's a perfectly valid hypothesis. Has Gerard ever had normal relations with a woman?'

'What?'

'I mean a normal relationship with a woman?'

'How should I know.'

'We know - you yourself know very well - that he has an unhealthy fixation on Melanie. And the only other close relationship with a woman of which we are aware concerns this possibly mythical Sarah. And by Gerard's own admission this was a strange, unfulfilled affair. An incestuous fixation with his mother would explain his inability to form normal relationships with women, as well as being a tenable explanation for the onset of schizophrenia.'

'This is preposterous.'

'Are you aware of Gerard suffering from some form of bodily defect - some abnormality?'

'How the hell should I know!'

'You've never seen him naked, then?'

'What the fuck do you take me for?'

'I must have access to the facts. If you haven't seen him without his clothes, then...that could have been very useful. I don't suppose Melanie might have...'

'Are you being deliberately funny with me?'

'I must have information. I must have the facts. I need to be able to picture very clearly exactly what the possibilities might be. Because you see if, and I stress if, there were some form of, shall we say, genital incompleteness...'

'What the...'

'...in the form of, shall we say, cryptorchism or monorchism - do you know what I'm talking about, Robbie?'

'I've never heard such - '

'Studies have shown that where emotionally disturbed boys suffer from this condition, particularly within the context of a disturbed parent/child relationship - and we have substantial grounds for believing this to be the case with Patrick/Gerard - then profoundly detrimental consequences may result. Hyperactivity, compulsive toying with physical danger, social inadequacy, a tendency to exaggerate, to lie, to fantasise. An interest in architecture as a symbolic substitution for the missing organ. Practically a blueprint for Gerard's character as we understand it to be.'

My one pressing desire at this point was to escape - escape from Fraulent and his fevered imaginings. His desperation to find a sexual explanation was perverse in its intensity, disturbing and repellent.

'An American child analyst has reported that his young monorchid patients have a desire 'of an almost frantic or feverish type' for redesigning and reconstructing buildings, hoping to quell anxieties about defects in their own bodies by making other kinds of structures whole. You see, Robbie, how perfectly this theory fits Gerard's preoccupations. This compulsion to erect perfect structures, systems, works of art - indeed the preoccupation, bordering on obsession, with aesthetics would be entirely consistent with a desperate need to compensate for deep-seated anxieties and feelings of inadequacy.'

'So you're saying that all great artists, from Wren to Beethoven to Picasso all derived their drive from physical abnormality?'

'Beethoven's art certainly became more intense and personal following the onset of deafness, and it could be said - '

'Okay, forget Beethoven. Bad example. Bach, Raphael, da Vinci, Shostakovich…'

'Dmitri Shostakovich certainly composed within a psychological context of fear and - '

'For fuck's sake, why do people insist on making sweeping generalisations from the narrowest of evidence.'

'Compose yourself, Robbie.'

I'll compose a sonata on your beard with my fist in a minute, Fraulent.

'This is only one theory and by no means the only possible explanation for the derangement of Gerard's mind. Let's look at syphilis, for example.'

Fraulent paused and peered at me over his beard. I stared back at him with increasingly combative dislike.

'What?'

'Suppose, just for a moment, that Sarah, rather than Patrick, is the substitute figure. That it's Sarah, in fact, that represents the expression of a key element of Gerard's psychological makeup. Now, let's look at a striking and unusual facet to this Sarah character - particularly pertinent in this context - the dislike of personal contact. Practically, in fact, a refusal to touch or be touched, even by her supposed boyfriend. Gerard's inferred explanation for this was Sarah's mystical, spiritual nature, wilfully and consciously detached from everyday concerns and preoccupations.

'But what if, and I stress again if, Sarah is an invention representing, shall we say, Gerard's own inability to form close ties, to physically get close to anybody. Have you ever actually seen Gerard touch someone or embrace them - have you ever in fact seen him embrace Melanie?'

Thrown out of kilter by Fraulent's earlier, more feverish ramblings I cast around in my mind for good examples of Gerard wrapping himself around Melanie. Then it struck me that he'd never touched her, to my knowledge. Ah, but wasn't that precisely the point!

'How the hell do I know what they get up to when I'm not there. God knows what they do when my back's turned.'

'This is one of your principal worries and preoccupations, isn't it Robbie? Your mind is constantly in turmoil imagining, I would suggest in some detail, precisely what Gerard and Melanie might be doing when you're not there. Gerard is, in fact, shall we say, always on your mind. In fact, do you not - '

'Don't you dare try and turn this around and make me the subject of your diseased and perverted - '

'Robbie, Robbie, I was seeking merely to reassure you that whatever your concerns and worries regarding Gerard and Melanie, I think it a distinct possibility that Gerard is psychologically and also possibly physically incapable of having a normal relationship with a woman. And that Sarah is both an inversion in the sense of gender and also a substitution, an imaginative expression if you will - and I think you demonstrated considerable perception in picking up on this, Robbie - of Gerard's own shortcomings.

'As to causal links, let's explore a possible hypothesis. Let us imagine Gerard at eighteen or nineteen - a shy, awkward young man with an intense, obsessive personality. He finds it difficult, perhaps impossible, to form or sustain friendships, especially with girls or women. So, having normal physical desires he seeks release for these impulses in consorting with prostitutes. But then he's unlucky. One of these ladies, perhaps through some sordid encounter one rainy night down a semi-derelict back street of, shall we say, Bradford, turns out to be infected with syphilis and transmits this disease to Gerard. Now, syphilis is a serious and progressive disease which spreads through the lymphatic system to affect almost all body tissues, and in its final tertiary stage causes mental derangement. Imagine the effect upon Gerard's already highly strung mental state at the discovery that he's been given this illness. And imagine - '

'How many more of these revolting theories have you got up your sleeve?'

Fraulent now appeared to me like the sinister proprietor of some dark, old-fashioned sweetshop, pulling down great jars of candies off the shelves. Lovingly caressing the bottle while extolling the flavour and texture of the contents.

'Not at all, Robbie, not at all. In fact I can offer you one final plausible explanation, and in many ways the best possible match, as it precisely mirrors Gerard's known characteristics. Have you heard of encephalitis?'

'What about it?'

'It means inflammation of the brain. And what interests us here are widespread reports of profound personality changes in patients affected by an epidemic viral form of encephalitis characterised by extreme drowsiness. The technical name for it is *encephalitis lethargica* - you would have heard of it as sleeping sickness. Now the really interesting characteristic of this condition is that years after recovering from the physical symptoms of the disease patients suddenly begin to manifest disturbing personality changes. Terms such as 'moral imbecility' and 'moral insanity' have been used. The condition itself is known as post-encephalitic sociopath. Now, I wonder...'

He rose and went to a bookcase laden with catalogued files, box files, journals and textbooks. The beard wandered in barely contained excitement, ranging over the material, seeking...

'Ah, here we are.'

Fraulent produced a document of several pages from a file, glancing swiftly through it as he returned to his chair.

'Yes - now this is an article written in 1930 entitled 'Zur Kriminalitaet der Encephalitiker' which I extracted from the journal Acta Psychiatrica. Now listen to this - I'll read just a few extracts which the author believed characterised the symptoms of this condition.

> *The post-encephalitic moral imbecile is often possessed of cleverness and brilliance...an exceedingly plausible and ready liar...knows neither shame nor gratitude...a coldly egotistical, vengeful, base, vile impertinence...truly explosive outbursts...criminal actions...wanton destructiveness... mythomania...malicious enunciations...grandiloquent and ecstatic states...inclination to lie...to confabulate past adventures...to simulate and deceive.*

'You see, Robbie, how perfectly these symptoms fit Gerard. And what is particularly interesting here is how they, that is the symptoms, illuminate the schizophrenic nature, and I'm using the word here in its informal sense, of Gerard's thought-world. On the one hand we have conscious, cynical manipulation. Of Melanie, in his attempt to turn her against you and win her for himself. Of you, Robbie, in his story about Sarah where he cleverly attempts to divert you from his true purpose and make you feel sympathy for his supposed suffering.

'And then, on the other hand, there are those times when Gerard appears to be under some kind of spell - strange, ecstatic states of almost unconscious possession, as you described in your encounter with him the other day, which mirror so accurately the visions and visits from the messenger of Hope of Sarah, or as we surmise, in fact Emily Brontë. This is what is so interesting here - the duality of Gerard's character and of his thought-world.'

I looked pointedly at my watch.

'I must be off, Mike. I've taken up too much of your time already.'

The beard gave a convulsive twitch at my attempt to escape prematurely from its clutches.

'Not at all, Robbie, not at all. My time is at your disposal. In fact there were just one or two areas which I thought it might be constructive to explore.'

Reluctantly I remained seated.

'Now, I must ask you just one or two more questions, Robbie, which I hope you will be able to answer as straightforwardly as possible. I wonder if, firstly, you feel a degree of frustration at your lack of achievement, especially in relation to Melanie's conspicuously successful career?'

'What's that got to do with anything?'

'Then you do acknowledge a measure of frustration at the imbalance?'

'No, I don't. I'm perfectly happy doing what I do. If other people think I'm underachieving that's their problem.'

'Is that what Melanie thinks, Robbie?'

'I really wouldn't know.'

'Hmm...hmm...Robbie, I don't want you to take this the wrong way, but...' At this point Fraulent's voice became soft, low and sympathetic. '...does Gerard in fact really exist?'

'What?'

'Well, let me put it this way. Have you ever been aware of hearing voices? Voices telling you to do certain things? Perhaps whispering poisonous ideas and insinuations directly into your mind? Have you ever had hallucinations, Robbie? Have you ever seen things or people that in your rational mind you know could not be there? Have you ever, for example, seen Melanie and Gerard together, perhaps acting inappropriately - in each other's arms, perhaps - possibly even engaging in some form of foreplay, even when in truth you knew it wasn't possible?'

It was like witnessing a replay of Gerard's feverish, ecstatic performance of the other night.

'Robbie, are you aware of a tendency to echo words spoken by others, in our discussion today for instance?'

'Echo? What on earth are you talking about?'

'There - you're doing it now.'

'Doing it now - doing what now?'

'You're doing it again, Robbie. I'm sure it's unconscious, otherwise I suspect you'd be aware of the tendency. Now, Robbie, you must let me have the facts. My question to you is of singular importance. Tell me about your intimate relations with Melanie. What makes her happy, Robbie? What positions does she prefer? What gives her real satisfaction? What really gets her excited? What would you say gives her maximum pleasure?'

I looked at the fevered, intense expression on Fraulent's face. Enough was enough. I stood up and walked swiftly out of the room. He came running after me from the house.

'Robbie...Robbie! I need the facts! I must have the facts!'

The air was cool and fresh in my face - a blissful release from confinement. I jumped quickly into the car, activating the central locking just in time to prevent the inflamed psychiatrist, his face now pressed against a side window, from gaining access. He jumped back as I put my foot hard on the throttle. The tyres squealed as the car shot forwards, but only when I'd reached third gear and put a safe distance between myself and Fraulent did I risk glancing in the mirror. He was still standing in the road, arms outstretched imploringly, the beard waving forlornly in the afternoon breeze. The image gradually receded to a speck before disappearing completely from view.

   I drove for several miles, then pulled into a deserted lay-by. Turning the engine off I sat back, eyes closed, basking in the silence. Ten minutes passed, and then I started the car and drove slowly home.

19

It was difficult at first to pinpoint where the screams were coming from. An intermittent high-pitched wailing rising from somewhere deep within the house, punctuated by banging and muffled shouting. And then the screaming began again. This time its pitch and intensity produced a cold stab of fear. I jumped up and ran to the door, almost colliding with a wide-eyed Melanie.

'Did you hear that?' she said, her face pale and strained. 'Where do you think it's coming from?'

These were almost the first words she'd said to me all morning, and I'd yet to account for the stony silence. As another scream ripped through what had been a quiet and peaceful Saturday morning, our eyes met, then our heads turned in concert towards the basement door.

Melanie was the first to react, moving swiftly down the stairs, while I followed more cautiously. The scene that greeted us was extraordinary even by Gerard's standards. He was down on his hands and knees on the basement floor, thumping the ground with a clenched fist. Becoming aware of us, he raised his head like a wounded animal, the face distorted, the mouth horribly open and twisted, a dark gash from which poured a wordless agony of groaning, followed by sudden high-pitched screams. The fearful sight and noise were frightening in the confined space of the basement. He began to beat the floor with both fists, the hair a ragged curtain over his eyes, burying his face. His body like that of a beetle, its head pushing into the ground.

Melanie knelt beside him, spreading her arm protectively around his shoulders. Murmuring tender, consoling words, applying her calming touch. At first to little effect, but after a while the screaming subsided, though the sobbing continued, his face pressing into her arm.

Then, as the heaving, wracking sighs abated, she began to whisper gentle words of comfort and enquiry.

'It's okay, don't worry, everything will be alright.'

No response.

'What is it, Gerard, what's the matter? We're here to help you.'

Then his body jerked upright, free of Melanie's hold. She leant back, still on her knees, looking up as Gerard leapt to his feet, the tear-stained face suddenly naked with rage.

'This!' he said, the word alive with hatred, disbelief, contempt. 'This!' Snatching some crumpled sheets of newspaper lying on the floor and brandishing them at us. His arm outstretched, violently shaking the bits of paper as if to cast out the evil within.

'What is the point of my creating beauty?'

His voice was harsh, metallic, and increasing by the second in hysterical intensity.

'What is the point of sacrificing my life in pursuit of artistic purity when this scum - this dirty, evil, lying scum persist in destroying all I value most at every single opportunity? Every time my back is turned I am betrayed! Why do I waste the precious years of my life if this - this is to be my only reward?'

Then the screaming stopped abruptly, and with an unwittingly amusing gesture he threw the sheets of paper onto the floor. Now trembling, now swaying, his eyes rolling theatrically, I thought for a moment he was about to faint. But then he gathered himself up and staggered off to one side, collapsing into a chair, his face in his hands.

Melanie stood transfixed, as if by a great piece of theatre, which perhaps it was. I stooped to pick up the scattered sheets, smoothed them out and reassembled them. It was the remains of *The Aire Gazette,* a local paper which I never bothered to buy or read. The front page was devoted entirely to an image of some large commercial building burning down. Massed windows lit by a deadly glow from within. Great sheets of flame, and above the flames black smoke expanding skywards. From two openings in the building, high up towards the eaves, bright rivulets of flame played around the lintels.

The structure itself was dark, brooding and immense. The roofline a series of triangular gables, like classical pediments. The cumulative effect of the doomed building, the intense yellow and orange of the flames and the restatement of black in the enveloping cloud was a composition of astonishing beauty. Marred only by a tall, shiny lift and ladder with a platform at the top from which someone was directing a thin pinprick of water into the inferno.

'Is this what it's all about, Gerard?' I said, holding out the picture towards the huddled form. 'Is this what's upset you?'

Gerard didn't move or respond.

'Let me see,' said Melanie.

I passed the paper to her.

'I know this place,' she said, studying the photograph carefully. 'It's an old bonded warehouse down by the river. They were going to convert it into flats. I remember seeing an article about it. They had an artist's impression showing what it would look like. I think there were going to be something like a hundred and sixty luxury flats with dramatic views overlooking the river. It sounded wonderful.'

'It does sound very wonderful, but I'm afraid the conversion won't happen now. It says the place is so unstable a breath of wind could bring it down. They're going to have to demolish it.'

An anguished, guttural wailing began, rising quickly to an animal scream. Gerard had slid off his chair, and was now lying half on his side, propped on one elbow, feebly pounding the floor, tears streaming down his face. Melanie gave me an accusing look, then spoke quietly but precisely.

'We're going to have to get away for a while until things have calmed down.'

'Get away? What do you mean?'

'I mean get away from here - from Leeds. Get right away somewhere for a while.'

'Where? For how long? I can't just leave work without notice.'

'Don't you think the important thing at this point is to care for Gerard?'

Was this just another level of performance - a level that perhaps even he hadn't reached before - another stage in some strategic plan? I looked once more at the little master's pathetic, broken form. How could such a mundane event as a fire at a disused warehouse create such a spectacular emotional reaction unless he was either insane, or putting it on for purposes unknown but highly suspect. It was difficult to conceive of a third alternative.

'We are not responsible for him, Melanie. If he has problems we can't cope with, we need to inform the proper authorities.'

'So that's what you were doing, was it?'

Her expression made me nervous.

'What do you mean?'

'Never mind that now. We'll discuss it later.'

Her features assumed a calm, but still premonitory aspect.

'I must go and visit it immediately.'

Quite miraculously he'd risen, composed his tortured soul and managed to make his way over to us. Now standing looking directly into our faces with those pleading, shiny eyes, like a starving puppy.

'Are you sure that's what you want to do, Gerard,' said Melanie gently. 'You might find it rather upsetting.'

'The building must be saved! It shall be saved! Such things are treasures too precious to the national psyche to allow these vile criminals to besmirch and destroy! I need to see the damage this scum has done.'

'Okay, Gerard,' she said, looking with respectful compassion into the distorted little face. 'We'll go and have a look, and then we can see what can be done.'

I looked coldly at the pair of them, then shook my head in exasperation.

Gerard was agitated as we approached. Craning his head this way and that to catch a glimpse of the warehouse. We couldn't get close in with the car - all the roads in the area were barricaded off. But we found somewhere to park, and he was away and running before Melanie had locked the car. We followed at a distance, silently, side by side.

She had a composed, set expression - one of calm but inflexible determination. An expression which discouraged investigation into the reason for the wall of silence. It was obviously some offence beyond the normal compass of offences, but aside from the visit to Fraulent, which I'd never thought to mention, the cause remained a mystery.

We emerged from the dark, pressing dankness of a tunnel under the mainline railway. Past a few decomposing red brick commercial buildings - disused Victorian workshops and offices. Along a narrow lane where the surface in places had peeled away to reveal the smooth stone setts beneath, and already the air was heavy with the tang of destructive fire.

And then we were looking down on it from the same level as a fire engine, parked over to our right in an area of waste ground. The fire long since extinguished, the machine was still sending a precautionary stream of water into the heart of the building.

A forlorn, desolate hulk. The roof entirely gone, collapsed into the outer walls. It was difficult to see how, even before the fire, such an age-ravaged structure could possibly have been salvaged to produce accommodation. The brickwork was uneven and badly corroded, the stone detailing around doorways equally worn, and in places the structure showed abrupt changes in level where it had subsided.

The lane gave access to a series of loading bays. There was a huge elevation change from the front to the rear of the warehouse, allowing easy loading at the rear to the upper levels of the building. The ground then sloped steeply down to the main road below, which paralleled both the front of the warehouse and the river.

Flying down this slope went Gerard, hair streaming wildly in his urgency to view the building's precarious façade.

I'd wanted to spend some time watching the parabolas of water jetting into the empty shell, but Melanie had already started down the path after Gerard. So I followed, arriving at the cordoned road to find the pair together, Melanie's arm tight around the little master's shoulders.

By stark demolition signs in bold red lettering, Gerard was clinging with both hands to the barricade, staring through the rectangular gaps. I could sense that awful noise threatening to emerge again as he surveyed the ruined warehouse, twisted mouth pressing against the steel wire divisions of the barrier.

I found the sight distasteful, and took a number of steps back to distance myself from the pair of them. And from this position, standing back a little, the full impact of the façade was revealed. Seven stories high. And though ruined and blackened by decades of city smoke, and now the fire, the doomed warehouse still managed to cast a defiant, brooding presence over the modern buildings around it. And it was difficult not to be impressed both by the sheer scale of the building and the arrogance of ambition which must have prompted such an undertaking.

Now there were gaping holes in the structure. Bricks and debris lay in the road. Halfway up the façade the stump of a loading door flapped helplessly. Some stunted remnants of saplings which had found a foothold at roof level had somehow defied the heat of the blaze. Birds flew in and out through the many openings at will.

I shivered in the chill, unfriendly air. The place was eerie and desolate enough by day. By night, in its dark immensity and with those rows of round-shouldered portals, it would resemble some citadel of the dead, drawing in lost souls who, once immured, would never emerge.

This unsettling feeling was confirmed by the sudden appearance at my side of Melanie. Unseen by me she'd left Gerard and was now standing close.

'So you went anyway,' she said, speaking quietly but distinctly.

I looked at her, and saw at once that it was useless to deny it. Her expression was unambiguous.

'How could you do that when you knew my feelings on the matter?'

The wind cut suddenly between us.

'How do you know?' I asked.

She smiled a small, secret smile, as if I'd made a weak joke, then shook her head. Gestures I found intensely irritating.

'Okay, I see that you know. I'm asking you how you know.'

'I know because Mike Fraulent called me and told me all about your secret visit.'

That little bastard.

'When?'

'It doesn't matter when.'

Her voice as cold as the wintry air.

'I can't believe you would go behind my back like that.'

'I was trying to help him, for Christ's sake. God knows he needs help. Look - what the hell's he doing now?'

Gerard had wandered off, and was now balanced on top of a barrier, his back pressed against a high wall adjoining the warehouse. Poised for a second with his feet on top of the barrier, he then stretched out his arms and jumped, landing in the prohibited area directly in front of the warehouse.

'Jesus, what's he doing?'

The only security on the site seemed to be a small guy drinking tea in a little hut just next to us. With a sideways glance to confirm that he was occupied, I ran with Melanie over to the barrier.

'For God's sake, Mel, can't you see he needs help?'

'Oh, never mind that now. Come on and give me a hand.'

'I can't get over there. What are you doing? We're not supposed to cross over that barrier. It says quite clearly...look, just be careful, will you...mind you don't...'

But then looking up at Melanie I temporarily lost the power of speech, such was the glory of her physique when viewed from that particular angle. And then she leapt, and landed with panther-like, force-absorbing suppleness. She went to Gerard without a backward glance.

Pride forced me to follow suit. With a quick look around, I scrambled up, forcing myself precariously against the wall, cursing Gerard meanwhile. I landed with an unpleasant jolt and joined the other two. We were standing directly underneath the highest and most fragile part of the building. Probably the most dangerous location in the entire city at that moment.

Gerard had his hands pressed against the dark brickwork. He seemed to be weeping. The hands were exploring the irregularities in the bricks, like a blind man reading Braille. As if he could read the meaning of the building through its texture, somehow discover its destiny. Melanie stood silently by.

'All over the country,' the voice came shrill and abrupt, 'there are grasping little bastards with brains the size of maggots, throwing all this away. Throwing it away!'

His voice caught in a crescendo.

'Destroyed forever! Forever, do you hear me?'

The screaming bounced dully off the empty warehouse, and then he began to beat with his fists against the brickwork. A couple climbing from a taxi beyond the barriers looked towards us, then hurried inside an expensive-looking hotel. Melanie had her face in her hands, stifling sobs.

'Oh God, Gerard. I'm so sorry. It's too terrible to contemplate.'

I found it all too ridiculous for words. For Gerard to find meaning to his miserable existence in the fantasy concept of a vanished world was sad enough, but to drag us into that fantasy was beyond tolerance. And Melanie's back turned towards me was further provocation.

'That little fuck Fraulent had no business calling you,' I said, loudly enough that there could be no question of her pretending not to have heard.

She cast a backward glance, the look on her tear-stained features suggesting surprise, as if she'd forgotten I was there.

'Oh?' she said. 'I thought he was your friend.'

'Did you? Well I thought...'

'You're not allowed in this area!'

Two men were striding towards us, and the voice carried a distinct warning tone. Surveyors or contractors, or possibly council officials, kitted out in hard hats, yellow reflective jackets and builder's boots.

'Do you not realise you're in considerable danger standing there? Could you leave the area immediately, please?'

'You!' said Gerard, spinning round, his finger pointing and eyes popping, '*you* are in considerable danger!'

He literally spat the words, before wiping his mouth with the back of his hand.

'You dare to tell me what I may do and where I may go when you - you filthy, degenerate scum' - each word enunciated separately and distinctly - 'are responsible for this destruction. You dare to lecture me!'

The guy who'd spoken, big as he was, stopped dead and rocked back on his heels, shocked by the fierce heat of Gerard's hostility. Melanie stepped forward and took Gerard's arm, her expression one of deep concern. She ignored the two officials.

'Come on, Gerard. Let's get away from here.'

'Why?' said Gerard, voice shrieking hoarsely, struggling to free himself from Melanie's grasp. 'Why your so-called security now? Why now, when this building, this glorious icon of our industrial past has been left, unprotected and undefended, for years? Years! Do you hear me? Why now? Such concern, such interest, when all that is left is a scarred shell!'

The pair moved in a little closer, and I took up a position more squarely behind Melanie.

'Look, I'm going to have to ask you...'

But then she turned and directed her gaze directly into the face of the one that had spoken, and the effect of confusion and disorientation was entirely predictable.

'We're leaving this area now,' said Melanie, looking deeply into his eyes, 'but I hope a lesson has been learned here, that our industrial past needs proper care and protection.'

I could have laughed out loud, had my face not been fairly rigid with tension and cold. To hear her singing so boldly, so clearly, so transparently and with such concise precision from the Gerard songbook was such sweet consolation. The poor guy's mouth was gaping, as well it might given the aggregation of assaults upon his senses.

Both stood mutely to one side as Gerard, directing one last heavy-duty glare towards them, began to stagger on Melanie's arm towards the barrier. I smiled a tight, conciliatory smile as I passed.

Part of the barrier had been pulled to one side, and we left the cordoned area and reached the deserted road. But it seemed that Gerard hadn't finished with either us or the warehouse. Bent almost double in anguish, he began to weep again.

'Look,' he sobbed, twisting round towards the ruined building. 'Look at it now.'

'I know. I know.'

'This is all nonsense!'

'I know. I know it is. But hopefully in the long run…'

'What hope is there for a world run by moral degenerates?'

'I know how hard this is for you.'

'A world fit only for mental defectives.'

'You must keep faith, Gerard, no matter what - '

'To think that such beauty, such symbols of human achievement, such landmarks of industrial history, should be lost in such pointless, pointless…'

He was bent over in such a paroxysm of emotion that I was afraid that any moment he'd be on his knees again, pounding the road.

'You know, I'm getting really cold standing here,' I said, trying not to shiver too melodramatically. 'Do you think we could go soon? I mean, you do accept that all this is too fatuous for words?'

Melanie looked at me, her expression combining amazement and disgust.

'Yes, we certainly must go. Make whatever arrangements you need to make.'

'Arrangements? What do you - '

'I told you quite clearly before. Gerard has been affected more deeply by all this than you seem to realise or care. What we need to do is get right away from here, right away from the city. For at least a week, perhaps more.'

I looked around me, searching for something that might give meaning to our life together. Gerard was now lying in the road on his side, his knees pressed up to his chest, his face completely hidden by his arms. Seeing him there, on that deserted road, where normally a constant stream of traffic would pass, and with the strange, sculptural remnants of the warehouse as a backdrop - suddenly the boundaries of possibility and reality seemed to dissolve. Or perhaps instead, like the universe itself, they were constantly, infinitely expanding. And whatever I'd once accepted as normality was in a parallel state of constant turmoil. Constantly redefined, overtaken, overturned, turned inside out, passing beyond the boundaries of perception. And perception itself gave way - bent, distorted by the bizarre nature of external events and appearances.

What to believe - that was the problem. What was it possible to hang on to, or take as reference point. How to make sense of our relationship, and the dynamics of our life with Gerard. I knew that Melanie, in my position, with her analytical ability and close, reasoning mind, would identify or superimpose a coherent structure, and identify the logical position and function of the constituent elements. She would achieve an overview, yet see all necessary detail.

But I was not Melanie. And trapped within my own limitations, and with no-one to turn to for guidance, I felt lost and alone. Trapped in a maze with no signposts or directions which might allow at least the possibility of freedom.

'Did you hear what I said?'

I turned blankly to Melanie.

'No, I wasn't...'

'I said - you'll have to phone Caroline. Tell her you need to take the week off for personal, family reasons.'

'He isn't family.'

'For God's sake show some initiative for once! Phone her when we get back and tell her you can't come in this week.'

'How is she supposed to cover my shifts without any notice? It's not as if - '

'That's the function of a manager, for goodness sake. I can't see any difficulty in reassigning responsibilities and adjusting internal staffing dynamics.'

'Great. What would that achieve except to show everyone I was surplus to requirements in the first place? Get other people to cover my job and it's soon going to occur to someone that they could do without me entirely.'

'I do wish you wouldn't be so defeatist all the time. The alternative is that I take Gerard away somewhere for a week by myself. I was hoping for your support.'

'Fine. Fine, I'll phone her. And what are you going to do?'

'I was planning on working from home for the most part this week in any case - I need to complete a couple of reports. Look, give me a hand to get Gerard home, and then we can get ready to go.'

We walked towards the prone figure.

'I just don't know what you're hoping to achieve by going away. It's not going to solve anything. He needs professional help.'

Her eyes flashed warning signals and with them, quite abruptly, my last barriers of defence seemed to dissolve. From this point on I determined to take the line of least resistance.

20

Little more than an hour later, we were heading for Scotland. I'd suggested Sutherland, somewhere along the main road up the east coast. At the back of my mind was some forlorn, last-ditch hope of convincing Melanie of what our life together could be. Sitting in the back as she drove north I had time to reflect on the futility of that hope, and in reflecting felt utterly passive and defeated. My will was drained, inadequate at the best of times to combat both Melanie's focused determination and events with a momentum beyond my control.

And I knew before we set off that the journey would be an endurance test. Gerard's powers of recovery were extraordinary. Subdued to start with, he became increasingly vocal as we left Yorkshire behind and headed for the Borders. And looking at the side of his head as he turned frequently to Melanie, seeing his hands caress the air, I wondered once again at the artifice behind the increasingly violent outbursts.

Symbolism, art, symbolism in art, aesthetics, architecture, terraced housing, stone setts and all the other detritus of his mind were paraded in extended review. And when the topic veered into the desperate waters of feminism, my irritation increased further.

'It is fundamental to the concept of a new, equitable society that feminine values flourish.'

The countryside rolled mutely past.

'However, in this society those values are not associated exclusively with the biological fact of being female. My definition of feminism is, indeed remains, unique and all-embracing.'

No, no. Say it isn't so.

'On one level it is the rejection of any preconceptions of a person's talents, character or predispositions on the basis not only of gender, but of race, age, physical appearance and so on.'

Please. Oh, please make it stop.

'On another level it is the making of a conscious choice that what are conventionally regarded as feminine characteristics or values - the caring, nurturing, compassionate, non-aggressive…'

I'm begging you now.

'…should be embraced by all, regardless of gender, and thereby freed from the straitjacket of gender association. They will become the bedrock of all human behaviour and social interaction. All other forms of behaviour will be seen, quite simply, as aberrations.'

'Gerard!' cried Melanie, her driving as swift and flawless as ever, 'that is such a masterful and radical definition. I take it that that is the underlying philosophy of A New Society?'

'Certainly,' replied Gerard, with his trademark smirk.

It sounded to me suspiciously like a sneaky repackaging of the New Man posturing that seemed largely to have died a welcome death.

'The trouble is, Gerard,' I said, trying to keep my voice level and conversational, 'human nature can't be overturned by pseudo-social theorising. Women don't like men who behave like women. When push comes to shove women prefer what they regard as real men, however repugnant that idea might be.'

'Robbie.'

I could see her in the mirror, smiling coldly and ironically, and braced myself.

'What on earth qualifies you to speak on behalf of women? Don't you think it a little presumptuous of you to generalise in terms of what women do or don't like?'

'Not really. I'm so in touch with my feminine side it's almost unnatural.'

'Since when has sitting on the settee watching snooker while drinking substantial quantities of lager been signs of affinity with one's femininity?'

I laughed.

'Hey, that's good!'

'Well?'

'Well? Do you really see me as completely one-dimensional?'

'I sometimes think, Robbie, that even one dimension would be an improvement.'

My laughter this time was of semi-hysterical wonder - like someone dying of thirst having a pint of cold, foaming beer thrust into their hand.

'I'm sorry,' said Melanie, smiling at my reaction despite herself. 'That was uncalled for.'

Wondering meanwhile at the golden softness of her hair, and the strong, yet feminine sweep of her shoulders, and the soft, warm skin of her arm, and the delicate way her hand gripped the wheel.

Her hostility seemed momentarily forgotten, or put aside, or deflected, or perhaps merely postponed. Or perhaps it was a generous, genuine attempt at good humour - an emotional release from the day's frenzy. Yet in all the long months that followed we seemed often to communicate from either side of a glass wall. A strange, intangible divide.

I wish now, as I wished then, that I had some concept of what she thought, and specifically what she thought of me. It's not the sort of thing you can really ask somebody and hope to receive an honest answer. Whatever she was, her essence, remained cocooned inside her head, and what she showed to me was little more than a public face.

Tied, both of us, by the very act of writing this narrative, to a past best forgotten, and still we continue to exist in a vacuum. A place analogous to the empty spaces of our small friend's mind. Spaces he'd filled with redundant, vanished objects - the derelict warehouses, street lamps, factory chimneys, endless lines of terraces. Empty, sad, senseless dreams. Symbols of a mind in chaos, seeking order in the midst of ruin and confusion. The burnt-out warehouse simply one more clue in some cryptic puzzle.

'We ought to stop somewhere soon and have something to eat before we carry on,' said Melanie.

I was for pressing on for as long as possible. We'd crossed the Forth Bridge and were making good progress in Melanie's inspired hands. I was still dubious of us reaching where we were aiming for in time to find somewhere to sleep, and sleeping in the car with Gerard was not such a desirable option. But then she spotted a sign indicating a scenic loop leading from the main road. We turned off and after a mile or so came to an obscure, straggling place, a street of low stone houses with grey slate roofs, occasionally enlivened by pink pantiles.

'What about there?' I said, pointing out a long, low, white-painted public house in the centre of the village, nestling among a few tired shops. 'It's open, anyway.'

The Waggoner's Arms Public House and Restaurant had a car park round the back, pretty much empty. Gerard climbed from the car, gazed at the darkening sky and began sniffing the air. Like an orator entering an auditorium, sizing up his audience, gauging the mood by some strange process of telepathic transference. He walked to the back of the pub, and began to commune with it, according to his custom, rubbing his hands along the stonework. Melanie was putting on her jacket, slipping the strap of a bag over her shoulder.

'It's not too late, you know,' I said quietly.

'What isn't?'

The central locking clicked shut, and she dropped the keys into her bag.

'This whole ridiculous trip. Look at him. He's so bloody weird he gives me the creeps. And he's not family, he's just some guy who lodges in our house. We have no responsibility for him whatsoever.'

'If he's not family, he is at least our friend. Can't you see he needs some recovery time from the emotional trauma of that warehouse fire.'

'He's not my friend. He might be yours. And what the hell's he going to get up to next? He's out of his comfort zone up here, not to mention his mind. At least in his lair he's got his wretched paintings and all the other rubbish to keep him occupied. Here he's got nothing. His mind's going to just freewheel itself to destruction. And you'll be responsible.'

She just glared at me in the dim light. The lack of any verbal response surprised me. I assumed she was tired from driving.

We collected Gerard and wandered round to the front of the pub. I pushed the door open to the public bar. Nobody took much notice of us coming in. A morose, elderly man was nursing a whisky whilst holding an almost unintelligible conversation with the landlord, squat, round and bald with fierce blue eyes, though placid enough. Perhaps it was the subdued pitch of tone which confused me, but for half a minute or so the only consecutive words I understood were, 'A've star'ed a new system. De y'see, it's because a've star'ed a new system.'

He didn't seem excited by it as such, merely a statement of fact. More low exchanges ensued culminating with the landlord exclaiming, 'Well, it's all happening! So you're all square then!'

'Aye. Like a say, it's because of ma system.'

I caught the eye of a pleasant, middle-aged woman behind the bar, and ordered our drinks. A young guy on a bar stool, all sideburns and stubble, was texting intently. A van driver having his tea, shaven head and trainers, studied the horoscopes in a tabloid spread open on the bar. The barmaid smiled with friendly interest as she handed me the change.

On shelves around the walls stood an assortment of dusty green bottles. Paintings of racehorses, a jockey's shirt in a frame. Long settles round the walls. A couple of outsize fairy lanterns gave off a yellow glow. Melanie and I went over to a corner of the room by the windows, slipping our legs under the table, relaxing into some tired leather-covered seats. Gerard had wandered off.

'I really don't want to eat here,' said Melanie, her voice low, looking at the mottled surface of the table. 'It doesn't look clean.'

'That's because it isn't,' I whispered back.

The walls and ceiling were yellow with cigarette smoke. A man with a red face took the landlord's attention.

'There were these really rough lasses there. Swearing like troopers.'

A fire burned brightly, close to the flat screen TV in the corner. Dust hung heavily in the light from the bull's-eye windows.

'Aye, they'll be Davie McCallister's lasses.'

I studied the adverts, before a lilting voice began to call the odds on runners and riders.

'Oh aye. A know him. He owns three houses on the front street.'

A man with hair sticking out the back of a flat cap was looking gloomily at the majestic animals and brightly coloured shirts. Curved nose, big moustache, receding chin, muddy boots, overalls. Bony elbows perched on the bar. As if he knew what was coming, had put money on it, and suspected the worst.

'A'm gan a different way home tonight.'

A round of laughter.

'Aye, Allie came in on Saturday night and said you were the only one in.'

'Look, why don't we just have one drink, then go somewhere else for a meal?'

'You wouldnae want to meet 'em on a dark night!'

Another scatter of laughter.

'Well, we could.'

I picked up the menu I'd taken from the bar, and quickly found the cheapest item.

'But, on the other hand, we could have a nice cheese toastie.'

'That's what you always have.'

'Well, I could have it again. You could have one as well.'

'Robbie, I really don't want to eat here.'

'We wouldn't have to eat in here. They've got a restaurant section just through there.'

I pointed to a sign on the wall next to the jockey's shirt.

'I didn't mean that. I mean I don't want to eat in a place where everything's covered in dust and stains, all of which look as if they've been there a very long time. If it's like that in here why should the kitchen be any different?'

'Why indeed? But I'm afraid I'm not up to that level of philosophical enquiry tonight. All I want to do is sit down, relax and have a drink.' I looked across to the bar. 'Now what's he up to?'

Gerard had already found an audience. He was standing at the side of the bar, talking to the man with the red face, while the thin man with the cap looked on from the other side. I watched with mild interest as others began to turn in their seats, drawn from quiet conversation as the performance gathered momentum.

'You're in top gear, you're coming down Bray Hill. You're setting off with a full tank of fuel, you're just a foot or so off the kerb at 160 miles an hour. Now you just roll it a little bit through the traffic lights in top. But as you come down the hill it's absolutely flat. Even if you're not pulling maximum revs at this point you're certainly flat, and you're going pretty quick.'

He was indicating the throttle movements with his hands, miming rolling it back, then opening the bike up to full throttle.

'A big jump, then another one. Okay - everything feels good. We're on the way to Quarter Bridge. Brake in good time, you need an early apex and then you drive the bike out of Quarter Bridge.'

The intense light of fanaticism was burning brightly once more. Of course I'd heard the TT story before. So I knew that in unabridged form it lasted for over half an hour. Every corner, every gear change, every braking point, every line dissected in excruciating detail. I was surprised yet again as to just what people will take on trust, accept as truth. Swayed so readily by the force of rhetoric. And he was good - you couldn't take that away from him.

'Brake in good time for Braddan Bridge. There's a lot of traps on the TT course that can catch you out if you're unwary.'

'Aye, a can imagine. A've - '

'The section on the way to Union Mills is somewhere you can make up time. It's quite important to keep to the left hand side as you're coming down to get a good line through, because it's quite a steep hill on the way out of Union Mills. It's important to get a good, fast, smooth line. Now you're on the climb to Ballagairie. You're back in top gear. It's a very fast right hander - remember, with a full tank of fuel the bike's going to handle very differently. You get your head down, your elbows in…'

'So we're staying here for a meal, then, are we?'

'…your knees in, your toes in…'

'Look, I really can't be bothered to go anywhere else, Mel. It might be ages before we find somewhere, and we've still got a hell of a long way to go. And look - Gerard's in his element. In fact he looks fully recovered to me.'

'Adverse camber on the exit. You just roll it and drive it. The secret of the TT course is driving the bike as hard as you can out of the bends.'

Gerard was holding the red-faced man in his thrall, speaking with all the concentration and intensity as if he'd been addressing the chief executive of a multinational company. Among the audience was someone I hadn't noticed before, a big guy with grey beard and check shirt, eyeing Gerard coldly from a stool at the bar. I felt a surge of warm emotion towards him, as if he could very easily become my best friend.

The barmaid came over to us, glanced at Melanie, then smiled at me with lips and eyes.

'Can I take your order now?'

'Yes, thank you, that would be great. Could I have a cheese and tomato toastie, please?'

'Of course you can. And would you like salad with that?'

'Well, why not. No harm in living dangerously, is there.'

She laughed pleasantly.

'I assure you there's no danger at all.'

'I'm sure there isn't. And why don't we really push the boat out and have chips with that.'

'A side order of fries.'

'Well, fries if you prefer. I'm really not fussy. If I was I probably wouldn't have come in here in the first place.'

She laughed again.

'It's just as well I don't take what you say seriously.'

'It certainly is.'

'Now,' she said, turning to Melanie and still smiling, 'what can I get for you?'

'I'll have the same,' said Melanie shortly.

'The cheese and tomato toastie?'

'Yes. Thanks.'

'That's fine, thank you. Anything to drink?'

'We'll order some more drinks later, thanks,' I said.

'Right. Is that everything?'

'No, there's another to our party. If you could just ask him what he wants, please. All to go on the same bill.'

'Of course. Who…'

'The guy over there - the one giving the speech.'

She glanced round, then turned back and smiled sympathetically, letting her eyes rest on mine for a second or so longer than necessary.

'Right you are. Your dinner won't be long.'

'Thanks very much.'

We exchanged another friendly smile, then she walked over to Gerard before returning to the bar. I turned back to Melanie and smiled an equally friendly smile.

'Does that woman know you?'

Her tone was cool.

'Who?'

'The barmaid, of course - the woman you've just been speaking to.'

'No. Why?'

'Oh, no particular reason. She just seemed to know you, that's all.'

'No, she doesn't know me. At least, as far as I know she doesn't know me. I certainly don't know her, or at least I'm not aware of knowing her. Not before tonight, at least, and even then...'

'The second is very difficult on a 750 - on a 600 it's absolutely flat. It is on a 750 too, but it takes a lot of practice...two trees here on the right hand side...left-hander, early apex, drive it hard...two apexes, one going in, one going out...burst out under the trees, things are starting to happen very quickly now...adverse camber, very bumpy...impression of speed because of the closeness of the houses...top gear bend, just about flat on a 600...power off, power on, big jump...just use the light at the end of the tunnel, that's all you've got to aim for...two bends that look alike, the first one's quite quick, the second one's tight and slow...climbing rapidly up the mountain any mistakes you make are multiplied...use the first left-hander as the apex, after that the bend just opens out...you know when you get them right you're making up time...you can do it but you need to be on line...very quick on a 750...second left-hander as the apex, drive it all the way round the outside…ignore the first one, peel across for the second one, apex the third and drift out for the fourth…flat on a 600…adverse camber, the bike just drifts wide…over the tramlines, then hard on the gas…early apex, the bike just drifts wide…very difficult on a 750, flat on a 600…'

'Robbie, I…I don't want to lose contact with you.'

Startled, I looked into her eyes. The depth in those bounded meres of ultramarine, sapphire, forget-me-not, lavender was unfathomable, infinite.

'I don't want to lose the closeness that we had. I feel we've drifted so far apart in the last few months, and I really want to try to recapture the feelings we once had for each other.'

Was it Melanie saying those words - words I had so longed to hear?

'I sometimes feel we stand on distant shores, looking across at each other, but it's too far to reach out. Too far to touch. The mists cover the water, and sometimes the sea is raging, sometimes so calm it's as if the reflection of our images could rest on the water, perfect and unchanging, for ever.'

I reached across the table. Her hands were cold to the touch. I held them to my face, my vision coloured with tears. For some time I couldn't speak. A slight pressure from her right hand and I released it, still holding her left tightly. She lifted her hand to my face, ran her fingers across my forehead, through my hair, pushing my hair to one side, as a mother might to her child in a gesture of pure, disinterested love. My voice as I spoke was hoarse and unsteady.

'I was trying to connect with you in Liverpool, Mel. You made it impossible for me. I felt so lonely and isolated.'

'I'm so sorry if I made you feel like that, Robbie. So sorry. I've thought about it since, and I know how much what you were saying meant to you. And I was so dismissive. I'm so sorry, Robbie.'

'It doesn't matter now, now we're so close again. You are everything to me, Melanie. You're such a beautiful person,' my voice trembling and uncertain. But Melanie's smile was warm with boundless love, her eyes searching my face.

'You're such a beautiful driver, too.'

She laughed.

'Oh Robbie, I love you so, so much. You're so funny, so wonderful. Yes, I know you like the way I drive.'

'Do you really not know how good you are?'

'I really just…I don't really think about what I do, or why.'

'I know, I know - that's what makes it so incredible. You don't know what you're doing, and yet you achieve perfection. You're just the most pure, perfect talent imaginable. You're like Jim Clark or Ronnie Peterson - just pure, sublime natural talent.'

'I've never heard of either of them, Robbie.'

'You must have heard of Jim Clark, at least. We passed not far from his birthplace on the way up. Oh Melanie, you are everything to me. You're the sun and the moon and the stars, and all the infinity of space. I couldn't exist without you. I love you so.'

She put her hand on my cheek, looking intently into my face, her eyes on mine.

'Robbie, we must never lose this closeness. Whatever happens, we must keep this feeling, this depth of love for each other. It's something so precious and so rare. You know you mean so much to me.'

We leant across the table and exchanged an ecstatic, lingering kiss, oblivious to anybody around us.

After a while, our hands still tightly clasped, each fell into a private reverie, some spell of deep contentment. It became clear to me, though perhaps no revelation, that only through my love for Melanie did any aspect of my life have meaning. And as I looked around, I saw the interior of that pub as the most beautiful place I'd ever seen, and the people in it the wisest, kindest folk I'd ever met. And even Gerard's voice was part of the perfection of the moment.

Then conscious thought took hold again, and I began to listen more carefully. And then my contented smile turned to broad delight as I realised he was lost. Whatever he'd memorised had become jumbled in his mind, and though his bluster carried him through, it was an increasingly incoherent account.

'He's getting mixed up. He's getting it all out of sequence. He's forgotten his script.'

'What do you mean?'

'I used to watch the TT on the telly. Anybody who knows anything about the course knows that Windy Corner comes after the Gooseneck.'

'Does it really matter, Robbie?'

She looked with kind, compassionate eyes towards Gerard.

'He really doesn't mean any harm, you know.'

'I know, I know. But don't you think…you see, it just proves that he was never there. He's never even been to the Isle of Man, never mind raced there.'

'Even if that were true, does it matter?'

'I have no doubt it's true. And of course it matters. That's why I went to see Mike Fraulent.'

Her expression clouded for a moment.

'Don't you see - everybody exaggerates a little now and then, and talks themselves up. It's human nature. But with Gerard it goes beyond any normal limits. He's describing the TT course as if he's ridden it, and won, on numerous occasions. But he's just got it all off a video. He's never in his life even been to the place, yet here he is claiming he showed David Jefferies the correct lines. What's he going to do for an encore? He'll be claiming next he gave tips on counterpoint to Bach, invented the Fosbury flop, perfected a technique of parthenogenesis in mammals, yet still - still found time to give Shakespeare handwriting lessons.'

Melanie put back her head and laughed. A wonderful, abandoned laugh that seemed to go on for some time. At last she stopped, composed herself, still smiling with transparent affection.

'That's not very constructive, Robbie.'
'Isn't it?'
'No.'
'I'm sorry.'
'Are you? What are you sorry for?'
'I'm sorry for everything.'
'Then you take responsibility for everything?'
'Certainly.'
'You sound just like Gerard.'

And she burst out laughing again. And though I couldn't help joining in her amusement, I was genuinely shocked. Never before had she betrayed any hint of insight into the depth of his self-delusion. But possibly it was simply confirmation of my suspicion that she had a very low tolerance level to alcohol.

During dinner Gerard spoke of symbols, that through the eyes of humanity everything within infinity has potential symbolic significance. And so he ranged over natural phenomena, from wind and rain, and sun and stars, and rivers and mountains and deserts and all the walking, crawling, sliding things that cover the Earth. And then the creations of the human mind - bridges, books, tunnels, spaceships, symphonies, the visual arts, cities and cathedrals. And then abstractions - mathematical forms, geometric shapes and scientific formulae. And finally the juxtaposition of unrelated symbols forming new and dense aggregates of meaning and significance.

But I wasn't interested in what Gerard was saying. I was ecstatically happy in a perfect, enclosed place of my own, where I knew that the only symbol with any meaning was Melanie herself. The symbol and epitome of beauty in the human soul. The pure, wistful face. Exquisite, perfect body. Twisting torrents of golden hair. An ideal - a place among the clouds, the pinnacle of all things.

21

Something about her smile that morning. A kindness in her eyes, warm interest in her expression. Sweet, sweet closeness. Magical empathy. All I'd wanted when we'd got there was to go to bed with her. Nothing else mattered.

She came out of the bathroom, fully dressed after a shower, opened a curtain and looked down at the street below. A cold light bisected the room. She pushed the curtain further back, leaning slightly to her right, her gaze lifted, perhaps glimpsing the sea over the tops of the grey-tiled roofs.

'Did you see the look on that woman's face last night?' I said. 'I thought she wasn't going to let us stay.'

Love, admiration and longing in my voice. She turned and smiled.

'I know. I don't know what she was thinking. Something unpleasant, perhaps.'

'Two men and one woman! Her little mind was running amok. Good thing they managed to come up with separate rooms.'

'Yes, and wasn't it a good thing we managed to push the beds together!'

She laughed, her expression obscure in the glow of gold and white.

'Come here, Mel. Please.'

She turned from the window, walked round to my side of the bed, knelt down, still smiling, and took my outstretched hands in hers. I felt the subtle warmth of her skin. I saw the love light in her eyes.

'Melanie, I love you so much.'

She knelt forwards and kissed my forehead, my ear, my stubbly cheek.

'Oh Mel, you're so considerate and gentle. You always respond in such a kind and subtle way to people's feelings.'

She released a hand and pushed back the bed covers, so that I was lying naked before her.

'Don't ever leave me, Melanie.'

'Of course I'm not going to leave you. Why do you say that?'

'You're all I have in my life. I think about you all the time. Every second I'm apart from you is like a living death. I never quite believe I'll ever see you again until you're there once more.'

'Robbie, you don't have to worry. I would never leave you.'

Her hand caressed my neck, my shoulders, my chest.

'I've never had people in my life that matter to me. I never really knew my mum and dad.'

'I know, darling.'

'Before you there was nothing. My life was empty and meaningless. If you left me, there would be nothing again.'

'I'm not going to leave you.'

'Whenever I have to say goodbye to you, when you go away somewhere, I die inside. There's just an emptiness. This horrific sense of complete desolation. I can't begin to tell you what it feels like.'

'Robbie, please. I've told you, you don't need to worry. I'm always here.'

She wiped the tears from my face. Slim, gentle arms. So fair, so beautiful, caressing me. Yet I knew fear was there too, waiting calmly. Saturnine, urbane, a cold, sardonic smile. A figure of shadows and hidden places. I was never free of its silent, watchful gaze.

I climbed from the bed, needing to embrace her. I knelt down next to her as she turned to face me. My face was in her hair, her arms around me, feeling her warmth, our legs somehow interlocking. Entwined.

The moments passed, and still I couldn't let her go. Then fear suggested another path.

'Melanie, what will I do if you have to go abroad?'

She pulled back a little, so that we were looking directly into each other's face.

'Abroad?'

'Didn't you say that Lundy's were looking to merge with some Italian supermarket chain? What if you had to spend time in Italy? My life is here, in this country.'

'That's...I don't know if that's going to happen, Robbie. It's something that's been talked about as a strategic opportunity, but as far as I'm aware it's at a very early and tentative stage. It's not something I'm particularly involved in. I really wouldn't worry about it.'

'I need the environment of this country. It's where I feel at home. I need the noise, the beer, a game of pool, the changing seasons.'

'I know you do, Robbie. Look, darling, we've got all week to spend together. And Gerard seems better already. By the end of the week I'm sure he'll be well enough to go back home.'

A coolness descended. I felt suddenly absurd and vulnerable. Detaching myself from Melanie I got up and slid back under the covers.

'What was he on about last night,' I said. 'I was concentrating on driving and trying not to listen.'

'Do you mean about the seer?'

'It was something odd.'

'Well, apparently this seer is a celebrated local personality. Somebody quite famous as a visionary, a soothsayer. He gets visits from all over the world from people wanting help or advice.'

'Since when has Gerard listened to anybody else?'

'He just wants to find him and speak with him.'

'Christ, that's all we need. An eccentric, or charlatan, or charlatan posing as an eccentric, filling Gerard's mind with all kinds of nonsense.'

'I'd like you to go with him, Robbie, if you would.'

'Me? Why?'

'I've got just a little work that I must get done this morning, and then I need to find somewhere to fax it to the office. If you wanted to do that with Gerard this morning, Robbie, then we could do something together this afternoon.'

We entered the deserted breakfast room, choosing a table in the corner. I looked around the room. There were various knick-knacks on the mantelpiece - a fisherman with a long brass rod, a sheepdog, a horse. A picture on the far wall of Highland cattle in light mist, or possibly driving rain, caught my eye. In the background was a conical, heather-covered mountain. I studied the painting for some time before redirecting my attention to Melanie. Her chair faced the window, and she was gazing wistfully towards it. I wanted to concentrate entirely on her beauty, but something was niggling away, refusing to relent.

'I don't know what the hell he's doing, going in search of this seer character. He's always had this sense of mission, yet now he's seeking out some prophet, mystic, holy man, witch doctor. Why? That's what I'd like to know. What's he trying to find out that he doesn't already know?'

'I suppose he's just...'

She lapsed into silence, her face thoughtful.

'I don't really know why he's going, Robbie. Curiosity, perhaps?'

'No. No, it's something more than that. He always claims to have such sure instincts, as if following a purpose commissioned by some divine entity. He's always claimed to be the prophet of his own destiny. So why should one prophet seek out another? It seems to me he has nothing to gain and everything to lose. Christ, we haven't even been here twenty-four hours.'

The woman who'd received us at the desk the previous night appeared and approached us, tight-lipped. Her hair was scraped back severely and securely tied.

'Good morning. What would you like for breakfast?'

Her eyes, at least, were expressive. I smiled, and ordered a cooked breakfast. Melanie pursed her lips before choosing muesli and fresh orange juice.

'Just the two of you?'

I managed to keep a straight face.

'No, I think we'll be joined shortly by the third member of our party.'

The eyes glinted as she nodded curtly, then withdrew.

'That was good,' I said, smiling, as the door closed behind her.

'Robbie, I don't really follow what you're saying about this seer. Why do you think it matters if Gerard meets him?'

'Look, if this seer character merely confirms all his notions of destiny then his detachment from reality will be more complete than ever. He'll never settle for anything that we might understand as normality. But what if, on the other hand, this so-called prophet destroys all Gerard's illusions? Would he be able to cope with the dismantling of his thought-world by someone with the supposed gift of second sight? Would he? His manic performances, the stance of unshakeable conviction and all the rest of his bag of tricks - it's all concealing desperate self-doubt. It's like a house built over a disused mine shaft - sooner or later something's going to give, and when it does the whole lot will fall into the abyss.'

Melanie's expression had become solemn.

'You seem to assume self-doubt. I see none.'

'Really? I think the doubts are profound. You have to look beyond the visible and see what lies beyond - hidden, invisible. And if there are doubts, and if he encounters a will more powerful than his own, then I think he will be very vulnerable to suggestion from this superior will.'

'Robbie, I think you're worrying too much. Gerard has always seemed to me very sure of his purpose.'

'Yes of course he's always tried hard to give that impression. But behind the outer façade is a black hole of doubts, fears and insecurities. And these in turn fuel his often absurd behaviour.'

'Were these ideas put into your head by Mike Fraulent?'

The mention of his name was like being hit by a cold wet sponge.

'No, they weren't. Fraulent had many strange theories, but what I've just proposed is all my own work.'

She looked thoughtfully at me.

'What exactly did you talk about? Your attitude towards Fraulent since your visit has been noticeably negative.'

'I'd like to know first what he told you over the phone.'

Unpleasantness was averted by the appearance of an elderly, smiling couple, followed almost immediately by Gerard. He was clean shaven, and his hair was shiny and carefully brushed. Gone was the smoking jacket, and instead he was wearing a smart dark suit with white, open neck shirt. Quite the little man about town - a pocket Hugh Grant.

'Hello, Gerard,' said Melanie, smiling, 'how did you sleep?'

'Very well. Very well indeed.'

It was clear he was nervous, fidgeting in his chair. Without invitation he abruptly launched into a detailed catalogue of all the things he disliked about the human race - its vile habits and pastimes, capacity for violence, greed and deception. As if he were merely an observer, an outsider.

'But you're a member of the human race as well, Gerard.'

He looked at me slowly, his expression uncomprehending.

'Well, you are, aren't you?'

Melanie smiled. There was a clink of cutlery and quiet conversation from another table.

22

The road along Strath Dalabrog was single-track, narrow and winding. I drove slowly, enjoying the austere scenery despite having Gerard sitting beside me, twitchy and excited. It didn't take long for him to launch into monologue.

'I sense a new beginning, Robbie. I feel a fresh impetus to both my political and artistic work. I see the threads of all my creative impulses coming together and meshing into one all-embracing pattern.'

I opened my window, breathing in the pure Highland air.

'All I need is a sign, a portent that now is the time of a great new beginning. That the time of preparation is finally over.'

I pulled into a lay-by to let a 4x4 go past, then turned reluctantly to Gerard.

'What if this guy doesn't say what you want to hear, Gerard? I don't see why you need the sanction of a stranger if you really believe in what you're doing.'

The hills rose around us, bleak and bare. I set off again.

'This would merely provide confirmation, Robbie. I need no sanction. Yet I believe the Fates will provide a sign, clear and unmistakeable, that I am the one chosen by Destiny to lead this victorious crusade. Just a sign, Robbie - nothing more.'

There were deep-seated doubts there, for certain. Doubts which had been well concealed until now. He had both arms stretched out in front of him, hands resting on the dashboard, fingers drumming in nervous agitation.

The river was glittering, pursuing wide sweeps to our left. Around us the contours of the hills became broad and profound. The brown of dying bracken on the rounded slopes washed into the heavy greys of cloud. In places closer to the road impenetrable clumps of spiny gorse appeared, a vivid green against the mottled browns. Small groups of oak and birch grew between river and road, among them bright flashes of rowan berries.

'There! There it is! There can be no doubt.'

A small grove of birches, tall and straight, was sheltering, almost obscuring, a large bungalow, bright blue against the subdued pastels.

'Stop here, Robbie! Just here! This will do fine.'

I drew the car in to the roadside on a large sward of green, receiving an incurious glance of welcome from the sheep closest to us. The house was set back a little from the road. Grey smoke was rising slowly from the single chimney. The many dark sash windows and black corrugated iron roof drew my gaze.

'Don't you think we ought to try and phone first, Gerard? Just to, as it were, introduce ourselves.'

'I don't think that will be necessary,' he said, setting off with a determined stride. Reluctantly I followed, approaching the house along a grassy track threading between areas of gorse.

Suddenly behind us the quiet valley filled with a low, throbbing expression of power. I turned and watched a passenger train glide as if from one dream to another across the landscape. The rumble of its diesel engine gradually faded to a distant murmur, and then to nothing. A breeze wandered softly through the bracken.

I turned back to the house, searching each window in turn, a cold tension in my stomach. The place appeared to be in darkness. No sign of life save the smoke still twisting upwards.

My sense of foreboding intensified. The spectral train, empty landscape, pressing cloud cover. The strange, lonely house. Whatever my sentiments towards Gerard, I sensed that no good could possibly come of this encounter.

'I don't think anyone's at home, Gerard. In fact I'm pretty sure there isn't. Come on, let's go. We can always call back some other time.'

My anxiety was in direct contrast to Gerard, now bouncing around in a state of great excitement. We'd reached the house, and ignoring my words he jumped onto the ranch-style veranda and pushed his face against a window. Silently, the door leading into the house from the wooden decking swung open.

At first there was just a void. A deep, thick emptiness seemed to spill from inside. Then, slowly, a head appeared. My eyes were fixed on it in anticipation, and I was certain that for just a split second the eyes caught my own, before sliding quickly away.

'Who is it?'

Gerard spun round as if on a spring. The voice was soft, low and beguiling, with just a gentle Highland lilt. The head from which the voice had issued was characterised by a long, pointed and in places discoloured white beard. The white hair on top of the head was combed back in furrows from a high forehead. A body shuffled into view to join the head, and with dragging steps made its way towards us, stopping directly in front of Gerard, now visibly quivering with excitement.

The figure reached out both hands to Gerard, who took them in his own. The eyes of the seer, for such I took it to be, were now closed, yet the head moved as if searching his visitor's face.

'Ah!' said the old man at last, nodding slowly. Nothing more, just that single, quiet exclamation.

It was clear from the outset that this was a class act. Without a word, the seer released his hold, turned slowly around and shuffled away in a pair of maroon carpet slippers back into the house, followed closely by Gerard.

I shut the door behind me, but so disconcerting and suffocating was the darkness, so tangible the sense of menace, that I turned in panic, stumbling and feeling my way back to the door, pulling it open and gratefully drawing in lungfuls of the pure, sweet air.

At that moment, standing just beyond the threshold, all my instincts were for flight. It would have been so easy just to jump in the car and drive away, leaving Gerard to his new friend and his fate. But despite my occasional bursts of anger I knew in my heart he was a vulnerable, damaged soul. And my desire to help was genuine, whatever Melanie might have thought.

Reluctantly, I stepped back into the house, this time leaving the door wide open. Pausing for several seconds to allow my eyes time to adjust, I began to make out a corridor, at the end of which came a faint glow. I worked my way slowly and cautiously towards it. The door was partially open. I pushed it back, revealing a dimly lit scene.

They were facing each other, either side of a heavy, dark table. A log fire cast a subdued glow. The seer's hand was grasping for a box of matches lying on the table. He located it, fumbled a match from the box and after several attempts managed to strike it. The face became a pale, bloodless mask, the eyes unflinching before the sudden glare of the match. He lit, then trimmed an oil lamp, the mantle glowing yellow at first, then as the glow became brighter settling to a white, even hiss.

'I don't need the lamp myself,' he said, lifting it slowly onto a hook in the ceiling, 'but I like to spread a little light upon the heads of my visitors.'

He chuckled to himself.

'Sit down, sit down. There's no sense in standing around like statuary. Now, will you join me in a warming glass?'

'No,' said Gerard, 'thank you. In fact I never drink.'

The furniture in that light had the appearance of strange, sculptural forms of indefinite mass. One would have been no more surprised to see them float, as disappear through the floor in a cloud of dust, leaving the occupants hanging grimly to the curtains. A table, sideboard, glass-fronted drinks cabinet. And in the corner a spinning wheel.

'Never drink, eh? Never is a word I use sparingly.'

The seer drew a bottle and glass from the cabinet.

'This is a cold place in the winter months,' he said, shutting the door of the cabinet firmly, and placing the glass and bottle on the table. 'It suits my purposes, however. I have a woman comes in every so often, to cater to my needs. She does for me, as you might say.'

And he chuckled again. The dark-spotted, deeply-veined hands were like claws as he tipped a generous shot of the pale liquid into the glass. The skin was thin and taut, the bones beneath all too visible. He took an audible gulp. A thin, yellow dribble found its way into his beard.

I sat to one side in the shadows, ignored by the seer. His concentration was solely on Gerard. The paraffin lamp cast a pool of light, while the fire glowed a dull orange in the background. A log occasionally crackled and spat. The bottle stood between them on the table.

If demeanour was any guide, then the seer held all the aces. I'd never seen Gerard so submissive, head bowed and subdued, his hands quietly folded on the table in front of him.

For long periods as the seer spoke his eyes remained closed. I was drawn to the face, awaiting the moment when the lids might lift. And when they did, abruptly and unsettlingly, the large pale eyes would glow in the restricted light, wandering constantly and randomly. Yet always resting momentarily upon Gerard, sitting directly across the table, held in some inexplicable web of attraction.

In a light voice, the pitch rising and falling, the seer indulged in a long, meandering preamble, touching on many matters of no discernible relevance to his guest. Then abruptly his tone became crisp.

'You came up yesterday.'

It was a reasonable assumption. Gerard looked up, cleared his throat, and replied clearly that we had.

'There is another - one more to your party, perhaps?'

This was better. I assumed that the seer had picked up on the distance between Gerard and myself - a lack of closeness reinforced by the fact that I hadn't placed myself by his side at the table. No doubt the deduction that at least one other person was necessary as a conduit between us was a relatively simple one to a skilled performer.

'Yes. A friend. A woman.'

'Ah, yes.' He mused for a moment. 'Melanie.'

I sat upright in my chair, eyes wide. Had I heard correctly? He'd almost whispered it under his breath. I couldn't tell if Gerard's surprise matched my own - he showed no visible reaction.

'So, what do you expect to receive from me?'

The voice was soft and, I thought, ironic. Gerard lifted his head, and looked across at the seer. His hands were now tightly clasped.

'I need to know whether there is hope.'

'There is always hope. Even for those who are merely of the common run, there must always be hope.'

He paused. The fire suddenly crackled and spurted a new flame. By now I was beginning to doubt my own recollection.

'But there are those for whom there is more than hope, more than desire, more than ambition. For a few, a very few, there is more than all of these. Fate itself will take a hand for those that are chosen for some great task. Are you such a one?'

'How can I tell?' said Gerard.

'How can you tell?' mused the seer in sing-song repetition. 'How can you tell? Do you need proofs? Do you not feel an inner conviction that you are the one chosen for the appointed task?'

'You have knowledge of the future. Tell me: am I the one?'

'Oh yes, I can see. I can see far and clear, even into distant corners of the future where none have ventured, and few would dare look. Nature bows before my vision.'

The face wore a strange smile as his hand reached unerringly for the bottle once more. Was it all a pretence, or was the precision simply the result of long practice? He tipped the glass back slowly - not hurriedly or eagerly, but with considered exactness, then set it back on the table, and wiped his mouth and beard with the back of a hand.

'Fate favours the chosen few. And Fate will favour only those who already possess exceptional abilities. Those whose willpower is already highly developed, whose spiritual development is already advanced. Fate does not bestow its favours on barren soil, but only on those who already have absolute faith in themselves.'

The seer bent forward across the table. His beard trailed at a tangent upon the surface.

'Only on those who believe in their destiny with unswerving resolve.'

There was a long silence, then the seer sat back in his chair and sighed.

'Your past is shrouded in darkness.'

Gerard's head seemed to drop a little.

'You were troubled. You were unhappy. Your father...'

He stopped. The eyes opened and their pale glow reached across to Gerard, sitting slackly in his chair.

'Much of your past is concealed from me. There has been loss, and much loneliness. The loss of a loved one - one especially dear to you. And a great darkness.'

He paused. Gerard nodded, almost imperceptibly. Of course it was all a conjuring trick. The seer was feeling his way with extraordinary perception by interpreting all the little signs. Tics in the muscles of the face, small nuances of body language. And doing so with all the delicacy and precision of a ballet dancer. To a suggestible subject, no doubt the effect was overwhelmingly powerful.

'And yet, out of the darkness will come light. From chaos and confusion will come order and authority. Are you willing to put your trust in my vision?'

His voice was now a low whisper.

'You know that is why I came.'

'That is not enough. You must surrender your doubts. You must let my knowledge be your faith. Let it inform your will. Surrender your doubts.'

He paused, and a deep and awful silence filled the room. Stillness and silence. Only the dancing of the flames.

'For you are the favoured one.'

So, finally, the anointing. The voice suddenly warm and caressing.

'For you, all things are possible. You are the one chosen by Fate to fulfil a divine mission.'

Gerard sat bolt upright in the chair, his hands gripping its upholstered arms.

'I see unparalleled success awaiting you in the future. Great power, great wealth and influence shall be yours. You will be venerated and revered in every corner of the world. And in the Highlands your name shall be spoken in awe for a particular achievement.'

'Is it to do with a building?' asked Gerard, his voice filled with ecstatic eagerness.

The seer nodded.

'Among many great deeds, this will be remembered above all.'

Gerard now beside himself with excitement.

'This is where my road was leading! Through all the days of doubt! My destiny shall be fulfilled!'

He jerked backwards in the ecstasy of his conceit, the chair creaking a thin cry of protest.

'Everything that happened has happened for a purpose! Everything! And so this is where it shall be built. Amid this great natural splendour shall be constructed the greatest artefact of human imagination.'

'Then you know to what I refer?' said the seer.

At this Gerard began to outline his plans with all the passion at his command, while the seer sat silent but alert. The artist's head was now erect, his posture commanding. He sat upright in the chair and spoke, not with the rabid insistence of old, but with a new calm authority. What before had seemed a construct, a façade uneasily maintained by will, now appeared like a natural assumption of authority, doubts cast aside like discarded skin. I felt I was witnessing the final stage of a metamorphosis, as all the silent uncertainties dissolved and the messianic persona emerged intact and fully formed.

The seer began to rummage in a drawer beneath the surface of the table, at length producing a sheet of paper, which he placed on the table top.

'I have something for you,' he said, reaching out a finger and catching the side of the paper, sending it pirouetting towards Gerard.

'What is this?' asked Gerard, picking up the sheet, which had come to rest in front of him.

'Land!' replied the seer. 'Land by the Dalabrog of just the size and level nature for the construction of a large building.'

'I shall need nine acres,' said Gerard.

'By a loop in the river - two, three miles along the valley, is a large area of flat, well-drained grassland. Perfect for the purpose. The price…'

He appeared to search Gerard's face, as if estimating a likely figure, then adding fifty percent.

'…the price is ten thousand pounds.'

'Ten thousand pounds?'

'Yes. Just ten thousand pounds. And all you are required to do is sign the document that's in your hands.'

Gerard looked down at the paper.

'A deed of covenant. Sign that paper and you shall have full rights to the land.'

'I'm sorry,' Gerard replied after a long hesitation, 'I just haven't got that kind of money at the moment.'

'How much have you got?'

The voice had acquired a sudden harshness.

'Well I…'

He stole a sideways glance towards me.

'I think I could manage possibly…two thousand pounds? I mean as a deposit, of course.'

There was a long silence.

'As a deposit that would be acceptable. You will need to sign that covenant, however.'

The paper was in Gerard's hands, and a pen had appeared and was now poised above the so-called covenant.

'Gerard. Don't sign that paper.'

He turned and looked towards me, his expression uncomprehending.

'Don't sign anything now. Give yourself time to think about this whole thing before you commit yourself to anything.'

For the first time during the meeting, the seer turned towards me, the latent malice now unconcealed, his eyes fixed menacingly on mine.

'Would you like me to tell you what is in your future? Or perhaps you'd prefer not to know.'

A dangerous light was in those pale eyes, and I began to fear for my safety despite his apparent frailty.

'Come on,' I said, rising and crossing to Gerard. 'We're getting the hell out of here.'

I took Gerard by his arm and pulled him from his chair. The seer had also risen, and was shaking a bony finger at me, apparently speechless. His face, now red tinged with blue, was twisted with rage. As we reached the door to the passageway, he suddenly found his voice.

'This is nothing to do with you! You are nothing! There is nothing in your future! You are an outsider!'

He began making his way round the table, his breath coming in shallow gasps, trying to reach us. My heart was thumping wildly as I ran Gerard down the corridor, desperate to reach the faint light, aware of the force of concentrated hatred behind us. Gerard complied without resistance, otherwise I'm sure we'd never have made it out of the place.

The air was fragrant and fresh beyond belief after the atmosphere of claustrophobic menace. I kept both of us running until, as we neared the car, I dared to look back. There was no sign of the seer, either outside the house or at any of the windows. And then I had a sudden vision of an old, blind man tripping and falling in his haste and hatred. Lying alone in the darkness.

Christ, I wasn't responsible for his actions. God knows what might have happened if I'd gone into that place again.

I needed Melanie. To feel her warmth, and draw strength from her strength. To take consolation from our renewed love and loving closeness. Such an unforeseen event. The strange workings of fate and human emotion. Now that it had happened, madness would never come between us again.

We sat in the car. Still breathing heavily, I glanced at Gerard, who was gazing straight ahead through the windscreen, a rare and inexplicable smile of utter contentment on his face.

'Gerard,' I began tentatively, 'I think we should be getting back now. Melanie will be expecting us.'

He looked round at me, still smiling.

'This is where it shall be built, Robbie. Why did I not think of it before? What a setting! A setting worthy of that sublime vision, and a scale fitting as a frame. At last! At last my life's work is beginning! It has been a long and difficult journey, Robbie. A journey with its share of doubt and disappointment. But now the way is clear. The path has been revealed, and I am prepared. From this moment on, no obstacle can arise that cannot be overcome. No foe that cannot be vanquished. No doubt that cannot be silenced. The way is clear. Now is my time. Now it shall begin.'

I expelled a breath slowly and glanced once more towards the lonely house. It appeared as desolate and deserted as when we'd arrived. I found the complexities of life increasingly overwhelming and perverse. A wilful, conscious annoyance when simplicity was such an obvious and attainable option.

'Gerard, I...look, I might as well just say this. I really don't think that building your cathedral is a realistic proposition. I wish it was, believe me. Nothing would give me more pleasure than to see it built. But we have to accept the realities of the situation. There's not the remotest chance of getting planning permission for such an enormous structure. And there's no point buying land that you can't afford when the prospect of building it is, frankly, zero. Look, why don't we just go back to the hotel?'

His smile was now patient and benevolent, the smile of a man sure of his purpose, and therefore tolerant of weakness in others.

'It would only take a few minutes, Robbie. It's only a couple of miles further down the valley.'

I didn't reply.

'It really wouldn't take long. I know exactly where to go.'

A piece of paper fluttered in his hands.

'What have you got there?'

'It's a map of the land.'

'Where did you get it?'

'I took it from the seer.'

'Took it?'

He paused momentarily.

'It was in my hand.'

After all, it would only take half an hour or so, and that would be an end of it. Perhaps better to play the farce out to a conclusion and make a clean break. Still, humouring a man disturbed in mind went against my better judgement and instincts.

A mile or two beyond the seer's house, the valley opened out. Just before a broad sweep in the river a large, flat area of grassland appeared.

'Do you think he means here?' asked Gerard, craning round anxiously, then examining the map.

I wasn't so sure. I didn't think we'd travelled far enough, though it would have made an impressive setting. Perhaps, however, some of the grandeur and sense of scale of the building might have been lost, given the height of the surrounding hills.

Another two, maybe two and a half miles further on the aspect opened out, as if passing through an amphitheatre into something more passive beyond. A mountain in the middle distance, diminished by perspective, provided a suitable backdrop as light through broken cloud played gently on its curving body. A largely symmetrical view framed by hills on either side sloping to the valley floor. We came to a broad expanse of rough pasture of sedges and grasses and moss, to our left the river, white and blue and green and grey, hugging close the pine-covered flanks of one slope.

This was surely it. And it was the perfect setting! God help me, but as I sat in the car I could see Gerard's cathedral in this sublime place. An extraordinary, meaningless vision, on a scale remote from the volume of people who would ever use it, meaningless also as an expression of faith in a largely secular society. Standing in surreal isolation from both its original location in the centre of a busy city, and from any sacred function it might ever have had. An insane indulgence, or art for art's sake in its purest and most extreme form.

And while these thoughts were chasing each other through the empty vastness of the hills, Gerard had jumped from the car, scrabbled down a bank and was now walking briskly towards the gently waving sedge, random locks of hair blown back from his forehead by the oncoming breeze.

I followed, trying to suppress my imagination, wandering after a while off the track, my shoes squelching between the thick clumps of sedge. He stood by the river, gazing intently into the distance. And the truth is a part of me wanted to see it there, just to experience the extraordinary spatial effect.

After a period of silence he turned towards me.

'That will have to go,' pointing to a whitewashed cottage at the side of the road.

And as I looked at the cottage, then imagined the logistics of building anything there, I saw the madness of false dreams, and was angry with myself for having agreed to go there at all. I made my way over to Gerard and stood beside him as he gazed around. He turned to me once more, smiling proudly.

'This is just a beginning, Robbie. This shall serve as the symbol of my entire philosophy. That aesthetics, the quest for beauty, is paramount, and must underpin every aspect of life, every action, every waking hour.'

'Gerard, it can't be done. For Christ's sake, can't you see that? Look, by all means start a political party. Spread your ideas. You're a very talented bloke. I genuinely think you're capable of achieving great things. But leave this. Yes, it's a beautiful idea. But its time has passed and…and it's just a distraction when you should be concentrating all your energies on achievable objectives. Leave it, man. Forget it, at least for now. Come on, let's go.'

'Robbie, I shall never compromise. If just once I compromise, then I am lost. My quest for aesthetic perfection is concerned with absolutes only. There is no room for compromise, no happy medium.'

'Perfection isn't possible. It never was, never can be. Not on this earth. For God's sake, you have to temper your vision with realism.'

'I know how to raise the money,' he said suddenly.

'What money?'

'The money to buy this land.'

Oh, for the love of God.

'It's quite simple, Robbie. All we need is two thousand pounds.'

'I know that. That is if you really believe that old guy actually owns the land. In any case it's two thousand pounds you haven't got.'

'Ah, but I know how to raise it.'

I took a deep breath.

'Go on then - I'll buy it.'

'A road race, Robbie.'

'What?'

'We post it on the internet, and we charge a fifty pound entry fee. We'd only need forty entrants to raise - '

'You can't organise a road race. It's totally illegal, it's highly dangerous and it's completely bonkers. And as for thinking you'd get anyone to pay fifty quid to drive on a bit of public road…'

He was shaking his head with an expression of patient fortitude.

'Robbie, Robbie. We must take a leap of faith. We must believe that all things are possible before dismissing the options open to us. Perhaps we should go back to the hotel now and discuss the idea with Melanie. She'll certainly know more about the technical possibilities of doing this using the internet, as I suspect we're both fairly equally computer illiterate.'

Please, dear Lord, you've been so good to me over the years. Well, that's not strictly accurate, of course, but still I would be grateful if you would kindly bring your great compassion to bear on me in this, my hour of greatest need. Thank you very much.

I think it was my birthday. I had a sense it was some special day. I took the things carefully out of the boxes. Some were quite heavy, but I could feel the fractured parts within the wrapping. Two large boxes, maybe packing cases. I took things, presents, out of them and unwrapped them. But whatever I opened was cracked or broken. Toys with broken parts. A plant, withered, its stem snapped. My mother was by me, crying.

23

Captivated by the sight of someone doing something beyond the scope of normal capability. Taking flight in a way which passes beyond instinct and talent into the realm of pure art. When Melanie took the wheel of a car I was transported, literally and figuratively.

All my protestations had been swept aside. He sat there taking notes, unaware, unconscious. There was one occasion - she had a clear sight-line around the corner, a fast downhill left-hander, travelling quickly under braking. What happened next was almost too quick to register. The back end of the car crept out, her left foot controlling the slide, her right still on the throttle, and we were heading downhill with a rock face ahead of us, rising ever higher behind a length of rusty barrier. Then the car miraculously straightened, and she was braking heavily, easing the brakes on the slippery surface, swinging the car the other way for a tightening right-hander, the car sliding and skittering on the poor surface, kissing the apex. Then accelerating fiercely up the hill towards the next series of corners. Left, right, sliding the car with exquisite, careless control on the shiny road.

Then another fast downhill left-hander that seemed to go on forever. She kept the car almost flat through the corner, rushing down the hill at well over a hundred. We came up behind a slower moving vehicle. Imperceptibly she widened her line, and without lifting or pausing overtook the car, swiftly leaving it in our wake. Achieved with instinctive precision, her left hand meanwhile fiddling with the heater controls. Such was my faith in her ability, sitting back, riding the roller coaster, feeling brave, though rationally you know it's perfectly safe.

Looking across at Melanie. She was calm and relaxed. It was all so easy. You could imagine her pausing to flick a few wayward strands of hair back behind her ears. Ability of such a high order that the extraordinary display was nothing to her. Yet such a waste. If only she'd been strapped tight into some single-seater...

He'll destroy us if he can. Little fuck-shit. Reach back through infinities of time and space - death itself, destroying us. His shadow upon us even at this distance.

Evil deceiver.

'Those people you're referring to are highly regarded colleagues. They've achieved more in their careers...'

The sudden bitterness was disconcerting, but I was riled by the wilful detachment.

'Oh, come off it, Mel, they were the biggest bunch of losers you could imagine. You've got more ability in your little finger than that lot could ever dream of. And as for Gerard impressing them...'

'You do say some ridiculous things sometimes, Robbie. Whether it's just deliberate antagonism, or an enjoyment in being provocative, or what it is I don't know.'

'Don't you? Then there is actually scope for improvement? You surprise me, in the sense that…and here was me thinking you were the very symbol of perfection.'

Her eyes searched my face, her expression one of infinite sadness.

'What is it about me that you dislike so much, Robbie? I'd really like to know.'

Of course I saw the pain there clearly enough. Yet so much had come between us now, so many unresolved issues, so great a gulf, that I felt incapable of bridging it. Once I would have moved swiftly to her side, put my arm around her, caressed her, felt her by degrees give way and melt into me.

'Do you remember that wonderful party we had, the one where Gerard made such an impact?'

It was such a ludicrous thing to say, so obviously detached from anything…that little fuck-shit. Almost a year now since circumstances had benevolently rid us of him. A whole year.

'Oh, you must remember. I invited some of the top people from work for drinks and dinner.'

Fairfax House. So alone.

Alone

'Why won't you tell him that it's madness? He might listen to you.'

Gerard had been in full flow, more at peace than he'd ever been. As if all his agonised longing and perplexity on the nature of beauty had been resolved. Serene, as in his mind he contemplated the first active step towards the realisation of his dreams. A step of unimaginable madness.

'Robbie, Gerard knows what he's doing.'

'For God's sake, how can you say that? That's the one thing he doesn't know. Since he's seen that old faker he's more convinced of his divinely inspired destiny than ever. Any lingering rational doubts have disappeared. We have to pull him back from the edge of the abyss before it's too late.'

'Oh, Robbie. You always see things in such wonderfully melodramatic terms. I don't suppose anyone will even turn up for this race. And if they do, it'll just be a bit of fun. It would take place in the early hours of the morning, anyway, when nobody's about.'

'Look, he's in no fit state in his present condition either to make rational decisions, or to drive a car - especially my car.'

'But we've already established that it's insured. You allowed him to drive it when we were down in Liverpool, remember?'

'It wasn't insured then,' I said.

It was Melanie's turn to look on disbelievingly.

'It was important at that moment that I had some time alone with you. Or have you forgotten?'

'No,' she said, 'I haven't forgotten.'

At this point Gerard returned, slipping onto his seat alongside Melanie, and the exploration of my rationality, which would doubtless have followed, was postponed.

'This is a world fit only for savages,' he resumed. 'The result is, unsurprisingly, a world of base and savage acts. But I shall create a world of timeless beauty, fit for civilized beings. And a civilized, peaceful society will surely result.'

I tried to block it out. The pub was empty apart from a couple of guys playing darts in the bar. I sat close to the fire, looking into the flames. I could see no future there. Everything had been obliterated. Just an infinity of nothingness.

'It is not the beauty of the individual that matters. Personal beauty must necessarily wither, decay and die. What matters is maintaining the beauty of landscape in perfect harmony with the human soul - unchanging and eternal. Beauty of mind can only flow directly from this source.'

There was more, always interminably more on his shining vision of purity and beauty, and he became progressively more ecstatic and confused. At length, after several twists and turns, the monologue ground to a halt. In the silence that followed, my attention was absorbed once more by the dancing flames, my emotions put on hold. Then I felt a gentle touch on my hand.

I looked up into Melanie's face, which had an expectant, almost pleading expression. It was clear she wished to avoid unpleasantness. And I knew she wanted me to make some positive noises about the idea of a road race, the idea of him using my car. She was unaccountably sleepwalking in the face of disaster. The danger was so obvious, and Gerard's lack of talent in particular was blinding. How could I give sanction to such lunacy? How could I bury my conscience?

Gerard had seen a possible route on the map. A triangular circuit that began and finished in Westerhaven on the main road. It was clear that the road was unsuitable, little more than a single-lane track. I'd suggested a radical alternative, never intended as more than a flippant aside - in my naivety I thought it would underline the madness of the whole business.

I took the map from his hands, and saw that the main road up the coast was the only route in the entire area wide enough for the purpose.

'Why not use the main road,' I said. 'Head north from Westerhaven. Then after reaching, say, Crabhead, turn round and race back south the way you came. Through Westerhaven again, through Roadside, down to Murkle or Olrig, then turn round again and back to the finish in Westerhaven.'

'That's ridiculous,' cried Melanie. 'The drivers will be racing in opposite directions along the same section of road.'

'Well, they'll just have to be careful, then, won't they? They'll have to be given strict instructions to keep to the left at all times.'

She was just about to respond when Gerard leapt at the idea, and insisted on checking out the route straight away. Melanie made no further protest. It was all so stupid, and it was only ever meant as a joke.

She agreed to drive so that Gerard could make notes on features of the route, record distances, work out likely average speeds. He seemed not to realise that Melanie's average speed and his own would be very different. Then he insisted on trying out the route for himself, asking Melanie to time him.

'I'll just leave you to it, then,' I said, reaching for the door handle as we drew into the kerb in the centre of the little town.

'Aren't you coming?' asked Melanie, turning round in her seat.

'No. I think I'll go and get a coffee instead. I'll see you when you get back.'

In hindsight I should have worried about that archlunatic let loose on such a quick and difficult bit of road. And alone with Melanie in the car. But at the time, I simply wanted at all costs to avoid being driven by Gerard.

The route altogether was just under sixty miles. Melanie's average speed over the complete course was phenomenal. I allowed almost double the time for this run, and enjoyed a leisurely coffee, then a walk around the harbour. A few small fishing boats were tied up. The Merry Wanderer, Brora Lass, other unnamed craft. Whitewashed cottages almost at the water's edge. A patch of untidy grass, rusty equipment, nets.

I'd seen the cottage along Strath Dalabrog. Low, thick, whitewashed walls, more brown than white. Ivy creeping over door, windows and roof, the door glimpsed through the covering, a sad and faded blue. The land all around it overgrown with gorse, brambles, nettles. Another winter, perhaps two - no more than that. Wide cracks in the chimney, around a window at one end. The roof rusting, gaps where flakes of metal had washed away with rain. Another winter, then little more than a ruin on the hillside. No children's voices raised in play.

I was looking in the direction of the river, and towards the cottage. By chance I saw the car in a queue behind a lorry on the main road, and began to walk to meet them.

The car was already parked by the guest house, Melanie on the pavement beside it, one hand resting on the roof. Her face a shade of white. Gerard was still sitting motionless behind the wheel.

'What's wrong?'

'Nothing. Nothing. Gerard just needs a little more practice,' she replied. Her voice trembled slightly.

'Are you okay?'

'Yes, I'm just…I could do with a cup of tea.'

'I'll make you one. What's he doing, by the way?'

I peered in through a side window at Gerard's head. It was held quite still, and fixed straight ahead, his hands gripping the wheel.

'He said he wanted to stay in the car for a while to visualise the route. He said visualisation was a useful mental technique in motor racing.'

She managed to say this without a smile.

24

With frightening swiftness the thing had achieved a momentum beyond my control. That evening, at Gerard's bidding, she created a blog with details of the race - route, times, the optimistic entry fee. She posted messages on the home pages of various bikers' websites among others. Race start was set for 4.30 a.m. the day after next. All I could hope at that point was that nobody would read the messages or turn up.

That he genuinely believed himself guided and protected by some divine power had seemed apparent even before his encounter with the seer, so frequent were references to providence and predestination. So I was surprised at the display of nerves as the time for the race drew nearer. Alternately sitting mutely, then talking without need to draw breath, all the while clenching and unclenching his fists. His voice had assumed an unusual, nasal quality.

If his belief in divine ordinance was sincere, then surely that would confer the benefit of divine protection, and there could be nothing to fear until his mission was complete. Yet in conversation he studiously avoided discussion of the coming race. Under pressure of nervous tension the veneer of confidence was unravelling. A pressure created by fear. Fear of the race itself - possibly fear of exposure. All the talk of motorbike and car racing exploits had always allowed the potential for public humiliation. He'd effectively boxed himself in, and there was no exit route now except ignominious flight.

'They are an essential part of the fabric of urban society. If they insist on destroying the fabric of society why should they expect any more than they receive? Take Victorian gas lamps, for example - such a perfect, classic design. Elegant, yet functional...stone setts, setting off so perfectly...detailing...'

Taking refuge in all the old standards.

'There were little tobacconists at street corners.'

Really it was tragic.

'Don't you see - it was a community. A true community.'

But aside from street furniture the cathedral remained the true catalyst for all this madness. Two thousand pounds for some old charlatan who'd probably pulled a similar scam a hundred times before. But then if it hadn't been that, it would have been something else.

We rose early, long before sunrise. When I answered a tentative knock on the bedroom door, his eyes were tired and bloodshot, dark crescents beneath each eye. Melanie made him a cup of tea and some toast while he sat silently on the bed.

Christ, it wasn't my fault. What was I supposed to do? Should I have taken the car keys and thrown them into the sea? But then we were only there at all because a warehouse had burnt down. What was that to me?

I went to the window. Beyond the glow of street lights dawn was still several hours away. A white sheen of frost had appeared on the roofs of the cars. I thought of telling them to abandon it. It was my car after all. But our love had just rekindled, and in a state of pathetic gratitude I didn't want to risk that, so I said nothing.

We left the guest house soon after four. We'd fixed the start for four-thirty, reckoning half an hour sufficient to brief anyone who'd turned up, and collect any entry fee. The air was sharp and fresh, the street silent and deserted. No lights were burning behind closed curtains.

There was a clear, starry sky, and light from a pale moon. I looked to the silhouette of the hill whose bulky mass overlooked the west side of the village, pure black against the lighter sky. Wishing the effect of vivid unreality, unique to early morning, could be consigned to a dream, and that I would wake. And she would turn and open her eyes, smile, sigh, and we would embrace and make love.

Instead I slid into the cold seat of the car, which started reluctantly before settling to an even, low-pitched hum. I left the engine warming, got out and began to spray de-icer on the windows. Melanie and Gerard remained in quiet conversation on the other side of the street. Perhaps he was talking to her about street lamps, or maybe she was giving him some last minute tips about driving style. Her arm was around his shoulders. He looked like a child being coerced into going to school. I crossed over to them.

'Right. It's ready.'

I could see his hands shaking. He didn't stir from her side.

'We'll be right behind you, Gerard,' said Melanie softly. 'We'll see you at the start.'

At length he left her embrace and wandered disconsolately across to the car. He cast one last, pleading glance back towards her, before climbing slowly into the driver's seat.

'He'll be fine,' I said. 'He's got all his years of racing experience to fall back on.'

Before she could reply Gerard began to rev the engine in a way that made me glad I'd warmed it up first. The car gave a lurch, then stopped with a sudden jolt as the engine stalled. I had to look away and hide my face. After several attempts he managed to restart it, and at last the car staggered away.

It would take only a few minutes to follow to the designated starting point. Halfway down the main street I began to notice that even this early in the morning heavy lorries were passing on the main road.

'Christ. This is so crazy. I didn't think there'd be any traffic at this time.'

'There isn't much traffic. I don't think it'll be a problem.'

'You are so startlingly unaware sometimes. Of course negotiating traffic at high speed wouldn't be a problem for you. But we don't know how competent or otherwise any of these people will be, if there's anyone here at all which I sincerely hope there isn't. But what we do know is how incredibly incompetent at least one of them is. That's what you should be concerned about. In fact, I don't know what the fuck we're doing here at all.'

She turned her head away at my use of a word she disliked, and a more distinct gap opened between us. At this point I received another unpleasant surprise. Even as we walked I was aware of noise above any occasional traffic. An open space came into view just off the high street. A mass of vehicles had gathered - motorbikes, high performance sports cars, boy racers in Astras and Fiestas with the usual body kits and loud exhausts, some tired old bangers, even 4x4s. Engines were revving, vehicles manoeuvring, some drivers out of their cars chatting. Some must have travelled up through the night, and all must have been cold and tired at this time of the morning, the lowest point of the body clock.

Melanie's face was set and determined, scanning the vehicles around her. Seeing the Golf, she immediately made for it.

'What the hell are we going to do about this lot?' I said, hurrying beside her.

'What do you mean?'

'How are we going to organise all these vehicles? I didn't think anyone would turn up.'

'Why should they not turn up?'

'Why should…that's an impossible question to answer. Whenever I try to communicate with you I only end up feeling more confused than before.'

'Robbie, please…'

Gerard sat huddled in the driver's seat of the Golf. He looked round with wide eyes when Melanie opened the door, leaned in and spoke gently.

'Would you like me to collect the entry fees, Gerard?'

He nodded silently.

'Okay. I'll be back shortly.'

I glanced at my watch. It showed four-fifteen. Hardly time to gather in the seer's blood money. She approached a group of bikers. I saw one give an initial derisive grin. Then as he looked into Melanie's face the grin faded, replaced by an expression of wonderment, and a sudden searching of the pockets of his leathers. He said something to his mates, who similarly began feeling in pockets and compartments. Notes of various denominations appeared and were handed to Melanie. I saw her say something, presumably words of thanks.

Standing on the pavement a little apart from vehicles and drivers, it was a process I was able to observe repeated a number of times. Contrary to my expectations, people seemed willing to pay for the privilege of using a public road. Willing to pay Melanie, at any rate.

I couldn't think how the local police hadn't arrived yet. And perhaps the same thought had occurred to Melanie. As the time neared four-thirty she approached me, clutching a bundle of notes.

'I think it's time we got this under way.'

'I'm surprised we haven't been arrested yet.'
'Do you want to start it off, Robbie?'
'Me?'
'Yes. Would you like to start it off?'
'Don't just repeat the same thing. No, I wouldn't like to start it off. The whole thing's madness, as I've said repeatedly, and I don't want anything to do with it.'
'Right. Well, thanks for the support.'

An eerie, expectant quiet had settled over the assembled competitors. All the drivers were back in their cars, and the bikers were gloved and helmeted astride their machines. All engines had been switched off as if by common, subliminal assent. We'd suggested in the web message that the event be divided into classes, with the quickest vehicles going first to have the best run at a clear road. In practice this meant the motorbikes would lead off, followed by the quicker cars, with the rest to follow on behind.

It was one of the few logical aspects of the whole business, and with this idea presumably in mind, Melanie again approached the bikers, exchanging words with the guy from whom she'd first extracted an entry fee. After a few moments he nodded, flipped down his visor, checked his machine and fired it up. The peace was shattered by the sound of a large-capacity sports bike insistently revving, followed and augmented by a dozen or more similar machines.

I ran to the side of the main road to get a view of the start. The bikes set off quite slowly towards the junction, paused briefly, then blasted away, singly and in small groups. Using both sides of the road, they jostled for an early lead, several pulling extravagant wheelies, a light haze of exhaust smoke drifting slowly inland. Standing directly behind them, I received the full effect of the raucous, screaming racket as the revs soared. And though they quickly disappeared from view, the counterpoint of high-pitched motorcycle engines continued for some time. The cars followed on, joining the road with much gratuitous tyre-squealing.

The last of the slower vehicles had set off, and at first I thought everyone had gone. And then I saw the Golf still parked, lights extinguished, the interior in darkness. And I cursed angrily, and took a few steps towards it. But then, in the stillness of the night the vehicle awoke, the lights came on, and after another pause tentatively poked its nose onto the main road. I watched it recede until, cresting a rise in the road, the tail lights disappeared from view.

25

The regular hiss and tumble of waves breaking along the shore, like a slow heartbeat. I found Melanie close by. As I moved to close the gap between us, without a word she turned towards the sound of the waves. I followed, and we found ourselves walking silently together at the water's edge. Already chilled by the early start, and disconcerted by the uncomfortable silence, I took no pleasure from the bleak and rocky shoreline.

I tried to bury conscious thought in mental calculations. I knew that from Westerhaven to Crabhead and back was roughly thirty seven miles. It was difficult to imagine how quickly the quickest bikes might cover that distance. Maybe an average speed of ninety or so might be optimistic, but taking that as a rough guide I worked out that it would be at least twenty five minutes before the first machine appeared. And probably three-quarters of an hour or more before the stragglers came through.

We reached a headland of rock pushing out into the sea. Unable to continue without negotiating a steep cliff face, we turned. Still without more than a word or two passing between us, we returned to the starting point.

Twenty minutes had passed. I chose what I thought would be a good vantage point, behind a barrier towards the southern end of a wide, constant radius section of road, still within the thirty limit around the town. Melanie made a point of standing some distance away.

After several minutes shivering and kicking my feet against the barrier, I became aware of a distant scream, rising and falling in pitch, gradually increasing in intensity. A light appeared, cutting around a headland beyond the town. As the high-pitched whine of a bike at speed approached, two more beams of light appeared at the same point, chasing each other through the darkness. Then it was on us in a blur of light and noise, driving hard through the corner, the machine leant well over, using the boundaries of the road to the full. The rider was taking a real risk, relying on the absence of oncoming headlights as proof of a clear road.

We stood there for another twenty minutes or so watching the bikes and then cars race through, with many intense private battles. Then with the last of the slower cars and 4x4s the road went quiet. We waited another few minutes as an increasing number of heavy lorries passed by travelling northwards.

'Where's Gerard?'

She was beside me, her face expressively anxious, and I realised then that I'd managed to blank him out of my mind entirely for a brief period. I thought of my car, and what he might have done to it, and also the fact that I'd neglected to put him on the insurance. And inwardly cursed myself, and him.

'Yeah, I'd quite like to know that too,' I replied.

'I'm worried, Robbie. I want to go and look for him.'

'How are we supposed to do that? We haven't got a car.'

'I know we haven't. We can hire a taxi or something.'

'At this time? It's not even half five yet. It's not like being in the city.'

Her look became intense.

'Will you please do something, Robbie? We need to find some way of going to look for him.'

'Okay, okay. Come on then.'

We climbed over the barrier, crossed the road and walked down to the high street. I was hoping to find a phone box with the number of a local taxi firm, and hoping also that they didn't give me too much abuse for phoning at such an ungodly hour. I found a box, and searched around inside it for a card or a number stuck up somewhere. As I came out I saw Melanie with her head poked through the open window of a white Toyota pickup loaded with milk crates. She extracted her head and cast a distant, preoccupied look towards me as I came beside her.

'This gentleman is kindly going to give us a lift.'

Without any further word she opened the passenger door and ushered me into the cab. I sat uncomfortably in the middle seat beside the driver. As we pulled away, I saw a bike returning, its headlamp blazing. The victorious rider probably wondering where the welcoming committee had gone.

The driver was an incurious individual. Perhaps Melanie had already told him the reason for the lift, but he never mentioned anything, or acknowledged me at all. Driving slowly northwards, he pointed out in a flat monotone where the road was going to be straightened and improved. I cast the odd sideways glance at the large hands on the wheel, the untidy tufts of grey hair escaping from the sides of his flat cap and the dense clumps of hair emerging from his ears.

The road was a mixture of fast, narrow straights, swooping, dipping curves, kinks and rises, deceptive delayed entry corners, in fact every type and combination of hazard you could imagine. And as we trundled along at forty at best, I thought of Melanie sight-reading this road with such consummate pace, poise and command, and was overawed once more simply through recollection.

After a few miles I became aware of an ominous absence of oncoming traffic. There was nothing at all coming the other way. I glanced at Melanie. Wrapped in her own thoughts, she didn't return my look.

Along the narrow, curving road, the sea to our right glistening as dawn approached. I could see ahead of us flashing blue lights and a line of stationary vehicles. Melanie noticeably stiffened beside me. The milkman muttered something as we slowed to a halt at the back of the queue.

Almost before we'd stopped Melanie had jumped out and was running towards the lights. As I shuffled across the cab to follow her, I wondered whether to offer to pay for the lift. He was busy complaining about the difficulty of turning round on the narrow road. Either he wouldn't be able to turn round, or he'd be stuck there for hours, or else he'd have to reverse all the way back up the road to a side turning, which would undoubtedly give him a sore neck, and he already had a bad back what with constantly bending down putting out bottles and collecting the empties.

'I'm sorry about that,' I said, before hopping out and following Melanie.

Past a number of lorries. One guy, out of his cab and on his mobile, gave me a curious look. I reached the head of the queue. There were ambulances and police cars, lights a vivid blue in the dimness. I was met by the sound of an inconsolable wailing and screaming.

I saw the car lodged against a tree. It must have come down the hill, lost control and mounted the barrier. It was lying at a strange angle. The windscreen was broken, and a branch of the tree was impaling the car. As I tried to reach it a forceful hand came out of the darkness, pushing me back.

'I'm sorry, you can't go any further. This is an accident scene.'

I looked into the wide face of a robust policewoman.

'It's my car. It was my friend driving it.'

She hesitated.

'You can't go there at the moment. Look, hang on a minute.'

Distracted by answering a call on her radio, I managed to slip past. I climbed over the flattened section of barrier to where Melanie was kneeling on the ground next to Gerard, who was clearly dead. I was shocked to discover that the primeval expressions of grief were coming from Melanie.

She'd pulled back a sheet covering the body and was holding his hand, wailing, sobbing and weeping into what was left of his face. Her golden hair was flecked with blood from the knotted mass of hair, blood, gristle, bone and brains which constituted the top and side of Gerard's head. The eyes, uncannily, were open, untouched and staring straight ahead. I almost gagged at the horrific injuries. I had to quickly look away and take several deep breaths as paramedics gently tried to persuade her to allow them to attend to Gerard.

I knelt beside Melanie. Put my arm around her, trying to comfort her. Finally able to help her to her feet, lead her away from the scene. She was clutching me, weeping into my shoulder. We walked a few yards down the road with no particular sense of direction or purpose.

She abruptly drew back from me, wiping the tears angrily from her face. Her features contorted with rage, screaming at me.

'You wanted him dead, didn't you!'

I was in shock, unable to reply.

'You're glad he's dead, aren't you!'

I thought she was going to physically attack me. Then she started crying uncontrollably. Hiding her face, starting to walk away. I tried to follow, but she turned, and through her tears told me to go to hell.

26

The scent of paint and turpentine still linger in the stairwell even these months later   is it a full year

I can't do it   why should I   she'll never believe anything I tell her   but if I could just find something something tangible

A dark void   black empty space

I know he's there

Like pitch   where the hell's the   where is it God damn it   Jesus the light's thin   can't see any   those shadows treacherous little ghost   you know what I'm after   what I'm intent on finding. Proof of what you were about. And when I find it Melanie will know and then she'll know at the last what was in your perverted little mind and then I'll write the truth about you by God. Then we'll hear the truth at last

Somewhere here   somewhere   somewhere among all this damn clutter. And when I find it when I find it

And when I find it I'll make a bonfire of your ambitions I'll cast them into dust I'll scatter them to the four winds. Dirty dirty deceiver. Your fatuous pretensions will be laid waste as if they'd never existed

Piazzas   chimneys   guns   statues   warehouses   steam trains   your mind is just a clutter of junk   you dirty deceiver   all nonsense   all detritus   all posturing and formless mess of vanity and deceit   what is all this nonsense   pages   pages in the little masters hand scribbles and loops of nonsense and deceit

What can I find that I haven't found before   all this nonsense   wait   a secret stash   why hide things under here you little deceiver what can you have to hide   a paper file   Testament   what does that mean you unclean deceiver what did you have to leave   your so-called art   will feed the flames when I get opportunity   no   wait

this is no will   an attestation   a declaration of belief

beyond belief

I am the God of all that is, and all that shall be. Out of my body was created all things. Out of my hand was created Heaven and Earth, Future and Past, Seen and Unseen. I am the Church, the Temple, the Spirit and the Sacrament, the Clean and the Unclean, the Living and the Dead. I am the Father, the Mother, the Daughter and the Son. All things come from me, and of me all things shall be. That which is in me, is me, and that which is without me, shall be within me. And there shall be no boundary to my Dominion. From me and within me and through me was created Melanie, the Light, the Life, the Fount of all beauty and wisdom. From the depths of her eyes shines memory of that which is past, and knowledge of that which is to come. Her long, flaxen hair ripples like cornfields touched by warm breath of summer. Her eyes deep pools of wisdom. Her body

I will read no more of this   drivelling endlessly onwards now you will believe me   now we have the truth of the matter   insane deceiver   the fixation with Melanie neither more nor less than I suspected   that much at least is explicit   even delusions of divinity cannot be sustained without sidetracking thoughts of Melanie   her manifold charms   Not that I hold the little pervert entirely to blame for that. If she hadn't hung on his every word face lifted in eager anticipation of each pearl of wisdom trusting little features innocent blue eyes fixed on his with that dopey baby-doll expression, lips parted, practically salivating   I tell you the looks I got were from an altogether colder climate   that little bitch wouldn't recognise loyalty if it grabbed her by the hair and thumped her in the face

Enough   what's this

Filthy deceivers   together   so now we have the truth in my mind was it   you little prick   you lying cunt   you lying   lying   lying   deceiving   leave me alone   leave me alone   you

'Robbie, what is it? What's going on down there? Are you alright?

'My God, your hands are shaking. What is it, what's happened? Come here, come and sit down here next to me.'

'Are you feeling any better?'

'I want to talk to you.'
  'Yes, Robbie, what is it?'
'I said I want to talk to you.'
  'Okay. Well, I was just up in the bedroom sorting some clothes out. Why don't we both go up and we can talk at the same time. Are you sure you're alright?'
  'What would you like me to say?'

'Robbie, I don't know what this is about. Come on up and let's talk about it.'

Folding clothes. Bright, cold.
She reads the so-called Testament, her eyes troubled.
'You're saying you found this down in the basement? Where was it?'
'Does it matter?'
'Robbie,' looking directly into my eyes. 'You've just made all this up, haven't you?'
'No.'
'This is all absolute nonsense. Gerard never made any such ridiculous claims.'
'I haven't written it. He did it.'
'It seems to me that you're just trying to destroy his reputation when he's in no position to defend himself.'
'What reputation? The little bastard was a nutter.'
'How dare you talk about Gerard like that. He had more talent, more humanity, more genuine human feeling than you could ever imagine.'
Bitter anger and contempt in her voice.

Sitting down next to me, hands folded in her lap.
'Look, I'm sorry, Robbie. I'm sorry I said that. I didn't mean it the way it came out. But I've tried everything I can to help you.'
'Help me? I'm not a child, needing your help. What do you mean, anyway - help?'

'I mean I've tried to encourage you to do things like...well, like the Open University. I tried so hard to encourage you to do a degree.'

'I don't need a degree.'

'But...well, it doesn't matter now.'

'No, it doesn't, does it. Nothing to do with me matters, does it? Nothing matters but the little master and his precious legacy. Legacy of nonsense. Legacy of lies and deceit.'

'Robbie, why are you so hostile towards me? And why do you have to constantly undermine Gerard's memory and deride him all the time?'

'You disgusting, disloyal cow. You wouldn't know the truth if it jumped out and hit you in the face. Your mind is so twisted I'm surprised you can walk in a straight line. And as for that bloody stupid book I only wrote it because I felt sorry for him. For both of you for that matter. And as a joke.'

Melanie rose, pain and anger in her eyes, her mouth drawn down in a line of suffering. She left the room without replying, leaving me silent and alone.

Looking around at our life. Every object full of significance   portent. Books on a shelf. Pictures on the wall. Pattern in the curtains.

All leading here. Leading inexorably up to this one moment in time and space. No other. Just the here and now of this precise moment. The clock ticks seconds and minutes away. An hour. Sounds from the street, children playing. Footsteps on the stairs. The door opens, Melanie comes in. Asks if she can talk to me, I reply yes. She is hesitant, nervous.

'Robbie, this is difficult for me.'

Sits once more beside me on the bed.

'What is difficult?'

She pauses for a period of time an eternity.

'We've grown so far apart, Robbie. We just don't want the same things from life. I feel we've been on separate, diverging paths for a long time now.'

Nameless, predatory fear gnawing my insides.

'I'm finding it very difficult to cope with your jealousy.'

'What do you mean?'

'I mean it's bad enough to be jealous of a living being, though there never were grounds for jealousy. But to be jealous of someone who is dead…I just don't recognise the person I thought I once knew.'

'Yeah, well…maybe if you spent more time with me and thought about me a little more you might be able to recognise me. You might even get to know me.'

Melanie was silent for a moment.

'I don't think I want to. In fact I don't think we can stay together anymore.'

The words cut with a serrated edge.

'What are you talking about?'

'I don't want to be with you anymore. I'm sorry, Robbie, but I'm leaving.'

I looked into her face, desperately trying to read the level of intent.

'What do you mean, leaving? You can't leave. Don't ever say that. We belong together.'

'I don't think we do. I used to, but I don't any more. I just don't love you anymore.'

'You do. You do love me.'

I took her hand and began caressing it, pressing it against my face.

'I love you, Melanie. I love you so much. I need you. I need you here with me. We need each other.'

'I'm sorry, Robbie.'

She didn't withdraw her hand. I thought I felt answering pressure.

'I didn't think it would mean this much to you. You haven't given any indication for a long time that I mean anything to you.'

'For God's sake, you mean everything to me. Can't you see how much your love means to me, how much I love you? Look, it's all this bloody Gerard thing. That stupid book has just kept the feelings from those times alive when they should have been allowed to die and fade away. If only I hadn't been writing that damn thing all this time we could have moved on and put all that behind us.'

'This isn't really to do with Gerard. We've both changed. We want different things from life.'

'We don't, Melanie. We don't want different things. We've always wanted the same things. Like, we're going to have children together. We even made up names for them. We're going to have two, a girl and a boy. We made up funny names for them. Don't you remember?'

She was smiling sadly.

'Yes, I remember.'

'If it was a girl it was going to be Rosemary St. John Abacus.'

'Wasn't it Abigail?'

'That was another one. We had variants. The one with Abigail was Rosemary Abigail Griselda.'

'That's right, I remember now. And there was Rosemary Abigail Morningstar.'

'Yes, I loved that one. And for the boy it was going to be either Ferdinand St. John Abacus or Ferdinand St. John Milan Trevelyan.'

'Robbie,' she said, suddenly withdrawing her hand, rubbing her temples, her face hidden. 'Robbie, you're not making this any easier for either of us.'

'Why should I make it easy when all you're trying to do is destroy our life together, our future.'

'Robbie, the last thing I want to do is hurt you. You know, you're a strong person. You'll be fine. This may be what you need to go on and really make something of your life.'

'How can you say that when you're destroying me. Why do you keep on saying we're not going to be together when we are. We are going to be together.'

At this point my tears flowed freely, without check and without dignity. I had never loved her more deeply, more for herself rather than from feelings of physical desire than I did at this moment. And it was now, just at this very point when I understood my own emotions more clearly than at any time in the past, that she had suddenly and without warning closed her heart against me, finally, irrevocably. The helpless, exquisite horror of it overwhelmed me. There was nothing ahead of me that I could possibly contemplate wanting to be part of. Life without Melanie was a void of loneliness and despair stretching into infinity.

She knelt beside me. She touched my face, brushing the tears aside, running her fingers softly over my forehead, parting my hair gently out of the way.

'Robbie, I don't hate you. I still care about you very much. We can stay friends. Don't be so upset. I don't want you to be upset. It'll all work out for the best.'

I clutched her close to me, her hair and shoulders becoming wet from my tears. I held onto her desperately, feeling that if I let her go now I might never touch her again, my head in her lap, her fingers in my hair, stroking my head. I wanted only to lie beside her on the bed, to know that she was mine and mine alone.

'You've closed your heart and mind against me. You have utterly and completely devastated me.' I could hardly form the words, or speak them coherently. 'You've made up your mind before even speaking to me and now nothing I do or say makes any difference.'

'You never made me feel wanted or valued.' She spoke softly and kindly. 'That's all I ever wanted.'

'I did value you. I did want you. You can't expect everyone to behave in an ideal way, like some romantic ideal. You shouldn't put someone on a pedestal, then despise them for falling off, or see them as not deserving to be on it in the first place.'

'I never idealised you Robbie, believe me.'

'I think you saw me at first as being more than I am and then you felt increasing contempt for me for failing to match your expectations.'

'That isn't the case.'

'You had this shining vision of Gerard before you all the time. Renaissance man writ large whose phenomenal range of talents was matched only by the size of his ego. No wonder I appeared such a poor, lacklustre bastard in comparison with the great Gerard. That fucking lunatic. What the hell was going on between you two, anyway?' My voice rising shrilly. 'We might as well have the truth now, at long last. There doesn't seem much point in hiding anything anymore.'

Melanie rose to her feet.

'I'm not discussing this anymore.'

'You're not discussing it!' I shouted. 'Well, I'm discussing it. Perhaps you can explain these.'

I pulled the photos of her and Gerard out of my pocket and threw them in her face. She flinched slightly but didn't move, letting them fall to the floor, making no effort to retrieve them. Continuing simply to look into my face with an unreachably cold, inscrutable expression.

'Look at them, you bitch,' I shouted, falling to my knees and scrabbling for the photos. Now holding them up to her with shaking hands.

'Look at them and tell me there was nothing between you and that evil little fuck-shit. Take them, you bitch.' Getting to my feet. 'Go on, take them, or are you too ashamed even to look at them - you disloyal, cheating cow?'

Melanie coolly took the photos, glanced briefly at each in turn, then looked back at me wearing that same unreachable, expressionless mask.

'Well?'

'What do you mean - well?' I half scream, half sob the words. 'What do you mean - well? What does that mean? What does it even mean? What were you doing with that little fuck-shit? Why has the little fuck-shit got its arm round you? Eh? Why? What were you doing with that little fuck-shit? What were you doing?'

Melanie said nothing for a few moments, then ran her tongue over her lips before speaking quietly and calmly.

'I'm leaving now. I'll come back later to pick up my things, or I'll send someone round to pick them up.'

'You haven't answered my question,' I scream. 'You haven't answered my question. Answer my question.'

'I'm not answering any more questions, and I'm not taking this conversation any further.'

'You are answering my questions,' I screamed again, grabbing hold of her top in a desperate effort to prevent her leaving the room. 'You are answering my questions. I need to know why you're doing this. For God's sake, Melanie, don't do this to me. Don't do it to me, don't do it, it's not fair. Please, please, please...'

'Get off me,' said Melanie, removing my hand with a strong grip on my wrist. 'Don't ever touch me again. Do you hear me. We're finished. It's over.'

She left me huddled on the floor paralyzed with grief, crying uncontrollably.

27

I'm never going to think about that little pervert or bring any of its madness to mind ever again   ever ever ever again Bastard little prick   managing to reach out from the grave to finally destroy my life with your bastard lies

Melanie hasn't called since collecting her stuff   nine days now   nine whole days and nights   after so long together Just call me   please   talk to me. Tell me that you love me   just call me and talk to me   Please please you love me

Bastard pervert

It's cold tonight alone in the darkness   dead hand of winter already reaching out icy fingertips touching the late evening the wind winters melancholy companion protesting mournfully   there's nothing poetic about sitting alone in a cold, cheerless room. The place is empty silent. Melanie has gone and there seems little chance now that she'll ever return

28

There's a rumour the whole area's to be a housing estate. This place will be torn down. Nobody gives a damn about Victorian buildings. They're just throwaway objects.

If you'd ever seen the entrance. Marble everywhere. Mahogany handrails on the stairs, windows with leaded panes, stained glass on the landings. I saw them when I came in. Panelled doors I know they're panelled under the hardboard because I've looked. There's an oak floor in the dining room

If you could see the scale of the place. And the brickwork has such colour and texture. Bits will be ripped out and flogged. The rest will be bulldozed.

I don't care anymore. They can pull the whole thing down. They can demolish the whole fucking country and cover it with concrete for all I care. I've given up caring.

There's no point driving yourself mad about things you can't control.

Melanie thought my title for the book overly facetious. I had to explain to her that it might have started off as a joke, a facile play on words, but in the end it came to mean something different to me. It's just that you have to do something here, and the silence does pile up, like snow. Layer upon layer. Sometimes broken by a distant scream or shouting or people scuffling. Usually it's just silence. Especially where I am. Anyway, I agreed in the end and chose a straightforward, prosaic title. But I still like *Silence Snows* I think it sounds rather evocative.

I'm expecting Melanie soon. She usually comes around this time. Sometime in the next few minutes, I hope. She'll probably be dressed in some brightly coloured, buttoned shirt of thin cotton. The top two, maybe three buttons undone. You'll just be able to see the top of her breasts. The curve of each breast clearly visible as she bends towards me, caressing my face, her nipples showing through her shirt quite distinctly. Tall and beautiful, a serene Goddess, above earthly considerations. The Light, the Life, the Fount of all beauty and wisdom! Venus, sublime in her nakedness, Her soul and mind Love and Charity, her eyes Dignity and Magnanimity, the hands Liberality and Magnificence, the feet Comeliness and Modesty.

The whole is Temperance and Honesty, Charm and Splendour. Oh, what exquisite beauty! How beautiful to Behold!

And then Gerard will be along later, I expect. When Melanie's gone, I hope. Don't get me wrong - I don't care one way or the other if he comes. I just wish he'd keep his eyes off her. You can see him looking at her all the time. Little pervert. He knows full well she belongs to me. She's mine, every curve, every flick of the hair, every smile, it's all for me.

Of course, that's the trouble with this place, it does things to your mind. In the end you just don't know who to trust.

Acknowledgements

The author would like to acknowledge the works listed below, as providing information, quotation and/or inspiration. Any misunderstanding or misreading of the information derived from these sources remains the responsibility of the author.

Botticelli, Frederick Hartt, Collins, 1953.

De Chirico – The Metaphysical Period, Paolo Baldacci, Bulfinch Press (an imprint of Little, Brown and Company Ltd), 1997.

Emily Brontë, Winifred Gerin, Oxford University Press, 1972.

Explaining Hitler - The Search for the Origins of His Evil, Ron Rosenbaum, Papermac (an imprint of Macmillan Publishers Ltd, 1999.

Giorgio de Chirico, Magdalena Holzhey, Taschen GmbH, 2005.

Hitler – The Policies of Seduction, Rainer Zitelmann (translated by Helmut Bogler), London House, 1999.

Liverpool – In A City Living, Gerard Fagan, Countyvise Limited, 2004.

The Brontës, Juliet Barker, Phoenix (a division of Orion Books Ltd), 1995.

The Man Who Invented Hitler, David Lewis, Headline Book Publishing, 2003.

The Speeches of Adolf Hitler, April1922 – August 1939, edited by Norman Baynes, Oxford University Press, 1942.

TT Circuit Guide (video), commentaries by David Jefferies and Nick Jefferies, Duke Video, 2002.

Utopia, Ian Tod and Michael Wheeler, Orbis Publishing Ltd, London, 1978.

Finally, special thanks to Magnus Clarke, for his interest in the novel during the period of its composition, for reading the first complete draft and making a number of insightful comments which resulted in a substantially improved work in certain areas, and for technical assistance with the invisibility theory.

Printed in Great Britain
by Amazon